WHAT'S REALLY HOOD!

Payback with Ya Life
Thug Lovin'

CONTENTS

BLACK IS BLUE *by Victor L. Martin*   1

THE "P" IS FREE... *by LaShonda Teague*   57

THE LAST LAUGH *by Bonta*   123

ALL FOR NOTHING *by Shawn "Jihad" Trump*   183

MAKIN' ENDZ MEET *by Wahida Clark*   239

BLACK IS BLUE

BY VICTOR L. MARTIN

Raleigh, North Carolina
Present time

Desiree Eason was young, black and sexy and far from being a follower of the norm. You know the stereotype of a black woman: sexually wild, two or more kids by different men, a boyfriend that's locked up, willing to open her legs for a man based on his flashy whip. Nah, Desiree was above and beyond that. Her looks were conservative but easily sexy. She was a petite size five, standing flat-footed at five-two with clear mocha skin. Her brownish hair, which she usually kept in a simple ponytail, hung past her delicate shoulders. Her light hazel eyes were inviting and between them sat her cute pert nose. Her lips were thin and sexy and stayed coated with the lightest touch of lip gloss. Her measurements were 34B-23-34. Desiree was a certified legal assistant for Shaw, Barnes and Rivers Attorneys at Law. Not bad for a twenty-three-year-old single-by-choice black female. At the moment she was headed back to her office with her laptop in one hand

and her Donald J Pliner bag slung across her left shoulder while chatting on her Audiovox picture flip phone. Just as she reached for the doorknob while shouldering her cell phone to her ear, a rude comment easily gained her attention.

"Damn, she got a nice ass."

Desiree promptly told her roommate to hold on for a second. "Excuse me!" she said as she turned around, eyeing the four black men lounging in the waiting area of the cozy law office. The comment was rude, but in truth...the truth was told. Desiree was filling out her clingy tweed Calvin Klein pants mighty nicely. In truth, she had a lovely ass!

She eyed each one of the waiting clients and dared one to speak up. Sucking her teeth, she turned on the heels of her Via Spigas, then went into her office. She wasn't upset over the comment, she was just tired of seeing black men in trouble. She hated the senseless gang violence, black men killing each other over a red or blue cloth, and she saw no end to it. Entering her office, she kicked the door shut behind her, flicked the lights on, then headed toward her desk. Kicking her heels off after placing her laptop on her desk, she resumed her conversation.

"Where were we?" Desiree said as she placed her stocking-clad feet up on her desk. She wiggled her pedicured toes while relaxing back into the leather contoured chair.

"What was that all about?" her roommate, Jelena, asked.

"Some dude making a remark about my butt!"

"So," Jelena teased, "what do you expect? You prancing around with that tight booty."

"Jelena."

"Yeah?"

"Shut it up," Desiree said, crossing her ankles. "Anyway, like I was saying...I'm tired of seeing my people going through this system."

"I take it that the case didn't go well today."

"No, it didn't. They gave Jamal a life sentence." Desiree's voice was filled with pain.

"He did commit a crime," Jelena pointed out. "He's the one that did the drive-by in Durham, right?"

"Yeah."

"And then shot the police station up in Raleigh?"

"Yeah."

"Well...he can't be allowed to walk free, can he?"

"I'm not saying he should," Desiree responded. "It's... I just wish there was another way to curb this big problem."

"There is a way, Desiree."

"I'm listening."

"It's called common sense. Ain't nobody forcing us black people to kill each other. Just because I'm a college grad doesn't mean I don't see the problem. And plus we both know that the system is—" A knock at Desiree's door forced her to cut Jelena off.

"Go ahead and take care of your business because my minutes on this phone is already over my budget limit so I'll holla at ya."

"Okay, bye, girl," Desiree said, removing her feet from her desk as she rolled back from it. Pushing the END button, then flipping her Audiovox closed, she laid it on the desk, then went to answer the door.

"May I help you?" she asked in her professional voice as she looked up to the man standing before her looking like Michael Vick, sporting a nappy mini afro and chewing on a toothpick. He wore a cream-colored G-Unit leather jacket with matching jeans and a pair of white Air Force 1s. He looked into her hazel eyes, smiled, then looked down at her sexy feet. Desiree rolled her eyes as she realized she had forgotten to slip on her heels.

"Mr. Shaw told me to give you my info and stuff," he said, grinning around the toothpick.

"Come in," she said, nodding at the chair in front of her desk.

As she walked around her desk she heard him mumble something under his breath.

"Excuse me?" she asked, sliding her feet back into her Via Spigas.

He continued to grin as he took a seat. "Anybody ever tell you that you favor Christina Milian?"

She ignored his comment as well as his smile. "I think we have more important matters to tend to other than my looks, Mr. . . . ?"

"Polo . . . I mean Tyrone," he said, removing the frayed toothpick from his mouth.

"What's your full name?" she asked, with her slender fingers poised over the wireless keyboard to her computer.

"Tyrone Leon Bell, also known as Polo."

"Need a trash can for that?" she asked without looking at him. She was referring to his toothpick as she typed his name in.

"Nah, I'm good," he replied, checking out her ring finger to see if shorty was married. Nope. *Damn, she's fine as fuck.*

Desiree was strictly professional as she took all his info. He was hiring Mr. Shaw in the hopes that he could keep him out of prison for a gun charge.

"Do you have any pending charges?" she asked, removing her eyes from the flat computer screen.

"Nah. But I'm on probation."

"For what?"

"Drug charge."

Once she had typed in the info she asked him about his current charge.

"Po-po found a gun on me."

"I take it that you don't have a permit?"

"Hell naw, shawty…" He started to laugh but paused at the stern look on her still-sexy face. "I mean… um…"

"It's Ms. Eason," she said sternly. "Not shawty."

"My bad," he said, holding his hands up. Her take-no-shit mind-set was off the hook. *I wonder if she's the same in the bedroom? I can only dream because she might not fuck wit such a thug nigga as myself.*

"And your reason for having a gun?"

"I live in Durham," he answered matter-of-factly. "Shit, it's like a fuckin' war zone…" he continued.

"Is that what you expect the judge to hear?"

He shrugged his shoulders. "Yo...that's how it is, sh—I mean, Ms. Eason."

"So," she said, crossing her arms. "If the judge gives you some time, and say that's how it is...then what?"

Polo looked briefly into her eyes, then off over her shoulder at the wall behind her. Glancing at one of the photos on the wall, he gained the knowledge that she had finished college at Bowie State University.

Clearing her throat to regain his attention, she repeated her question. Polo shrugged his shoulders, then tried to look into her eyes. He could only hold his gaze for a few seconds before he again broke the eye contact. *Damn, shawty placing me outta my damn element. She must not know who I is. Dat nigga Polo dat fuck slow and stack dough.* He started grinning at his silly thoughts.

"Is something funny, Mr. Bell?"

Polo gathered himself as he erased his grin. "Nah... I was just thinking about something, that's all." *I'd eat dat ass fo' breakfast...word up!* he continued in his thoughts.

"How old would you happen to be, Mr. Bell?" she asked, uncrossing her arms to type in the info.

"I'll be twenty-one next week," he replied.

The rest of their conversation went on as it had started. Strictly professionally. When it came to the point of the payment, Polo pulled out his fist-size roll of colored bills. Fifteen hundred dollars were counted out, then placed on her immaculate desk.

"Do you think the case could be put off a few months?" he asked.

"You can talk to Mr. Shaw about that next week. But by looking at his caseload...the answer will nine times out of ten be yes."

"Good," he said, placing his frayed toothpick back into his mouth. Feeling cocky, he asked her if she had a man. That was a wrong move.

"Be sure to call Mr. Shaw next week," she said, ignoring his question about her personal life. She showed him the door with a forced fake smile. Polo kept his smooth composure as he came to his feet. As she turned to open the door for him, he stole another glance at her heart-shaped ass.

Whoever hitting dat is a lucky-ass nigga! he thought to himself as he exited her office.

Once Polo made it outside in the chilly November weather he zipped up his G-Unit leather jacket, then pimped down the crowded sidewalk. He started grinning as he neared his glossy candy-colored Duke-blue Dodge Charger perched on a set of twenty-two-inch deep-dish DUB Shoreline rims. Sitting on the hood was his buck-wild cousin Tink, smoking a Newport.

"Get the fuck off my hood!" Polo said, pulling out his keys.

"Fuck you!" Tink replied, sliding from the glossy hood. Polo paused to check for any dents as Tink thumped his burning Newport toward the gutter. None were found.

"Whut dey say?" Tink said, sliding his long twisted dreads from his face. "You goin' back to prison or not?" He laughed.

Polo waved Tink off as he keyed the remote to raise the Lambo doors in the air. Once inside, Tink held up his numb hands near the vent, waiting for the heat to blast. Conversation inside the Dodge Charger was pointless. Reason being, the eight square KICKER subwoofers shook Polo's whip with Three 6 Mafia's "Stay Fly." As Polo checked over his shoulder before pulling out, Tink reached into his waistband and pulled out a black .380 that he laid in his lap. With nothing on his mind he rapped along with the music.

"I gotta stay fly, ah, ah, ah, ah, ah, ah, ah, ah, till I die!" The system was hitting so hard that he couldn't even hear his own voice. Polo sped through the busy traffic as he unsuccessfully tried to push Desiree from his mind. It was something special about shawty. To Polo, she was the type of chick... wait, she was the type of *woman* to grace the cover of *Essence*. Deep in his mind he knew that she was not feeling him and his thug persona.

Leaving downtown Raleigh he wheeled his Dodge Charger toward Tink's baby mama's crib in Washington Terrace Projects. Tink's ears were still ringing as he stepped out of Polo's Dodge Charger. His baggy black Vokal jeans and white hoodie were his thuggish attire for the day. His .380 was now in his front pocket for easy access in case any drama popped off. He waited for Polo on the dirty sidewalk before heading in to check on his BM (baby mama).

"Ain't that Lil' Rick over there shooting craps?" Polo asked, walking up to Tink. Tink glanced at the group of hustlers in the tight game of craps. Tink nodded his head, as he easily recognized Lil' Rick's lanky six-two frame clad in baggy black jeans with a matching black hoodie.

"Yeah, dat's him, whut up?" Tink asked.

"Ain't nothin'. I just need to holla a'im later."

Tink shrugged his shoulders, then walked toward his BM's crib while holding up his sagging jeans. Polo followed, glancing back once at his tough-looking Dodge Charger.

Tink entered Trina's cozy crib to find her busy in the kitchen.

"Close the door!" she yelled over her shoulder while flipping over some pork chops. "My heat going out!" she added.

Trina wasn't your average project chick, not that she was hood. Trina was the same age as Tink, eighteen. Sadly, her parents had kicked her out when she became pregnant. She wasn't put on the streets, but her parents pulled a few strings to get her name on the waiting list and quickly into her own apartment. Their reason was firm and simple. If she was grown enough to have sex and get pregnant, then she was grown enough to live on her own. Luckily, Tink had been there for her and his baby boy since day one. His only flaw in her eyes was that he sold drugs. Trina stood at five-four and didn't favor anyone famous. She was just cute and a bit sassy when the mood would strike her. Tink came up from behind her, cupping her round butt and softly nuzzling the side of her neck.

She giggled. "Stop, Tink, 'fore I burn myself with this hot grease."

"Whut else you got cookin', ma?" he asked, stepping back so she could move freely at the stove.

"Hmm...macaroni and cheese, butter rolls and some potato pie...and yes, some cherry Kool-Aid that our son made." As soon as she spoke about their two-year-old son he came running into the kitchen, wrapping his arms around Tink's legs. As the three had a family moment in the kitchen, Polo was slumped on the beige sofa rubbing his temples. Trina yelled from the kitchen, asking if he was staying to eat. He answered yes as he chewed unconsciously on his toothpick out of habit. Polo was tired of being "dat nigga." He knew his luck wouldn't last long in the drug game. His hustle was strictly weed and he was content with it. He had a fly whip on twenty-twos with Lamborghini-style doors but he was far from, as they say, baller status. He had been harshly reminded at a car show in Greensboro when the author/entrepreneur Jaeyel Imes pulled up in an artic silver Porche Carrera GT. Polo was ready for a change. This gun charge was bullshit!

"I'ma get a job," Polo said to Tink as he entered the living room with his son, Cameron, on his back.

"A job!" Tink lowered his son to the floor, then sat next to his cousin. "Oh." He smiled, rubbing his hands together. "You gotta lick set up? Who you got in mind?"

Polo frowned, sucking his teeth. "I'm dead-ass, nigga! I'ma get a real job...legal."

"Why the change of heart?" Tink asked. He then told Cameron to go put his shoes on. Cameron skipped away while singing 50 Cent's "Window Shopper."

"Reason one." Polo held up his index finger. "Ain't tryna go back to prison for a muhfuckin' thang. I think I can beat this case. And if I do, I'm done with this street shit."

Tink could tell by the tone of his cousin's voice that he was dead-ass. "Where you gonna get a good job at?"

Polo shrugged his shoulders. "Shit, I'll work at Burger King before I risk my freedom again. I got a few grand in the stash and I'ma throw in the towel before I slip up."

Tink started grinning. "Let me find out you think dem alphabet boys got you under surveillance," he joked.

"Nah, I don't rate that. That's for that lame-ass nigga Kaseem and his team of yes-men," Polo stated sourly.

Tink was in a different situation from Polo. Tink had a family to feed while Polo's main concern was paying off his new whip. Tink sold weed for Polo on the side and also did his thing selling that hard. Nothing major, though, he only sold pieces on the block. If Polo stopped the weed, then Tink knew he would be in a bind. Maybe he could hook up with that jackmaster Lil' Rick and stick up some niggas that's already on.

"So what's up?" Polo asked, breaking Tink's train of thought. Tink shrugged his shoulders just as his son came skipping up the hall.

"Food's ready, y'all!" Trina yelled from the kitchen.

Polo removed his G-Unit leather jacket, then followed

Tink toward the kitchen, but both were turned around when Trina ordered them both to go wash their hands. It was clear that Trina was running thangs and Tink could care less because it was all love.

Later, around 3:45 p.m., Polo was leaving Trina's crib with Cameron to take him to spend the night with Trina's parents in Selma.

"Turn it up, Uncle Polo, please!" Cameron squealed as Polo shook his head, smiling. He loved Cameron like crazy.

"Aiight, but not too loud this time." Polo adjusted the volume with the controls, then filled the Dodge Charger with Common's "Testify."

At the same time, Desiree was in her office working on her laptop while talking to Jelena. Jelena's high-pitched voice filled her office as it flowed from the landline speakerphone.

"I just can't date no man with no felonies, girl, and I'm being honest with you," Desiree said, even though she was slightly attracted to Tyrone aka Polo. But that was something she wouldn't even confess to her best friend. Plus she was committed to Lamar and her stance was firm, she would not date a man who ran the streets.

Jelena laughed. "Well, you just as well put that label over seventy-five percent of the brothers in the US."

"I think that percentage would be higher and it don't matter."

"Why?" Jelena wanted to know.

"Hellooo, I gots me a man. A legal man at that," Desiree bragged.

"Yeah, whateva. Look, what's that author's website you wanted me to check out?"

"www.VictorLMartin.com," Desiree rattled off in excitement.

"Okay, I got it. Well, let me go make my rounds, I'll see ya tonight."

"See you the same," Desiree said before pushing the END button on the speakerphone. Just as she glanced out the side window she saw an eye-catching metallic black BMW 760Li with black rims backing into a slot beside her pearl-white Nissan Maxima. A smile quickly formed on her beautiful face as a chill ran up and down her spine. She was so wide open over her older man that she was close to speaking on that L word. Love! She had met the thirty-seven-year-old Blair Underwood look-alike at Club Black Tie four months ago. His name was Lamar Seagal and to Desiree he was the perfect man for her. Shutting her laptop off she became excited about what she was about to do. She was in the office building alone with all the lawyers out attending a conference. Really it was something that Jelena had placed into her head...office sex!

Her panties were slightly damp when Lamar entered her office with two dozen red roses. She was speechless as he walked toward her in a pair of brown leather pants by Gucci. His pullover was thick and also by Gucci, just like his loafers. When she started to thank him, he held his index finger to his lips, signaling for silence. After placing the roses on her desk, he moved his six-three frame behind her. Her hazel eyes glazed over as he moved his large hands down and over her soft breasts. He massaged them slowly through her clothes. She couldn't wait for him to strip her of her clothing. When his hands pulled away she started to complain but again he silenced her. Catching her off guard he tied a black silk scarf over her eyes. This was something new to her and it turned her on. He then stood her up on shaky legs. Slowly he undressed her. First he removed her heels, her pants, her stockings, her jacket, her blouse, and then her bra. He then helped her slip her beautiful feet back into her heels. He stepped back to admire her precious body. Topless and standing in a pair of heels. He smiled at the wet spot that stained her peach panties. Desiree stood blinded near her desk as Lamar removed his clothes. He stripped buck naked down to his silk socks. Desiree moaned out his name when she felt his tongue circling her erect nipple while he slid a hand under her panties. She was slick and hot.

"Lamar!" she shivered as she parted her legs. "Ooooooooohhh, Lamar." She gripped his shoulders as he slid his beefy middle finger into her moist pussy with her left titty filling his mouth. He was really working her pussy with his finger. She gave him all the access she could give by hiking her leg up his naked waist. The smell of her enticed pussy suddenly filled her office, mixed with the smell of the two dozen roses.

When he slid her panties down her legs she tried to

remove the blindfold but Lamar pushed her hands away. Instead, he guided her small hands to his engorged dick. She wrapped her hands around it, then moved her hands back and forth. When he laid his hands on her shoulders, she took the hint and went to her knees, licking him on the trip down.

"Ooooooooooohhhh, Desi!" he moaned as she slowly licked around the head of his dick. He looked down to see his pre-cum seeping into her mouth. She ran her tongue around his head while gripping his shaft with one hand and palming his ass with the other. Back and forth she began to slowly suck his dick as he palmed the back of her head.

"Suck it, Desi," he panted as she continued to slurp at his dick. "You do it so good, Desi." His words of encouragement spurred her on as her nails dug into the flesh of his ass. It also felt as if her pussy were dripping in the squatting position she was in. Lamar made her head spin when he somehow managed to scoop her up and turn her body upside down. She squealed with excitement as Lamar started tonguing her pussy and ass. He was able to hold her light body with ease as she squirmed and twitched. When the two carefully went to the carpet, Desiree quickly took over and mounted him. Squatting in her heels, she lowered herself on his dick, moaning with pleasure. With her hands planted on his eight-pack stomach she rode him with pure passion. She couldn't recall removing the blindfold but it was now off. Up and down she bounced on his dick, which filled her tight pussy properly. Spasms racked her body as he urged her on by talking nasty to her. She even gave in and slowly spun around to ride him with her back toward him. She later found her legs high up on his sweaty shoulders with his dick plunging in and out causing his balls to slap rhythmically against her ass. Sweat, lust and sex covered them both. His rhythm was set on cruise control, long-dicking her with his piston-like strokes. Desiree arched her back, digging her nails in his back, then felt her pussy explode around his end-lessly plunging dick.

"Lamar, yessss!" she yelled. She shuddered, rolling her hips to his dick as her body gave in. Her thighs were flattening her breasts and Lamar was pumping her steadily. When she felt him release inside her pussy it triggered another orgasm of her own. He slowly lowered his body on top of her after sliding her legs from his shoulders. He kissed her lightly on her sweaty forehead, then moved to her mouth for an open wet kiss.

"I...needed that, Lamar," she said. "I really needed that."

He merely smiled while caressing her naked body with his hands. "You coming to see me tonight?" He lowered his head to lick her right, then left, erect nipple. Desiree nodded yes while enticingly tightening her pussy around his semi-erect dick, which was still inside her. It made him twitch. She kept doing it until he became hard again. Without pulling out he flipped her over and took her doggy-style, ass up, face down, while gripping her small waist. His favorite position.

*   *   *

"Tink, Tink, Tink!" Trina panted while riding Tink. "I'ma cumming, baby!" Up and down, side to side, she moved her body over Tink's.

Tink was under her with his hands palming her small 34Cs as she reached her climax. Since they were struggling as it was to make ends meet, they were having safe sex. When she climaxed, she slid up off his hard dick, then moved up to his face for him to lick her out. Tink was more than happy to please his girl. Seeing that he was still hard, she spun around, rolled the rubber off, then pleased him via oral sex until he erupted inside her mouth. Later, after she took a quick shower, she came back into their bedroom to find Tink holding up his white hoodie, which Cameron had spilled some Kool-Aid on.

"I told you to put that in some cold water so that stain won't be so hard to remove," she said, putting on some deodorant.

Tink laid it on the bed, then stepped to the closet. Inside he saw the two new Sean John solid-color hoodies that Trina had bought at the Crabtree Valley Mall. One was blue and one was Syracuse orange. He knew he was gonna hit the block tonight so he went for the blue hoodie. He figured it was the closest he could get to black.

"You're not planning on hitting the block tonight, are you?" Trina asked as she snapped on her bra. As Tink removed the blue hoodie from the closet she took his white one and placed it in the bathroom sink, then plugged the sink to fill it with cold water. "You hear me talking to you, Tink?"

"Yeah, I heard ya," he replied, pulling the tag from the brand-new hoodie.

"You know how I feel about you doing that, Tink. I really think you should follow Polo's move and—"

"I'm not a follower!" he stated, cutting her off.

"Tink!" Trina explained. "You know I don't mean it like that, baby. But Polo made some good points and you know it."

Tink turned his back on Trina as he pulled the hoodie over his head. Trina sat on the edge of the bed and watched him. "I don't want you out there in those streets no more, Tink," she said softly.

"WHUT THE FUCK!" He spun around. "You want a nigga workin' at a fast-food joint flippin' burgers or sumthin'? Dat shit is lame as fuck!"

"No it ain't!" Trina stated, coming to her feet. "What's lame to me is coming to visit the man I love in prison for being hardheaded!"

"Ain't goin' to no prison," he said, throwing up his arms.

"Oh, it's legal to slang now?" she said sarcastically with a light roll of her neck. Tink blew hard through his nose while rubbing his face. When he dropped his hands he looked at Trina and saw her eyes were close to tears. He motioned her toward him but she shook her head from side to side.

"C'mere, girl."

"No...I'm pissed at you right now," she snapped.

Tink gave in and walked the few steps toward her. "You really love me?"

She rolled her eyes. "No, I just clean up after your funky behind like every day, plus I make sure the sex is on point. I take care of our son and I've been faithful to you since day one...do I need to add more? I can't believe you asked such a stupid-ass question!" She tried to hold it back, but a small grin formed on her face. Tink did the same.

"Look, baby, I'm sorry I bassed on you." He placed his hands on her waist. "You forgive a nigga?"

She shrugged her shoulders, then folded her arms under her breasts.

"I'ma sell these last five grams, then I'm done."

"Don't be telling me no lie, Tink."

"I'm dead-ass."

"For real?"

"Yeah. I figure I can get a job since I don't have any felonies...and you better not leave me for no baller," he joked while rubbing her panty-covered ass. She giggled and punched him playfully in his chest.

"What time will you be in?" she asked, wrapping her arms around his neck.

"As soon as I'm done."

"And don't re-up neither."

"Dat's a promise. Afta tonight I'm doin' it strictly legal."

"I'll wait up for you. I just got *A Hustler's Wife* by Nikki Turner so that'll keep me up." She glanced over his shoulder at the digital clock by the dresser. She knew it would be hours before nightfall and Tink wouldn't leave until then. Being in such a happy mood, she lowered his ear to her lips and whispered provocatively. Since she was already in her panties and bra she stripped naked with ease. Trina was gonna have raw sex with the nigga she loved but he had to pull out before he came...she hoped he could.

When nightfall fell drearily over Raleigh, North Carolina, Lil' Rick was pulling his solid-colored black hoodie over his head. He watched from the cut as his mark led two chicks toward a room at the Red Roof Inn. The two chicks were both white girls, college students, Lil' Rick figured, from their NCSU sweatshirts. He had watched the three from the second they pulled up in a black BMW 545i with black rims. Lil' Rick shivered when a cool gust of wind blew in his face. He waited a good twenty minutes, then removed a black .38 from his pocket and moved toward the room.

Datwon, the driver of the BMW, was breathing heavily as one of the white girls vigorously sucked his dick. Behind her was her friend, pumping away wildly with a black studded seven-and-a-half-inch strap-on dildo. The three had been using meth since they entered the room. The last time Datwon had tricked with meth he had stayed awake for four days straight! Even as the red-headed girl sucked him off, he had a glass pipe near the bed ready to smoke more meth. Around his nose were traces of meth that he had snorted off the two girls' naked bodies. The girl sucking him licked his shaft up and down while massaging his balls while her friend continued to fuck her from the back. He closed his eyes when he felt himself close to cumming but his concentration was broken when someone started banging on the door. His eyes shot open as the two freaks froze. His heart hammered in his chest: if it was the D's, then he was fucked. Not only from the meth in the room, but in the trunk of his BMW were two and a half keys of raw meth. Pushing the girl from his dick he rolled butt naked out of the bed. His hyperactive mood caused him to rush boldly toward the door.

"W-who is it?!"

"Me, nigga!" Lil' Rick said. "Hurry up, po-po was checkin' out your whip and—" He was cut off as Datwon unlocked the door and yanked him in. Lil' Rick was his nigga so it was all good. But before he could ask Lil' Rick about the police he was surprised with Lil' Rick's .38 pointed at his head. Datwon looked at Lil' Rick, then laughed. The meth running through his blood made him feel unconquerable. Lil' Rick smiled as he peeped the keys to the BMW over near the bed.

"Here's the joke, nigga." Lil' Rick lowered the .38 to Datwon's stomach just as Datwon tried to rush him. The two claps from the .38 were muffled because the barrel was pressed into Datwon's belly. As Datwon crumpled to the floor, Lil' Rick moved quickly toward the car keys with the .38 pointed at the two white girls, who hadn't made a sound. Lil' Rick wasn't planning on being caught for murdering Datwon, but if he were, it would be a black-on-black crime and drug-related. Hell, the max he would get…under seven years with a good lawyer.

But if he killed the two white girls...he'd never see the streets again. Picking up the keys he also found the two girls' college IDs. He quickly asked who had rented the room. They both pointed to Datwon.

"I suggest y'all bounce and forget about all this 'cause I'm sure y'all mommy and daddy won't be pleased to know y'all getting high and trickin', and if you do talk to the police..." He held up their IDs as he backed toward the door. Once he made it outside he paused, then walked quickly toward the BMW. A few seconds later he pulled off with the lights off and got missing.

An odd feeling came over Trina as Tink headed outside. The time was what made her feel funny about tonight. Six-forty-six p.m. She stood looking out the window as he walked away. His blue hoodie looked black. She watched him until he walked from her view. "Be careful, baby," she said softly to ease her mind and heart. Leaving the window she went to watch some TV to bring some sounds into the silent apartment. A smile formed on her face at the clumsiness of Tink's actions during their round of raw sex. By "mistake" he claimed he was unable to pull out...the three different times he had cum inside her.

"So did you do the nasty with Lamar?" Jelena asked Desiree.

Desiree glared over her shoulder by looking in the mirror above her dresser. "Like I'ma tell you my business," Desiree replied.

"I told you about the ménage that I did with Samuel and Ron, didn't I?" Jelena said, folding her arms as she sat on the edge of Desiree's bed.

"Yeah, you did, Ms. Freak of the Week. But you also volunteered that bit of sexual info," Desiree said.

Jelena smacked her balm-covered lips as Desiree stepped back from the mirror to check out her outfit. Jelena had to give her girl some points on how she was rocking a pair of Seven jeans and a cashmere sweater. On her feet were a pair of Giuseppe Zanotti–designed ankle-high stiletto boots. Her silky hair was hooked up in a French roll that showed off her sexy neck.

"Vera Wang or Euphoria?" Desiree asked, seeking Jelena's choice of which scent she should wear.

"Vera Wang," Jelena said.

"Euphoria it is," Desiree replied and Jelena rolled her green eyes.

"You gonna spend the night with Lamar?"

"I might," Desiree replied as she sprayed the scent on. "Why, what's up?"

"Just asking," Jelena replied as she shrugged her shoulders. "Being nosy. You know me."

Desiree was about to put on her earrings when her $5,700 Vertu Ascent pink cell phone started to chime. It was the first gift that Lamar had given her...before they even had sex. When Jelena saw how Desiree started to blush and giggle, she quietly got up and left Desiree's bedroom to give her some privacy with her call.

"How is the lady of my life doing?" Lamar's voice melted Desiree in her boots.

"Fine," she replied, looking at herself in the mirror. She was proud of what she saw. Mainly she was concerned about how Lamar viewed her. At times she was a little self-conscious about her small frame. She was not stacked like Jelena, who could easily give the video goddess Buffie the Body a run in the "make a nigga drool" department. In time, she had learned to accept her small frame and love herself.

"Are we still set for tonight?" Lamar asked her.

"I wouldn't miss it for nothing, Lamar."

"That's what I need to hear. By the way, what time do you have?"

Desiree turned up her wrist to glance at her gold DKNY watch. "Six minutes to seven."

"And I'll see you at—"

"Eight sharp," she said, cutting him off with a smile. "Oh, and Lamar..."

"Yes, baby?"

"How about I spend the night?" she asked in a sexy tone.

"That sounds deeply enticing. But I doubt you'll get any rest."

"I'd be let down if I did," she purred.

"So it's like that?"

"Any way you want it, Lamar," she confessed. "You know how I feel about you, baby."

"I would be a fool if I didn't."

Desiree knew in her heart that Lamar was the perfect man for her and it showed all over her beautiful face. They talked a few more minutes before hanging up.

Leaving her bedroom, she headed to see what Jelena was up to. As always, she was in her bedroom sitting in front of her Dell computer surfing the Web. In the background Jelena had Keyshia Cole's "I Should Have Cheated" pumping from her CD player.

"Damn!" Jelena exclaimed. "He's engaged."

"Who?" Desiree asked, standing over her shoulder.

"Victor, he's engaged to some lucky girl...hell, I can't pronounce her name."

"It's QuoVadis," Desiree said. "Click Photos and you'll see a picture of them together."

The two started joking back and forth about Jelena's fantasy to date a famous black author as the night moved on. Desiree made sure to stay up on the time because she would not be late for her visit with Lamar.

Lamar sat in his huge den in front of the roaring fireplace sipping a glass of Johnnie Walker Red Label on the rocks. After satisfying his thirst he placed the empty glass on a coaster, then picked up a remote. With a touch of a button a retractable motorized screen unrolled behind him just as the Panasonic HD home theater projector filled the screen with the sex act that he had filmed with Desiree. He had hidden a camera to record everything when he tied the blindfold over her eyes. Slowly he spun his camel contoured chair around to face the screen. He smiled at his devious act. Of course he had asked to film their sex act once before but she was strictly against it. Well, what she didn't know wouldn't hurt her. He watched with pride as Desiree took his dick into her mouth. Tonight he was ready to film her once again once they got behind closed doors. As he watched the screen, he couldn't help but wonder how sex would be with Jelena. At times he had wished that it had been Jelena and her juicy body that he had met at the club instead of Desiree...hell, he couldn't help it that he liked his women thick. But somehow Desiree had grown on him. He grabbed his throbbing erection through his slacks as he watched Desiree's sweet lips glide back and forth over his spit-shined dick. He couldn't wait for eight p.m., which was now forty minutes away. Just as the scene showed Desiree flicking her wet tongue over his balls, his Motorola headset started to chime. Without removing his eyes from the screen he reached over to pick up the headset and place it on his head. Sliding the mic toward his lips, he answered the call.

"Speak."

"We have a big problem," the male voice calmly replied.

"What kind of problem?"

Lamar listenened closely as his right-hand man told him what the problem was. His mood went from aroused to pissed.

"WHO THE FUCK TESTIN' MY GANGSTA!" Lamar roared as he shot to his feet with his hand in a tight fist.

"Lil' Rick."

"Lil' Rick, Lil' Rick." Lamar repeated the name, hoping to trigger when and where he had heard it.

"Datwon had him pushing for him over near Shaw."

"How is Datwon?" Lamar asked as he tried to level his temper off and think clearly.

"He'll make it. The two tricks he was with called me first instead of the police. Like I said, I then called Dr. Evans and he patched Datwon up as best as he could. Datwon's girl is with him at Evans's private office."

"I want this Lil' Rick nigga dead before the sun comes up!" Lamar ordered.

"I already put the wheels in motion."

"Good...look, meet me at Evans's office."

"Now?"

"Yes. I'm on my way now. I can't let niggas take me nor no one on my team for being soft!" Lamar stated. With his temper on the edge he yanked the headset off, then flicked the sex scene off. Five minutes later he was pulling out of his driveway in his black BMW 760Li.

"Remember, if you see Lil' Rick, call me as soon as possible and don't say shit to 'im," said Lamar's right-hand man, Mance. Mance sat behind the wheel of his quiet-running black BMW M5 with black twenty-two-inch Zenetti Blade rims. Sitting next to him was a cute but deadly-looking Teairra Mari look-alike keeping an eye out for the D's. The street hustler nodded his head at Mance, then gave him some dap. And just to make it stick in the hustler's mind, Mance nodded at the girl next to him, who reached into the open glove compartment to pull out four grams of coke. She reached over Mance and dropped the work in the hustler's hand.

"You find Lil' Rick for me and that's yours, plus a grand when I see you again."

"No doubt, dawg," the hustler replied. He knew he could sell the work and get four hundred and if he came across Lil' Rick...shit, he would have enough to cop some weight. As Mance sped off, the hustler pulled the fur-lined hood of his Rocawear houndstooth jacket over his dreads and went walking up the block. He placed the four grams in his front left jacket pocket, then reached into the right to feel the rubber grip of his nine-millimeter.

"Please, Tink," the crackhead by the name of Tanisha begged. "Why we cain't work out the deal like we always do? You know I'ma swallow."

"Cain't do it dis round, Nisha. Cain't take no shorts tonight," Tink said, squinting from the burning kerosene heater in the far corner. He knew Trina would be pissed when she smelled kerosene in his gear. Only two grams to sell and he could go the fuck home.

"Just this last time, Tink. I swear 'fore God I'ma come correct next time." She had the nerve to drop to her knees with her hands clasped together.

"Ain't no next time," Tink replied. "And get the fuck up."

"Please," she pleaded, remaining on her knees.

"No!"

"Please."

"No!"

"Please."

"Hell no, Nisha!" Tink said, standing up to peek out

of her front window. "I just gave you some shake a few minutes ago. Whatcha do? Eat tha shit like candy or something?" he said, about to laugh.

"Ha, ha, very funny!" Tanisha replied, sticking up her slender middle finger behind his back. She came to her feet, mumbling under her funky breath. Tink turned from the window to see Tanisha flopping down onto her flower-printed sofa. She rolled her eyes at Tink as he smiled at her.

"What time your friend across the skreet get off?"

Tanisha pursed her lips, shrugging her shoulders.

"You need to stop trippin'," Tink stated as he pulled out a Snickers candy bar from his huge front right pocket. Catching the pissed-off Tanisha off guard, he tossed her a nice-sized ten piece of hard. "Think fast!"

He may have thought he had caught her off guard but was proven wrong as she caught the crack in mid-air. Her face was instantly changed to "gonna get high soon" as she examined the crack.

"Thanks, Tink!" She rose to her feet. "You want me to suck your dick now or can I hit this first?" The way she asked with no touch of shame you would have figured it was an everyday thang for her...and sadly...it was.

"Nah, I'm good." He waved her off. "But don't ask fo' shit else!" Again she gave him the finger, then turned to head for her bedroom. She knew that he didn't like for her to get high where he could smell it.

"I got dem thangs!" Bizzy boasted as he hit the block. He walked up on the group of hustlers drinking Colt

45s, sitting on the hood of the dark green '84 Chevy Caprice Classic. Bizzy gave up some dap to everyone as he kept an eye out for Lil' Rick. Bizzy sold two grams for a hundred dollars, then asked how the block was tonight. It was colder than a muhfucker, but the money was coming nonstop. That also meant the jack boys were roaming, so Bizzy made sure to keep his hands in his pockets. Not only to keep them warm, but to keep that hammer in his grip.

When it neared ten minutes to eight, Bizzy felt the urge to seek some warmth and maybe some head. Tanisha popped into his mind. For a phat twenty piece he could get some pussy.

"Yo, I'll holla at y'all niggas later." And with his exit, he headed down the block in his tan Timbs toward Tanisha's crib. Minutes later he was rounding the corner and about to cross the street to Tanisha's crib when he saw a figure coming down her steps. Bizzy froze, then backed up. It was Lil' Rick. Bizzy had mistaken Tink's blue hoodie for black and since Tink shared Lil' Rick's frame...Bizzy was fooled. Bizzy knew that Lil' Rick was known to pay Tanisha a creep visit every now and then. Bizzy reached fast as he pulled out his cell phone to call Mance.

"Yeah?" Mance answered on the third ring.

"I see your man."

"Who? Lil' Rick!"

"Yeah. He walkin' up the street right now."

"He seen you?"

"Nah."

"Can you follow him without being seen?"

"Hold up, dawg. That ain't part of the deal."

"It is if I add another grand."

"Bullshit."

"Ain't no time for games, Bizzy. Will you do this or not?" Bizzy shifted his stance as he watched an easy two grand walking in the opposite direction. As the chilly wind bit into his exposed hand he made up his mind and told Mance he would do it.

"Shit!" Mance cursed as he walked up to Lamar aka Kaseem.

Kaseem stood up with his face still filled with anger. Yes, he lived a double life, a life of the street that Desiree didn't know about. "What's up?"

"That was Bizzy; he's trailing Lil' Rick over by Shaw."

"Well what the fuck we still sitting in this office for? I meant what I said so let's do this."

"I know, I know," Mance said. "But...I don't have my piece. All I got is the pump in my trunk."

Kaseem shrugged his shoulders. "Get it and let's go."

The two had already discussed that Lil' Rick would be made an example of. Kaseem could take the last of the meth that Datwon had been jacked for. Mance gave his girl a nervous glance as he popped the trunk to his BMW M5.

"Just take the car and go to Kaseem's crib," Mance whispered. She kissed him on the lips, then followed his request.

Kaseem pulled off seconds later in his black BMW

760Li, with Mance beside him with a twelve-gauge pump between his legs.

A puzzled look appeared on Desiree's face as she pulled up to Lamar's driveway. By now she was accustomed to his greeting her at either the door or his driveway, but tonight she was met with silence. She pulled up to his closed two-car garage, then switched her ride off. Figuring that he would come bounding from his crib, she took the spare second to primp in the vanity mirror. As two minutes went by and there was no sign of Lamar she started smiling. He was up to one of his games, she thought. Zipping up her leather coat she grabbed her purse and made her exit.

Lamar slowed his BMW 760Li at the red light when his car phone started to chime. With a simple push of a button mounted on the steering wheel he switched on the hands-free phone.

"Yeah!"

"Um…Lamar." Desiree's soft voice filled the BMW. "I know I'm not standing on your front step and you're not home? Please explain? It's eight-oh-five, Lamar." Lamar slapped his forehead with the palm of his hand. With the bullshit now at hand he had allowed Desiree to slip his mind. Thinking quickly, he told her the truth with a bit of lies. He told her a friend had been in an accident, car accident to be exact. He promised he would be home by nine. He then gave her the code to enter his crib. He told her to make herself at home and he promised to make it up to her.

"Damn!" he muttered when she hung up. "Forgot all about that bitch." When the light turned green he glanced over at Mance, who was back on the celly with Bizzy.

Desiree felt a bit awkward as she entered Lamar's crib. It was odd to be in his crib with him not there. She removed her leather jacket when she entered the den since the fireplace was roaring. She looked around and noticed that his place was cleaner than hers. Dropping her purse beside the loveseat she flopped down, then wondered if Lamar was up to something kinky. She loved how he was full of surprises. Tonight she wanted to have "the talk" with him. Heck, she figured he too was ready to take their relationship to the next level, and in her mind she couldn't find one reason not to. Relaxing back into the comfort of the soft leather loveseat she closed her eyes. She started grinning. A kinky thought of waiting for Lamar in the nude crossed her mind. Keeping it real with herself, she allowed her mind to drift to Tyrone. Him and his silly name, Polo. As quickly as he popped into her mind, he was pushed out as she replaced him with Lamar. Minutes later she became bored and thirsty. To take care of the latter she got up and headed into his sunken kitchen. In her search of his refrigerator she found a carton of pine-apple juice. When she was about to refill her glass again she heard someone coming through the front door. Walking quietly back into the den, she was surprised to find Mance's girl, Nikki. Nikki had received a call from Mance just a few minutes ago so she went along with the lie about one of Lamar's friends having a car accident. Nikki and Desiree got along fine since the two had been out on double dates a few times with Mance and Lamar. Nikki at times felt sorry for Desiree about her not knowing about Lamar's secret life. It just goes to show, don't believe everything you see.

"Turn some music on or something on up in here, girl," Nikki said. "And I know Lamar got something to drink."

"You handle the entertainment and I'll get us something to sip on," Desiree said. She figured she could hook something up with the Rémy Red Strawberry Kiwi Infusion that she had seen in the refrigerator. When she later took the two mixed drinks back into the den she found Nikki with the remote in her hand. They both sipped lightly at their drinks as the retractable motorized screen unrolled. Nikki loved to watch movies and she knew Lamar kept something worth watching in his movie section. When she pressed the PLAY button the screen filled with a graphic scene of Desiree riding Lamar. Desiree's mixed drink nearly came out of her nose as she choked up.

Tink, as usual, was walking with his head down. He was staying to his word and calling it a wrap after selling all his work. His girl was right, selling dope wasn't the positive move. Sure it paid the bills, but the risks weren't worth it. Yeah, Young Jeezy rapped about selling the snow, but that's all he did. Tink would rather say "Welcome to Burger King" than bend over for a jackleg corrections officer to conduct a body cavity search. Just as he strolled under a busted streetlight he heard a car creeping up behind him. He shot a quick glance over his shoulder, expecting it to be the D's. The sight registered quickly. A black car with its lights out and someone leaning out the window holding a pump. He bolted toward the grassy vacant lot to his right.

"Shoot 'im! Shoot 'im! Shoot 'im!" Lamar shouted at Mance. Mance licked his dry lips, aimed, then eased back on the trigger. BOOM! The loud report from the pump rang in Mance's ear as he watched his target stumble in the knee-high grass about twenty-five yards away. Mance aimed once more, then fired. BOOM! The target went down.

"GET THE SHELLS! GET THE SHELLS!" Lamar shouted.

"Huh?" Mance said, sliding back into his seat. Lamar shouted again for Mance to get the two shells that he had ejected from the pump. Luckily, he found them near the right rear tire. The second Mance was back inside, Lamar sped away with the lights off.

Tanisha just happened to be running up the block to catch Tink because he had left his cell phone by mistake. If it had been any other hustler she would have sold it the first chance she had. But Tink was cool. She was about a hundred yards away and seconds from yelling out Tink's name just as the black BMW rounded the corner. She saw it. She saw Tink take off running through the field and saw the muzzle flash twice from the loud pump. She didn't yell or scream. She just picked up her pace as the BMW sped off. Out of nowhere someone ran into her, knocking her flat on her ass. She was able to see Bizzy's face as he hauled ass in the opposite direction. It was obvious that he had done something wrong. Dismissing Bizzy, Tanisha rose to her feet and prayed that Tink was okay.

Moments later Polo was pulling into Washington Terrace Projects bumping Boyz n da Hood's "Dem Boyz." Just as he pulled into a parking spot Trina came flying from her apartment. She was hysterical when she ran into Polo's arms.

"MY BABY DEAD! MY BABY DEAD!" she sobbed.

Polo didn't know what the fuck was up. At first he thought she meant her son.

"Noooooo...Tink!"

Polo calmed her down and tried his best to get some sensible info from her. Once he did, he led her to the passenger seat, then ran back to the driver's side, got in and sped off. He couldn't believe what he had heard. Not Tink, hell fuck no, not his family.

Nikki knew the shit was about to hit the fan as Lamar pulled into his driveway. Desiree had refused to let her call Mance. In truth, Nikki wanted to see what Lamar would do. She wasn't feeling how he had secretly taped the sex act. But more personally, she knew there was a tape of her also. She had been fucking Lamar on the low for over a year and a half. She would never forget the night Lamar aka Kaseem had blindfolded her in his bedroom. That shit made her mad but the look on Desiree's face was . . . let's just say that it wasn't pretty.

Lamar entered his den with Mance behind him. Lamar glanced at his Rolex as he walked toward Desiree. Eight-fifty-three p.m. He was about to apologize for the inconvenience and hug her but Desiree snapped and slapped the blackness out of him.

"You grimy son of a bitch!" Desiree vented.

Lamar rubbed his stinging left cheek as he told Mance and Nikki to excuse themselves. If he had looked at Nikki he would have seen her grinning. Lamar had no idea why Desiree was tripping, but he sure as hell planned to find the fuck out. When he was alone with her he again stepped toward her but she took a step back.

"Don't even think about touching me!"

He froze, holding his hands. "Okay, let's talk, Desiree. Explain to me why I'm getting disrespected in my own house?"

"You got the audacity to even let the word 'respect' roll out of your mouth! You fucking bastard."

"What is this about, Desiree?" he said. "This can't be because I'm late."

"Nigga, you taped me having sex with you!" she shouted.

Lamar's mouth fell open. Damn, he remembered leaving the disc in the projector.

"How many other times have you done this, Lamar?!"

He started to rub his temples again. This wasn't a good night at all.

"I asked you a damn question, Lamar!"

"Baby, look, I…"

"Don't call me that! FUCK YOU!" she shouted. She picked up her jacket and purse. When she attempted to walk past him, he reached for her arm but she jerked away.

"Desiree, let's talk about this, okay?" he pleaded with her as she stormed toward the front door. "It's not what you think. I…I wanted to surprise you."

She stopped in her tracks and spun around with nothing but pure hate masking her face. "A surprise? Well I got one for you because I'm pressing charges!"

It was then that he realized that she had the disc. He thought about it. She would look trashy if anyone viewed the disc. He could say it was her idea but later she caught a scorned heart after she found him with another woman. He could make up that lie with ease. Hell, if she did press charges, he could even have another woman over when the police came to speak with him. The more he thought about it the less he cared. With a grin he pointed toward the door. "Leave." Desiree bit her last words off as she spun around and left. Everything she felt for Lamar was dead. Her tears didn't fall until she was backing out of his driveway.

*   *   *

The second Tanisha had gotten off the phone with Trina she had dialed 911. The block was now lit up with an ambulance and a half dozen police cars. Polo sat on the hood of his Dodge Charger as he watched a police officer help Trina into the back of the ambulance. He could also see the plainclothes detective asking the crowd for any tips but no one knew anything. Polo stood up as Tanisha made her way across the street. He motioned for her to get inside his car. He saw how she was shivering so he turned his car on to produce some heat.

"Thanks, Polo," she said. "How is Trina?"

"Stressed the fuck out and mad," he said wearily.

"I don't blame her. I know she love her some Tink."

"So what you got to tell me?"

Tanisha relaxed as the heat warmed her body. "I think one of Kaseem's boys did it. You know, all dem black BMWs look the same to me."

"Are you sure?" He sat up in his seat. She had his full interest now.

"Yeah. It had those black rims too. This one was a four-door. And Bizzy..."

"What about him?"

Tanisha told him she had run into Bizzy after the drive-by. Polo balled up his fists as his mind was filled with payback. He knew about Kaseem and how everyone on his team drove a BMW. All were black with black rims but no two drove the same model.

"Is Tink gonna be okay?" Tanisha asked as the ambulance slowly pulled away.

"Yeah. But he'll be off his feet for a minute. I heard one of those paramedics saying Tink was lucky because he was hit with birdshot and not slugs."

"I just saw all that blood on his back and plus he wasn't moving."

Tink was indeed lucky. But tonight would be a painful night with over thirty rounds of birdshot burning his back, his ass and the backs of his thighs. If the shots had been an inch or two higher he would have been hit in the back of his neck. Polo watched the crowd wander off as the ambulance rolled off. He then asked Tanisha if she had mentioned anything to anyone else.

"Nope. And you know I ain't talking to no police." She then asked him if he could take her to her cousin's crib across town.

"Mance," Lamar said, waving him to the den.

"What was all that about?" Mance asked. "Having girl problems?"

"Some bullshit," Lamar replied. "Look, Datwon's girl just called. I need you to go pick her up and run her home and back to the doctor's office. And while you're out, get rid of the pump." He gave Mance the keys to his BMW. "Leave Nikki here. It's better that this stays between us. I know you haven't told her nothing."

"No, but..."

"No buts, Mance. I know we can trust her, but roll with me on this one."

Mance nodded his head, took the keys, then headed

for the front door. As soon as Mance backed out of the driveway Lamar had his arms around Nikki's small waist. They kissed deeply as he backed her toward the sofa. When he laid her down she parted her legs.

"Wait," she said, pulling from his kiss.

"What?"

"You know what!" she said. "Don't lie to me...but I know you've been taping us fucking."

"Yeah...so what?"

She pushed him up off of her. "Why, Lamar? What if Mance sees one of them? All you had to do was ask me...but all this secret shit ain't cool." She frowned.

"Oh, so now you mad at me?" He sneered.

"No." She folded her arms. "My nose ain't stuck up like Desiree's." She smiled.

Lamar took her in his arms once more, softly nibbling at her neck. She gave in as she wrapped her arms around his neck. Within minutes he had her back on the sofa with her sweater lifted up and her bra unfastened. She palmed the back of his head as he sucked the erect nipple of her left breast. He was careful not to leave any passion marks. She laid her head back, closing her eyes when she felt her jeans being unzipped. Goose bumps formed all over her butt as Lamar tugged her jeans and her panties off. He was so keyed up that he had his dick out once Nikki freed one leg from her jeans. His pants were around his ankles when he moved his dick up and down the length of her pussy before he shoved himself inside her. Nikki dug her nails in his shoulders as he started penetrating her. They fucked hard and fast. Her one exposed breast jiggled erotically as Lamar rammed his dick in and out of her moist tight pussy.

"Ooooooooohhhh, Lamar." She panicked. "Don't stop, don't stop, oh, ohhhhh yes!" Lamar lifted her left leg on his shoulder and drove deeper inside her. Two minutes later he released inside her while calling out her name. Just as quickly as they had started, the two got dressed, then started kissing once more. Nikki knew she was wrong to be cheating on Mance, but it was so easy...so she did it. Mance saw Lamar like a brother, and he was blind to the way she acted around Lamar. She didn't have any feelings for Lamar...she just liked to fuck and that was that. Their kissing caused another erection, so she unzipped his pants, pulled out his dick, lowered her head and sucked him off with her eye-rolling head game.

Polo sat in his ride a few feet from Bizzy's crib, unsure how to step on Bizzy. What if Tanisha had been wrong and gotten Bizzy mixed up? Bizzy was known to carry his hammer at all times and wasn't afraid to use it. Polo touched the .38 snub-nose that lay in his lap. He wished he had his .45 but the D's had it. Tanisha's warning rang in his head.

Don't you go off doin' nothing crazy and end up in jail.

Polo refused to even think about jail. But damn, he had to do something. A nigga tried to merk his family. He knew Tink would be okay, but he still had to do something. Making up his mind to put the .38 in his pocket, he stepped out into the cold. Just as he was about to close the door, Bizzy snuck up behind him and stuck something hard into the middle of his back.

At the same time, Lil' Rick was in Goldsboro, North Carolina, in a hotel, eating a Pizza Hut pizza and watching TV. Datwon's BMW was at the chop shop being stripped, and the meth would hit the streets tomorrow. When his cell phone rang, he wiped his greasy fingers, then answered the call on the third ring.

"What it do?" he answered.

"Boy, shit is crazy," his cousin Melanie said.

"Whut, Kaseem lookin' for me?" he asked. Not that he really gave a damn.

"Don't know about that. But guess who got shot?"

"Who?"

"Tink."

"Word!" he picked up the remote and pressed the MUTE button.

"Yeah. My girl Lori just told me about it. Said it was a drive-by and that he was hit in his back."

"Is he dead?"

"Don't think so. You know Lori be twisting the facts and shit."

"Yeah, I know."

"So...you still gonna hit me off with some bread?"

"Yeah, and don't worry about me. Just keep your eyes and ears open on Kaseem and his boys."

"I got you. Well, I'll talk to you later, be safe."

Lil' Rick hung up, tossing the flip phone back on the

lumpy pillow. He thought about Tink. *Damn, what did he do to rate a drive-by? Nigga wasn't pushing no weight or nothing.* He bit into his pepperoni pizza and chewed with his mind on Tink. Lil' Rick considered Tink to be his nigga, and he knew how tight Tink and Polo were. He wondered if Polo was out to get some revenge, and if he was, Lil' Rick wanted to help. After his lick on Datwon, he now carried a Glock nine-millimeter... one that he was ready to use. Making up his mind, he turned the TV off, grabbed another slice of pizza, then headed out the door. His ride was a tan Toyota Camry XLE that belonged to one of his cousins who stayed in Goldsboro. Pulling out, he started to dial Polo's cell phone number but changed his mind on the last digit. He would just wait until he reached Raleigh. Drama was definitely in the forecast tonight.

Polo's heart skipped a few beats as Bizzy laughed in his ear and asked for a ride.

"Nigga, you need to be on point in the hood. Especially ridin' 'round in this fly whip."

Polo played along. If Bizzy had had anything to do with Tink being shot he would have made it known. When Polo pulled from the curb with Bizzy in the passenger seat he remained quiet. But not Bizzy.

"Yo, Polo...I gotta tell you somethin' but you gotta keep it on the hush. Can you do that?"

"What's up?"

Bizzy started from the beginning and told Polo how Mance had approached him about Lil' Rick. He explained how he only suspected that Mance wanted to rough Lil' Rick up over some money or some shit. Kaseem and his team had been in Raleigh for two and a half years and had yet to bust any guns. Until tonight.

"You know about Lil' Rick messin' wit my girl so I don't too much care fo' dat nigga and plus he robbed me and Dre last month," Bizzy went on saying. He then explained how he had followed Lil' Rick from Tanisha's crib and up the block until Kaseem and Mance shot him.

"I thought they was gonna scoop Lil' Rick up, yo. Before I could say or do anything, Mance started blastin' on dat nigga, yo. Shiiit, I nearly broke some chick neck when I turned around and haulin' ass, yo. Whut you think I should do? Like I said, I ain't feelin' Lil' Rick, but I wasn't down wit dat drive-by shit." He left out the part about Mance paying him.

"That's it?" Polo asked as he slowed for a red light on Capital Boulevard.

"Yeah. I feel about fucked up over it, yo."

Polo cleared his throat. "Blue ain't black."

"Say whut?"

"I said, blue ain't black."

"You aiight, my nigga?"

"Yeah, I'm straight. But it's you that got your colors mixed up."

"Whut da fuck you talkin' 'bout?"

"That was Tink you was following. Not Lil' Rick. Nigga, you nearly got my cousin killed."

Bizzy rubbed his face and spoke through his hand. "Say word, yo?"

"On er'thang I love, my nigga."

Suddenly, it dawned on Bizzy why Polo had been parked out near his crib. But how in the hell had he known...

"You did some foul shit, Bizzy," Polo said, breaking his thoughts.

"Is...is Tink dead?" Bizzy slowly moved for his hammer but Polo beat him to the draw. Bizzy stiffened in the leather seat as Polo stuck his .38 under his chin.

"I know you wasn't goin' for your heat?"

Bizzy shook his head no. "Nah, dawg...it...it ain't like dat."

Polo lowered his .38. "No, Tink ain't dead. Just gonna be off his feet for a minute."

"Good." Bizzy exhaled. "So...whut you gonna do about Kaseem and Mance?"

Polo shrugged his shoulders, then asked why. Bizzy started grinning and said he better make up his mind soon.

"Why?" Polo asked again.

Bizzy nodded, then pointed across the intersection. "There's Kaseem's Beemer."

Desiree was halfway home when she realized that she had left her cell phone back at Lamar's. She had too much personal info on it for him to have. She was now stepping out of her car in his driveway. She noticed that his 740Li was gone and that was even better. She walked quickly past Mance's BMW and up to the front door.

*   *   *

Lamar wasn't worried about Mance sneaking up on him and Nikki because he had instructed Datwon's girl to call him once Mance had taken her home and back to the doctor's office. From the doctor's office and back, it would take Mance a good twenty minutes. With this in mind, he was back between Nikki's thighs. He had her facedown, ass-up, pumping her steadily in front of his blazing fireplace. Both were butt-ass naked. There was loud moaning, skin slapping, that had caused both of them to ignore the knocks at the front door. Lamar was fucking Nikki like a pro. Her pussy was popping around his plunging dick as he palmed her butt cheeks, lightly spreading them apart.

"Kaseem, Kaseem!" Nikki chanted as she enjoyed his every thrust. Her body was dripping with sweat. She knew she was going to need a shower before Mance came back. She also knew they were taking a big risk of being caught...but, in truth, it turned her on. Looking back over her shoulder she told him to do it hard. He started to lean forward to lick the sweat off her back just when Desiree walked into the den.

Datwon's girl had been back at the doctor's office for over ten to fifteen minutes before she remembered to call Lamar. She punched in his number but hung up on the second ring when Datwon woke up asking for some water. Her mind was on Datwon so once she hung up she had moved to Datwon's side. Really, she didn't see any big deal in calling Lamar anyway.

*　　*　　*

As for Mance, he had made it back to Lamar's in record time. He shook his head when he parked behind Desiree's car. She must not have been too mad, he figured. He locked up Lamar's car, then walked up to the front door. He punched in the code, then stepped inside. The second he closed the door behind him he heard Desiree cursing and yelling. He rolled his eyes and headed for the den. He just wanted to get his girl and leave Lamar's drama-filled crib. But just as he reached the entrance to the den, he froze at the sight before him. Desiree had her finger all up in Lamar's face...who stood butt-ass naked. But what made his heart stop was the sight of his girl. Nikki was behind Lamar, clutching Lamar's shirt over her naked body. He blinked as he put two and two together. Mance rushed into the den, pushed Desiree to the side, then hit Lamar with a two piece. Nikki screamed as Lamar staggered backward before shaking Mance's two blows off. She stepped in between the two but Mance punched her in the face, knocking her flat on her back. Mance reached for Nikki's purse, dumped it, then picked up her .38. Desiree was about to make her exit when Mance fired a shot over her head. She screamed and fell to the floor. Mance backed up until he could cover all three with the .38. Desiree shook with fear. Lamar held up one hand with the other covering his bloody mouth. Nikki was still knocked out.

"This how you gonna fucking do me, Kaseem! Fuck my girl behind my damn back. After all the loyalty I've shown you...huh? Nigga...I killed a nigga tonight for your bitch ass!"

"Mance, listen," Lamar pleaded.

"SHUT THE FUCK UP, NIGGA!" Mance shouted. He looked down at Nikki's nude body. His hate for Kaseem rose as visions of them fucking popped into his head. He gripped the .38 as tears filled his eyes. He thought about how much he had given Nikki during their four-year relationship. How he had never cheated on her, not once.

Silence ruled the den until Nikki slowly regained consciousness. She rolled to her side, then slowly sat up. Her nose was busted. She was fully aware of what had happened. Tears traveled down her face as she looked at Mance. "Baby..." she sobbed. "I'm so sorry, I didn't mean to." Her head snapped back as the bullet from the .38 punched her above her right eye. Her body remained erect before it fell backward. Desiree screamed as her hands covered her mouth. Lamar just shook his head as the blood flowed from Nikki's head wound. Lamar started to plead his case. His angle was that Nikki wasn't any good.

"Yeah, I know," Mance said coldly. He lowered the .38 and saw Lamar release a deep breath. Lamar stood up but noticed the .38 was still aimed at him. Before he realized it, Mance had calmly squeezed off two shots at his groin area. Lamar crumpled, howling in torturous pain as he faced a slow death. Desiree's screams filled Mance's ears. Everything was moving in slow motion for Mance. He got tired of Lamar's moaning so he shot him twice in the face. He then walked over toward Desiree, stepping over Nikki's body. Desiree begged and begged for her life. Mance only smiled at her with tears in his eyes.

Polo and Bizzy had witnessed Mance's murder spree by peeking through the window. Polo had followed Mance but what he was seeing now was something he didn't want any part of.

"Let's go, yo," Bizzy whispered near Polo's ear. Polo took that as some good advice but he remained glued to the window when Mance pulled his last victim toward the fireplace. He squinted to get a better look.

"C'mon, Polo!" Bizzy had a touch of urgency in his voice.

"Wait…" Polo said, pushing Bizzy's hands from his jacket. "That's…Ms. Eason! Whut the fuck!"

"Fuck dat. Let's be out, yo."

Polo ignored Bizzy as he watched Mance place the gun against Desiree's forehead as she knelt in front of him.

"Please, Mance," Desiree sobbed. "I…"

"Shut up!" Mance said, pressing the .38 into her forehead. Behind Desiree the blazing fire was making a cruel thought burn its way into Mance's mind. He wanted to see her burn. He wanted her to suffer. He nudged her back toward the fire. When she felt the intense heat at her back she pushed forward but Mance started to choke her with one hand. He wanted her to burn alive. She raked at his face with her nails. She dug her nails in deeply to the white meat but he ignored the pain.

Toying with her, he raised her to her feet. He released his grip. She gasped for air. Seeing how light and small she was, he dropped the .38, then ripped her sweater off with his free hand. Desiree fought, kicked, clawed and screamed as Mance shoved her toward the fire.

Polo knocked the back sliding glass door out as Desiree's screams filled his head. He rushed toward the den with his .38 in his hands. When he reached the den he found Desiree fighting for her life with her back on fire. Polo rushed toward her, jumped over the sofa, landed on his feet, then shot Mance three times in his neck before he could turn around. He shoved Mance's body to the side, then pulled Desiree from the fire to frantically beat the fire out on her back. She passed out from the pain. Seeing that she would live, he called 911 on Lamar's phone, wiped off his prints and left it off the hook. He knew the 911 operator would send police sooner or later, and Polo would be missing by then. As he left with Bizzy he received a call from Lil' Rick. He made it a point not to mention Lil' Rick's name.

"Whut up?" Lil' Rick said. "My cuz tole me about Tink. Is he okay?"

"Yeah, got hit wit some birdshot."

"Damn. Any idea who did it?"

"Nah," he lied.

"Well...keep this on the low. But if you need a nigga, I'll be ova Candy's crib. Get at me, dawg."

Polo hung up. "Bizzy."

"Yo."

"That was Lil' Rick. Look, I'ma keep what you told me to myself and you do the same about what went down at Kaseem's crib."

Bizzy crossed his heart then kissed his finger. "Dat's a bet, my nigga. I'm not havin' no D's question me about nothin'." In truth, it was his fear of Lil' Rick. The deal of silence was sealed.

Five weeks later

Lil' Rick was now back in Raleigh pimping hard in his new sunburst orange Hummer H2 rolling on twenty-eight-inch DUB rims. With Kaseem dead and his team broken up, he had no fear of anyone retaliating for his lick on Datwon. Even Datwon had packed up and left with his girl. Shit, he was happy to be alive.

Tink was home now. He could walk, but no running, nor could he lie on his back. The good news was that Trina was now four and a half weeks pregnant with his second seed. Tink also had a job. He worked at a kiosk selling black-authored novels for Vic Mar Publications. It was legal and positive and Trina was proud of her man.

As for Bizzy, he got tired of stressing about Lil' Rick finding out about his deal with Mance, so he packed up and moved to South Carolina with his uncle.

Polo was still going back and forth to court for his gun charge—well, he only went twice but it was two times too many. Today he was waiting at his lawyer's office to speak to his lawyer. He nodded at the new white legal assistant who had Desiree's old office. Polo had been at Trina's crib watching the news when the story had broken about the three dead bodies at Kaseem's crib. He knew Desiree was okay when the reporter stated her condition but didn't mention her name. He would never forget that November night.

"Tyrone Bell," an unfamiliar voice called his name. He looked toward the door to see a fine shapely brown-skinned woman wearing winter apparel by Baby Phat from shoulder to feet. The woman walked toward him in her fur-lined boots and held out her gloved hand. Polo came to his feet.

"My name is Jelena," she said.

"How you know my government name?" he asked after shaking her hand.

"You mean the one your mother gave you?" She smiled. Seeing that Polo didn't return her smile she got serious. First, she thanked him for sending Desiree flowers when she was in the hospital. Polo lied and said it wasn't him. She waved him off. She explained in a whisper that Desiree hadn't mentioned his name to the police and that she now wanted to thank him for saving her life. Polo knew it was pointless to lie after Jelena had told him that she was Desiree's best friend and roommate.

"How is Desiree doing?"

"Fine. Just minor burns on her lower legs and back. She's a fighter."

"That's good."

"She was right about you." She smiled as she looked him up and down.

"About what?"

"Said you looked like Michael Vick." She then looked him in his eyes. "Polo, do you have a girlfriend?"

"No...nobody to stress me if I don't call or stay out. Why?"

"Like I said. My girl wants to thank you and I know she likes you and I'm just looking out for my girl." She then asked him to follow her outside. There was a light snowfall but Jelena was traveling in a well-equipped tan gold Lexus LX 470. Sitting in the passenger seat was Desiree, wearing a black mink coat and YSL shades. He got into the back as Jelena got behind the wheel. There was an odd moment at first until Desiree broke the silence. She turned slowly in her seat to look at Polo. She removed her shades and said thank you. Polo said it was no big deal. But it was a major deal to her. He had killed a man to protect her. She then asked if he wanted to go out to dinner later on that night if he was free. He accepted her offer.

It was nine months later when Polo gave Desiree his last name. He was now a married man with a legal job and everything was all good.

THE "P" IS FREE...

BY LASHONDA TEAGUE

ONE

The pussy is freeee but the crack cost money! Oh yeaaah!

Knowledge reigned supreme from the boom of Wiz's brand-new gold Volkswagen Jetta. It was kitted bumper to bumper and cruised the streets of Newark on gold BBS rims.

It was 1986 and Wiz was on top of the world, because the new game in the streets was making young nigguhs rich, damn near overnight. It was called crack or flavors, depending upon the vial cap color, and it was quickly becoming the answer to all the ghetto's problems. Poverty, abuse, despair, you name it, crack was the shoulder we collectively cried on. But for nigguhs like Wiz, eighteen and hungry, the only addiction to the drug was the money it made, which created its own high. Not even a year ago, Wiz was a tackhead dropout, stealing cars and robbing cats for sheepskins. Now he had a sheepskin in every color, with Ballys to match, a solid gold dookie rope with the dangling anchor medallion and a four-finger ring that read WIZ KID in looping gold letters.

He drove through the streets bumping KRS-One with

the windows down to let the spring air in. Every light he stopped at, his system turned heads. Nigguhs scowled and frowned, while women frowned upside down, from ear to ear.

It was his system and kitted Jetta that got their attention, but his looks kept it. Wiz never had a problem scooping females. He had a peanut-butter-brown complexion, chinky hazel eyes that shimmered behind his gold CAZAL frames and dimples that winked from his cheeks when he smiled. Wiz was skinny, but his bow-legs made the shorties melt when he walked.

Wiz definitely had his share of chicks, but none could claim his name because he was engaged to the streets with a summer wedding fast approaching. He had two crack houses, one on Goldsmith Avenue, the other on Chadwick, and was looking to open a third. Each spot brought in a grand on a bad day and Wiz stayed on top of his B.I., milking it for all it was worth. He pulled up to his spot on Chadwick, checking his beeper for the fifth time in as many minutes.

"Damn, this bitch on my dick." He sucked his teeth, faking annoyance that his pipe game kept the chicks sweatin' him.

He looked up, then got out of the car, and all he heard was:

"Yo, Wiz!"

"Baby, talk to Moe. I ain't got but eight dollars."

"Yo, Wiz! You still want them sneakers?"

"Wiz, I need to see you!"

The block seemed to be infested with shabbily

dressed zombies, moving to and fro, trying to feel that blast. He was annoyed at the way the feens were all over, making the spot hot. He had told Moe about keeping order, so he was vexed that his word wasn't being followed.

"Get the fuck out of my face," he hissed at the woman with eight dollars as he pushed past her and took the front steps of the two-family house two at a time. He had rented the basement and second floor from the old man who lived on the first. The old man was cool and didn't ask questions, because he was well paid for his silence.

"Yo, Moe! Moe! Open the fuckin' door!" Wiz yelled, ringing the doorbell repeatedly. A few moments later black Moe, the fortyish coon he had running the spot, opened the door.

"Oh what up, Wiz? I ain't know—" Wiz brushed past him and entered the foyer, slamming the door behind him.

"Yo, Moe, how many times I have to tell you to keep the fuckin' feens in line? You makin' the whole block hot!"

"Man, nigguhs and flies, Wiz, nigguhs and flies," Moe quipped with an irreverent wave of his hand.

"What?" Wiz sniped, because he was in no mood for Moe's coon talk.

"Nigguhs and flies I do despise, but the more I see nigguhs, the more I love flies." Moe chuckled and, despite his ire, Wiz did too. "Them mutherfuckas feenin', Wiz. I been out over an hour. Hell, I been beepin' you like crazy."

"Yeah, yo, I had to bag the shit up," Wiz told him, as he pulled a large Ziploc bag from the elastic of his Fila suit. The Ziploc was stuffed with small orange-topped vials rubber-banded together in groups of ten. He handed it to Moe. "That's thirty clips. I'll be back through tomorrow."

Moe turned the bag over in his hand. "Shit, you coulda saved time and just brought me the shit to bottle up."

Wiz adjusted his slight sag, freeing his boxers from the uncomfortable bind the Ziploc had put them in. He didn't respond because the truth was that Moe was in question. Moe was a grand hustler, but every time he let Moe bag the weight, it always came up short. So Wiz had started doin' it himself.

"Yo, I'm ghost, Moe. Beep me if you need something else before tomorrow."

Wiz stepped out on the porch. The feens seemed to sense the presence of their crystallized savior, because they had stopped wandering up and down the block. Now they all were basically in a line, eyes glued to Wiz standing in the door. A wave of remorse momentarily seized Wiz's emotions, seeing the intense expression of anticipation on the ashen black faces. Their eyes blood-shot, lips cracked, bodies shriveled, a total disregard for themselves as human beings. He looked into the faces of the women: many were still pretty. Young, old, it was all the same and it made him think of his mother. Even though she smoked, she still worked and Wiz vowed he'd never let her end up out here. "Nigguhs and flies," he mumbled to himself as he headed to his car.

*   *   *

"I raised you better than this, Crystal! Look what you're doing to yourself! I refuse to watch you destroy your future...your*self*! Not in my house, *not* in *my* house! Now, you either give me that mess or you and it can get out in the streets where it belongs!"

Her mother's words echoed in Crystal's soul, even though they had been spoken over a month ago. She just couldn't get them out of her head, and even though she knew her mother was right, she couldn't get crack out of her system. It was slowly consuming her, becoming the god she worshipped and the religion she devoutly practiced. Every step she took toward the crack house made her heart race faster and her self-respect drop lower.

Crystal had questioned herself many times about how she had reached this point in her life. She had good parents, a good home and two years put in at Rutgers University, but she had let it all go at a club party on Chancellor six months ago.

Flashing lights...movin' to the beat

The blue light blazed and sweaty black hormones grinded to the sounds of Secret Weapon, and Crystal was having the time of her life. She loved to dance, to be in a crowd of dancing people, passing joints and drinking Pink Champale. Her head was buzzing and her man of choice was fine enough to really make her express her rhythm. So when her girl Tricia showed her the slim glass cylinder, eyes glazed and shaky-handed, she didn't skip a beat.

"What's this?" Crystal yelled over the groove, as she took the pipe in her hand.

"Th-th-that's that shit," Tricia replied through her numbed senses. "And these nigguhs got plenty of it!" She gestured toward the cat whose party it was. A face Crystal didn't know, but you would know as belonging to Wiz.

Crystal looked at the rocklike substance stuffed in one end of the pipe, curiously, as the party continued around her.

Is it all over my face? Hell yeah! Cause
I'm in love dancin'!

She had sniffed coke before, and it really didn't faze her, so what she had in her hands didn't send off any warning signals about what she was doing. She put the pipe to her lips and the lighter to the opposite tip, illumining her blue-lighted skin with an ominous orange hue. The rock sizzled and snapped its way into smoke, curling and filling the pipe, tumbling toward her inhalation, and when it reached her...it spoke. *Crystal... welcome home, baby, welcome home...feel that? Yeah, you feel that...you know what that is?...me...don't I tingle?...tingle like a thousand kisses...let me in, Crystal, I promise* (it snickered) *I'll be gooood to you. Because I know...know. What you need, Crystal. I know your secrets. About the abortion no one else knows about. That you're afraid to be ridiculed for, shamed for. I don't judge you, I agree. You don't need a baby...all you need...is me.*

I'm caught up! In a one-night love affair...

Crystal's downfall was her sense of motivation. When she wanted something, she didn't rest until she got it.

When she wanted to run track, she didn't rest until she brought home all-city. When she wanted to go to college, she didn't rest until her SATs stood out. So now that she wanted to get high, she couldn't rest until she stayed that way.

Crystal had basically been homeless since her mother put her out. She slept in crack dens or crackhead's apartments on the rare occasion that she did rest. Her days were filled with chasing the pipe, boosting clothes and selling her body if all else failed. Nothing and no one would stop her from that blast. Not the streets, not her momma and definitely not the fool ganking at her in a gold-kitted Jetta.

She wasn't what Wiz's standards considered a fly girl. She was cute, no doubt, real cute. Her caramel complexion and doe-shaped eyes gave her face a sensual innocence that Wiz admired. Her shape wasn't ghetto thick but her firm breasts stood out against her T-shirt, tantalizing his gaze. It wasn't her gear either, because she was dressed average: T-shirt, windbreaker and sweatpants, along with a pair of electric blue 54.11 aerobic Reeboks. It was her style, the way she carried herself, head up, like a woman with a purpose, a direction. He had no idea which direction she was headed in.

He turned the corner and drove down Goldsmith to his crack spot. On this side of town the feens were less conspicuous, but no less plentiful. He watched his team of little nigguhs, Lil Mike, Nu-Nu and Pills, handle the customers one after the other. He ran Goldsmith differently from Chadwick. Here the house only served as a stash spot, while his team played the block. Pills held the money, Nu-Nu held the work and Lil Mike held the heat.

Wiz parked his car in the middle of the street, because Goldsmith was divided by a concrete partition that doubled as a parking lane. When he got out, his young team gathered around him.

"What up, homeslice?" Pills, the youngest at fourteen, greeted him while lighting a cigarette. "When you gonna let me push the whip?"

Wiz chuckled. "Mutherfucka, when you buy it."

Pills pulled out four large stacks of money, rubber-banded together. "Shit, I got the money right here."

Wiz took the money and put it in his glove compartment. "Yeah, you got *my* money right here." Wiz checked his watch. "And didn't I tell y'all to watch for truancy during school hours? They see y'all and come runnin' up in my shit. Y'all wanna drop out in kindergarten, so what, just don't get me fucked up too."

"Man, I'm in the eighth grade," Nu-Nu, fifteen, stated factually.

"*S'posed* to be in the tenth grade. Y'all don't never go to school," Lil Mike, fifteen, scolded them. He was the only one who did attend occasionally, even if it was only to show off his money, gear and jewelry.

Nu-Nu pulled out a modest knot of his own. "Man, *this* my school right here, and I'm at the top of my grade!" Nu-Nu and Lil Mike dapped each other and Wiz smiled proudly.

Of course they should be in school, but so should he,

so what could he really say? At least they weren't running around hungry and dirty, or worse, high.

"Yo, yo, Pills. Here she go!" Lil Mike whispered excitedly. They all turned their attention to the corner and watched Crystal turn the corner and head straight for them.

"Yo, yo, if she ain't got enough, tell her to see me. If she let me fuck her, *I'll* put up her high," Mike said lustfully. He and his crew had already learned the power crack gave them over women two and three times their age and what they would do for the drug. They all wanted Crystal, but none had managed to hit.

"Y'all some young freaks," Wiz accused, eyes still on Crystal. For some reason he didn't understand, he was disappointed that she was a smoker.

"Yo, Nu-Nu, come here," Crystal called. She stopped a few houses away with her hands in her windbreaker pockets, doing the crackhead shuffle.

"Yo, money, she smokin' that?" Wiz asked Lil Mike and Pills as Nu-Nu went to serve her.

"A hundred miles an hour," Pills confirmed, still fantasizing about the day she'd fall into his power. They always did.

Wiz shook his head, analyzing her up and down. He could see she couldn't be much older than him, pretty, and she had business about herself. *How the hell did she get caught up?* He wondered what made seemingly sensible people smoke after seeing the damage it could do.

As she turned to walk away, her profile sparked a vague familiarity in his mind, and before he knew it, he called out, "Ay yo, shorty! Hold up!"

Wiz bopped over to her, hearing Pills remark, "I git seconds, Wiz." He ignored the comment as he approached her. Crystal's mind was too preoccupied with the plastic in her palm for her to notice anything about Wiz, except for the fact he was holding her up, and only natural curiosity made her want to know why.

"Excuse me, but...where do I know you from?" Wiz asked sincerely, but to Crystal's ears it sounded like a hoochie "can I kick it" line, and a weak one at that.

She quickly dismissed him like, *no*, and walked away, leaving Wiz like a piece of brushed-off lint.

He started to say something slick, but he didn't want his young boys to think some feen had dissed him. He walked back over to the car, reached under the passenger seat and produced another Ziploc bag full of clips. He handed them to Nu-Nu, who quickly took the pack in the house.

"So what up, Wiz? What time we goin' to the LL concert tonight at Sensations?" Pills asked him.

"Don't know what time you goin', but I'm goin' at ten," Wiz replied, sliding in the driver's seat and closing the door.

Lil Mike leaned in the open window. "Come on, homeboy, let us roll wit' you. These feens can wait a few hours."

"See, that's the attitude that keep nigguhs broke. You think they gonna not get high? Hell no, they gonna go spend they money on Bergen. We ain't in business to miss money, nigguhs," Wiz schooled him, then started the engine.

"Shit, you ain't stayin'," Pills remarked.

Wiz smirked. "'Cause, lil' nigguh, I got you to handle all that, huh. Beep me." He turned up the system to let them know...

The pussy is freeee, but the crack cost moneeey!

TWO

Wiz! Wiz! Boy, you hear that damn phone! You know it's for you!"

Wiz heard his mother yell, bringing him out of a well-deserved sleep. Twenty-four/seven he stayed on the grind, so when he crashed, he crashed. He truly hadn't heard the phone because the ringer was off. Wiz reached over and picked up the receiver. "What!"

"What? Oh, it's what now? I been beepin' you all day. You can't call nobody?" the female voice belonging to Michelle hissed through the receiver.

Wiz rubbed his eyes, then checked his black Movado: eight-thirty p.m.

"Yo, I been busy. I ain't got the luxury of waitin' on a nigguh all day, aiight," he replied sharply.

"And what's that supposed to mean?"

He sighed, because the conversation was irrelevant. "You call to argue or you got something to say?"

Michelle sucked her teeth and rolled her eyes with the tone of her voice. "Anyway, is we still going to the LL concert?"

Wiz sat up like, *we*? "Why everybody think I'm a fuckin' taxi? Look, I told you I might take you. *Might.* But right now, I really don't feel like being bothered wit' you, so—"

Michelle cut him off. "Bothered! Oh, so it ain't no bother when you come to my house two in the mornin' to lay up with me! It ain't no bother when I'm suckin'—"

Click!

Wiz cut her tirade off in mid-stride and immediately turned his thoughts to what he would wear. He heard the phone ring up front, but he didn't bother to answer until he heard, "Wiz! Wizard, get in here, boy!" He sighed deeply, then made his way down their apartment corridor to the kitchen. His mother was sitting in the kitchen, still wearing her nursing outfit, smoking a cigarette. "Boy, what did you do to that chile?" she questioned.

"Nothin'."

"Nothin'? Well, why is she callin' my house screamin' 'I hate you' like she done lost her damn mind?"

Wiz leaned against the door frame. "Man, I don't know, ask her."

"I'm askin' you. I done told you about these females and emotions. If you don't want to deal with them, don't. But don't keep treatin' them like shit, because what goes around comes around, you hear me?"

"Yeah, Ma," he answered, like he'd heard it all before. "I gotta get dressed."

"Dressed? For what?" she asked, putting out her cigarette.

"Just out, man," he whined in annoyance, because he could see where she was going. She did it all the time.

"Well, before you go out, I need you to let me get a little somethin'. Shit, Momma wanna party too." She smiled, trying to take the sting out of her request.

Wiz sucked his teeth. "Ma. I just gave you some yesterday. What you do with that?" She got up from the table to take her meal out of the microwave.

"What the hell you think I did wit' it? What I 'posed to do wit' it?" she quipped, snatching her hand back from the burning edge of the Tupperware bowl.

"I wish you would just leave that stuff alone," Wiz mumbled under his breath.

"And I wish you would too," she shot back.

"Why? I ain't smokin' it," he fired back.

"No, you just sell it to people who do. Somebody's daddy, somebody's son and somebody's momma. So if it ain't good enough to get high on, it damn sure ain't right to get by on," his mother said, looking him dead in the eyes. "You wanna be grown, fine, so am I. You sell it; I smoke it, so fair exchange ain't no robbery." She scraped the leftover shrimp fried rice from the bowl onto her plate. "Now, you gonna look out for me, or do I have to pay for it too?"

Wiz looked at his mother. She was young, only thirty-five, and her pecan complexion still glowed with a girlish quality. But he could see how the drugs were beginning to take a toll on her beauty. "Yeah, man," he reluctantly agreed, heading to his room to get it. He dug in his wall stash, retrieved a ten-bottle clip, and returned to the kitchen. He sat the clip on the table without looking at his mother, then turned and walked out.

She wanted to call him back, tell him she loved him and that she was sorry things were the way they were, but what could she say that could make him understand her addiction, and her dependency on him for a steady supply of drugs that kept her from becoming another crack feen in the street? There was nothing to say, so she simply closed the kitchen door and got her pipe out of her purse.

Every hood has a club . . . not just any club, but *the* club. Sensations was it in Newark. Only the liveliest nigguhs hung at Sensations, and the hood legends rarely missed an attendance. So when LL Cool J came to Newark that spring of '86, nigguhs really showed out. Ask LL, he remembers.

Branford Place was lined with slick whips. No-top Wranglers with Louis Vuitton seat covers, Benz AMGs, with Ferrari kits, and, of course, various flavors of Suzuki bikes and Sidekicks.

Wiz pulled up and parked his Jetta on Halsey Street, then rounded the corner. He came alone because he didn't do the crew, and he didn't bring a girl, because that was like taking sand to the beach. But his presence was felt because his name was on the rise and he had legends in his bloodline.

Wiz slid through in a pair of white Calvin Kleins, baby blue silk shirt and matching baby blue Ballys. His forty-inch rope swung to the rhythm of his suave nonchalant stride and shimmered under the streetlights.

People were scattered everywhere. Girls in Chinese bobs, bamboo earrings and painted-on graffiti jeans congregated in cliques, flirting with the money nigguhs while the wild nigguhs stalked the shadows.

"Yo, Wiz! It's vic season!"

The tone was ominous, but anyone familiar with the voice would know the words were barked in jest. Wiz knew the voice well. It belonged to his older cousin Ali Smalls, notorious across the Brick. Wiz turned his attention to Ali, who was leaning against a green Eldorado with Al-Ameen and Ali Hubcap from Prince Street. He walked up, giving everyone a pound, and gave Ali Smalls a brotherly hug.

"Look at lil' cuz, yo. Muthafucka gettin' his weight up, love love," Smalls remarked, proudly checking Wiz out from head to toe. "What up wit' you?"

"Chillin', man, what up wit' you?"

Ali shrugged. "I told you, Cuz," he began, pulling a chrome bulldog .38 from his waist with a smile, "it's vic season. You see anything you want?" Ali questioned, gesturing to the large crowd, gold and diamonds everywhere.

Wiz knew Smalls meant it, because the nigguh was

treacherous. The type of nigguh to do drive-bys with a silencer, but to look at him, you never would've guessed this light-skinned pretty-type nigguh was so dangerous.

"Naw, yo, I'm straight," Wiz declined.

"You sure? Let me know love, I'm in the house."

Wiz nodded and walked off, heading inside Sensations. The air inside the club was suffocating. The place was packed, especially with females waitin' on Ladies Love, so Wiz was like a kid in a candy store. He knew from the eye contact he was getting from every angle that he would have his pick, so he told his dick don't worry, we fuckin' tonight. Once LL took the stage, he didn't disappoint. He was young and hungry, already out to prove he was the G.O.A.T. He blazed "Rock the Bells" and "Radio," made the chicks' panties wet with "I Need Love" and the nigguhs amped for "I'm Bad," but for some reason, the song that stuck in Wiz's head was . . .

Yo, Yvette . . . There's a lot of rumors goin' around
It's so bad, baby, you might have to skip town . . .

All he could think of was Crystal's face. He just couldn't shake it, because he wondered why a chick like that would choose to throw her life away over a ten-dollar high. He thought of his mother, Moe and all the cats he had seen get swallowed by the blast. What the fuck was this shit he was selling—but then again, why should he even care? *Shit, somebody gotta sell it, might as well be me*, was the last thought he had before he was brought out of his thoughts. "Excuse me. Excuse me, but umm, do you know what time it is?" the sweet soft voice asked him as he looked into the face of an angel. She was a sexy, short five-two in a pink tennis skirt, baby tee and white-on-white Lottos. Her ass was juicy, his eyes could taste it, and her thighs were so thick, his dick was already jumping.

"Time to show you where I'm parked," Wiz smirked, winking his dimples.

She giggled. "No, really. I can't find my girlfriend and I really ain't trying to miss the last PATH home."

"Oh, so you from New Yitty, huh? Where at?" he questioned, knowing damn well she wouldn't see wherever it was until morning, if he could help it.

"Harlem." She eyed his four-finger ring, "Wiz Kid," she smiled, "why they call you Wiz?"

"My magic wand," he joked, "I make dreams come true."

"Oh really?"

"Would I lie?"

She looked at him, licking her lips. "Probably, but I do too."

Wiz closed the distance between them to whisper in her ear. "Then you can trust me, 'cause I'm just like you. But believe me when I tell you, I got my car outside, and it's ready to take you wherever you want to go."

"What about the last train?" She quivered, already seeing it pulling off without her.

"I got you," he replied, meaning it in more ways than one.

She smiled her consent.

"So, yo...what's your name?"

"Damn, Veronica, let a nigguh wake..." Wiz's sentence drifted off incomplete as he gave in to the sensation of Veronica's mouth on his dick. He looked down at her head between his legs and her lips wrapped around his dick, letting the pleasure curl his toes. They had gotten a room last night and wasted no time in fucking the shit out of each other, then they had both collapsed into a satisfied slumber. He woke up to her uptown head game that had his Newark ass twisted.

"You like it, Daddy?" she purred between slurps. "Yeah, you like it, I bet your girl at home don't do it like Veronica, do she?" She licked tantalizingly slowly up his eight-inch shaft and all around the ball of his head.

"What girl at home?"

She climbed on top of him, gripping his dick, then squatted on it with a squeal. "Stop...Stop lyin'...Dick this good don't come without a leash," she stuttered, long-dicking herself into a zone of pure feminine pleasure.

Veronica's pussy felt like warm quivery Jell-O to Wiz, and he had to curl up his insides so he wouldn't bust off too soon. But when she reversed her position and rode him backward, just the sight of his dick disappearing inside her made him pound her furiously until they both came. She flopped down beside him, brushed the hair from her face with a satisfied smile and asked, "Don't Veronica know how to treat a man in the mornin'?"

"No doubt," Wiz replied.

She leaned in to kiss him, but he turned his face, so the kiss landed on his cheek. Wiz's rule was, he never kissed a chick on the mouth, especially not one he hit the first night.

Crystal lay on the mattress, staring at the cracks in the ceiling. She followed the crack from one side of the room to another while she waited for the old man to go limp inside her. He always did, which was one reason she didn't mind tricking with him. Every month he got his disability check, and every month like clockwork she and Tricia would trick him out of it. It was always the same story. He could hold an erection only for a few minutes, then before he ejaculated he'd go limp, grunt and roll over. He'd give them both twenty or thirty dollars, then go to sleep.

All it was was a business transaction. Crystal felt nothing inside because she was learning to separate herself from herself, and in the process she lost a little more of her soul each day.

The old man rolled over and flopped down on the bed, sweating like it had been three hours and not three minutes. "Whew! You young gals is gonna be the death of me one day, I swear. Where's your girlfriend? Why she ain't come?"

Crystal thought of Tricia with a mild degree of remorse. Tricia was supposed to come. It was a silent agreement that they worked the old man together. Hell,

Tricia had turned her on to the trick. But Crystal had lied to Tricia, telling her she had a ride to pick Tricia up. So instead of meeting her at the old man's house, Crystal was coming to get her. That was just an excuse so Tricia wouldn't come and she could get all the money, Fifty dollars, which he had given her before going to sleep.

Crystal pulled up her jeans and fixed herself in the mirror. It wasn't that she didn't like what she saw, she simply didn't care. Friendship no longer mattered; she saw Tricia as stupid, because if it had been her, she would have kept the trick to herself.

Crystal walked out of the small bedroom and through the living room. She eyed his stereo system, weighing it in her mind, but she decided against it. He was a steady trick, so why burn a stable bridge? She let herself out of the dilapidated two-family home and exited the rusted fence with a squeaking clink. The rain wasn't hard, but kept up a steady drizzle. Crystal put her windbreaker hoodie over her ponytail and headed toward Lyons Avenue to see who was holding. But when she turned the corner, all she heard was, "Bitch, you ain't shit!"

She looked up and watched a fuming Tricia heading straight for her, double time. The look on her face told Crystal that Tricia didn't want to talk, and before she knew it a razor came slicing through the air, narrowly missing her cheek. Crystal stumbled slightly, but she was able to grab Tricia's forearm and keep the razor at bay, while she dug into Tricia's face with her free hand.

"Argghh!" Tricia winced in pain, "I'ma kill you!"

Both Tricia and Crystal were small, but Crystal was quicker. She bit into Tricia's wrist until the razor fell from her hand. Tricia grabbed her by the ponytail and yanked her head back, causing Crystal to fall backward on the ground.

"Get the fuck off me!" Crystal grunted as she struggled to topple Tricia in their wrestling match.

A small crowd of guys were gathered around, yelling, "Go hard, shorty! Flip her over on her back with your knees!"

"Fuck that, pin that bitch arms!"

"I got my money on Red," one commented, referring to Tricia.

Both women were kicking, scratching and punching until one guy had the decency to break them up. He grabbed Tricia with one hand and Crystal with the other, holding them apart by the length of his arms. They struggled to get at each other. "Yo, y'all mutha-fuckas, help me!" he yelled.

Another guy grabbed Tricia as she continued the fight verbally. "You backstabbin' bitch! I know you fucked 'im, I know you fucked 'im!"

The guys ohhed and ahhed like it was a joke.

"Damn girl, you fucked honey girl man?" The guy who had the decency to break it up accused Crystal, but she ignored him.

Her nose was bloody, her hoodie was ripped and she had lost a shoe in the fight, so her left sock was soaked.

"Get off me!" she growled, snatching away from the guy and spotting her shoe.

"You gonna give me my money, Crystal! You hear me?! Where's the money?!" Tricia screamed, still trying to get at Crystal.

Crystal stepped into her shoe, fixed the heel and turned away like, *Bitch, fuck you! I don't owe you shit!*

Tricia was close to tears. She was so mad, because she wanted to get high and she felt betrayed. "You crack-smokin' bitch! That's all you is! A fuckin' ten-dollar whore!" Tricia screamed, knowing it hurt Crystal to hear it because it hurt Tricia to be one.

But Crystal took the insult in stride, letting the pain go where her self-esteem had drained into. Pure nothingness inside.

Wiz hated the rain. He was a summertime sunshine cat, so when it rained, it made him moody. He couldn't remember a time he hadn't felt this way, but he didn't remember the reason why. He had dropped Veronica at Penn Station, exchanged numbers and promised to call, which he definitely planned on doing. It wasn't just because of her banging head game; she also lived in Harlem, where he bought his weight.

So it was convenient to have an uptown layup, and hopefully he could convince her to mule his drugs back to Newark on the 107 bus while he drove back without the heat. Wiz sat at the light, watching the windshield wipers go back and forth, while the system pumped... *Sun showers bring light to the flowers loving you my baaaby.* Until his attention was attracted to the hooded figure crossing the street in front of him. He recognized the person instantly as the chick from Goldsmith. He watched her huddle her shoulders against the heavy drizzle, walking like every drop was an assault on her person, and he was moved to compassion.

He made a right on the light, then let down the passenger window as he drove slowly next to her. "Yo! You, shorty!" Crystal saw who it was but didn't even break stride, quickening her pace. "You act like I'ma snatch your purse, yo, where you headed? I'll give you a ride," Wiz offered, keeping one eye on the road and the other on her.

What does he want? she thought. "That's all right, I can walk," she replied without looking his way.

"In the rain? Come on, yo, get in. I said I'll take you," Wiz reiterated a little more forcefully, because he wasn't used to no female telling him no.

Crystal just kept walking. Recognizing him from Goldsmith, and remembering his comment about knowing her from somewhere, and because she felt the same, she avoided finding out from where. She didn't want to meet anyone from her past life, who remembered her as she had been and would then see what she had become. So she ignored him to avoid the embarrassment.

Wiz, on the other hand, was fuming. "Yo, all this here ain't even necessary. I was just tryin' to be nice to your dumb ass. Fuckin' crackhead," he spit, and the insult was the straw that broke the camel's back.

Everywhere she went she had to put up with being treated like a feen, but she wasn't about to be called out her name when she hadn't done anything to deserve it. Before Wiz could pull off, she turned to his car and blazed him.

"Nigguh, if I'm such a crackhead why the fuck you want me in your car?!"

Wiz hit the brakes and yelled back, "Bitch, I hope you drown out there! Mutherfucka can't even be nice no more!"

"Nice?! You ain't bein' nice, you just want some pussy! It's a shame you have to buy it from a fuckin' feen, you lame-ass bama!"

Wiz threw the Jetta in park and leaped out in the middle of the street, leaving the driver's door wide open. Crystal saw the rage in his eyes, and she hoped she hadn't pushed him too far, but just in case she looked around, spotted a forty-ounce bottle and smacked it against the pavement. She brandished the jagged edge like, *Nigguh, I wish the fuck you would!*

Wiz stopped short, took one look at her with that sad excuse for a weapon and busted out laughing. The bottle was jagged, but it only hung together by the glue of the label. One poke and it would only crumble to the ground. Crystal didn't see the humor, and despite the bottle's condition she still gripped it tightly until she felt a sharp pain in her palm. She looked down and saw that her hand was dripping blood. Wiz saw a red drop hit the pavement, and without thinking snatched the bottle from her hand and inspected the cut. "You need to go to the hospital, yo."

Crystal snatched her wrist away, wincing in pain. "I-I'm fine."

Wiz ignored her. He ran to his car, grabbed a New Jersey Devils hockey jersey he had bought recently and wrapped her hand in it.

"I told you, I'm fine," she repeated, but in a softer tone, allowing him to bandage her wound.

"Man, just get in the car," Wiz told her, leading her firmly by the elbow to the Jetta. They both got in, then he whipped a U-turn in the middle of Lyons Avenue and headed to Beth Israel Hospital.

Crystal and Wiz sat silently in the half-crowded waiting room. Wiz sat back with his head against the wall and his eyes closed. Crystal looked down at the blood-soaked jersey and thanked him in her mind. She looked at his white Calvins, which were spotted with blood and wondered why he had bothered to help her. He could've said, "Serves your dumb ass right," and left her leaking in the street, but he hadn't and that thought alone made her look him in the face for the first time. The first thing that struck her was his strong facial bone structure. Wiz had the type of jawline that sculptors tried to perfect. His lips looked juicy and suckable, and his eyelashes were feminine in length, but masculine in quality. Crystal could tell he was younger than her twenty-three years, because his skin was still baby-smooth, without a trace of hair, except for his fuzz of a mustache. She decided right then she had never seen him before, because she would've remembered his fine ass anywhere.

"I'm a fly muthafucka, huh?" Wiz smirked, eyes still closed.

Crystal played it off and looked away. "Huh? I was just looking over there, at that, umm, painting."

Wiz sat up and smiled, wetting her with the dimples. "Yo, every closed eye ain't sleep," he told her, then checked his watch. "Damn! We been here ten minutes already," he remarked, then crossed the room to the nurses' station to confront the old white nurse. "Yo, what a muhfucka gotta do, bleed to death before he get some fuckin' assistance!"

"Sir, please clam down," she replied in a nasal tone. "Where are you bleeding, and what happened?" To her it was all routine.

"Not me, dumb-ass, her! The whole fuckin' shirt is soaked!" he exclaimed, and pointed to Crystal.

The nurse, seeing the irate young black male, called emergency. A few minutes later Crystal was escorted to the back. Forty-five minutes later she woke Wiz up and told him, "I'm finished."

The doctor had given her eighteen stitches in her palm. Wiz stood up and said, "I'm hungry. Let's go get something to eat."

Wiz and Crystal sat in IHOP, talking, laughing and eating pancakes and eggs. It had been so long since Crystal last remembered laughing, and Wiz had never experienced conversation with a woman interesting enough to hold his attention. "So you nice? I mean wit' boostin' and shit? You say that's your main hustle, right?" Wiz asked, because he had a situation in mind.

Crystal shrugged and took a bite of her pancake. "I ain't never been caught."

Wiz looked at his watch, then said, "Well dig: I need you to boost something for me. Nothin' major, just an outfit. What you gonna charge me?"

"You mean now? This minute?"

"Yeah. You 'bout yo' business, right?"

Crystal could see a catch somewhere, an angle Wiz was playing, but she didn't detect any game. "Depends on the store."

Wiz stood up. "Come on, then, I'll show you."

Since the IHOP was in Elizabeth, they rode the few blocks to downtown. The streets were semi-packed with early-morning shoppers, stragglers and commuters. He led her to a clothing store called Mannings. They specialized in sports apparel, but they carried name-brand jeans as well. Wiz looked around the store at the clothes until he found the Levi's section. He picked out a pair of red Levi's jeans that were twenty-six in the waist. He handed them to Crystal, and she arched her eyebrow. "These can't be for you. I know you wear at least a thirty-six," she joked.

Wiz shrugged. "Birthday gift. Help me find a top."

"Who's it for?"

"This chick," was his only reply.

For some reason she didn't understand, she felt a little salty. He was having her help him pick out some skeezer's outfit, but business was business. "Get that." She pointed to the matching Levi's jean jacket and a white spandex top.

"Cool. Handle your business, yo."

Crystal grabbed two sets of each article of clothing and disappeared into the dressing room. While she was gone, Wiz bought a pair of white-on-white K-Swiss. She returned moments later with only one set, returned it to the rack, like, *It doesn't fit*, and headed for the door. Wiz took the shoe bag and followed her out. When they reached the car, Crystal pulled out the outfit and handed it to Wiz and said, "I hope she likes it," with just a hint of female attitude.

Wiz smirked, enjoying her jealousy. "She better," he replied, then started the car. "So what do I owe you?"

Crystal propped her elbow on the door handle and ran her hand over her ponytail, hesitant to ask Wiz for what she really wanted. How could she, after spending the last few hours in such normal things in male-female relations, like laughter, good conversation and companionship? She stuttered mentally to have to come back to reality. Wiz asked again, "Whut up? Fifty, a yard, what?"

"No, I, umm, you holdin'?"

"Huh?"

Crystal sighed. "You got work?"

Wiz just looked at her, hating his own reality check. "Yeah, yo."

Crystal looked out the window while Wiz looked at the back of her head for a minute, then put the Jetta in drive, turning up the system.

Boogie Down productions-uctions-uctions.

Will always get paid-aid-aid...

"Could you turn that down?" Crystal asked. The monkey was on her back, and she was getting irritable.

"Whut?" Wiz asked, irritable because she had a monkey.

Crystal sucked her teeth. "Never mind."

Wiz turned it down.

"If you heard me, why you say what?" Crystal quipped.

"I was turnin' it down so I could hear you," Wiz lied.

Moments later, he pulled into the Newark Airport motel. The same place he had had Veronica in. He still had the key from last night. Crystal narrowed her eyes on him, feeling her blood pressure rising like mercury.

Wiz pulled up in front of 202 and cut off the car. "Come on," was all he told her, one foot out the door.

"No. For what?" she wanted to know.

"Just come on, damn. I wanna talk to you."

"We can talk right here."

"You want the shit or what?"

"Go get it. I'll wait out here," Crystal declared, then added, "Why did you bring me here?" she asked, insulted because she hadn't expected this from Wiz.

"You comin' or what?"

Silence.

"Look," Wiz began, "I ain't tryin' to trick with you, aiight. I get pussy like most muhfuckas get problems. I'm tryin' to put you up on a trick."

She turned her attention.

"What kind of trick?" she wanted to know.

"You boost, right? I was thinkin' we could do business. Budget Rent A Car right next door. So I could rent you a car by the week so you can go out, load up, and sell it to me half price, you dig? Then I sell it and make a flip."

Crystal studied his expression, trying to detect a catch. "What's that got to do with the motel?"

"I figured you need a place to chill for a minute, you know? Room and board, yo...but it's comin' out of your check." He smiled, making her want to stick her finger in his dimple.

Crystal giggled. "So I work for you now?"

"I don't know, do you?"

Crystal viewed her options, of which she had none, and replied, "Aiight, Wiz Kid. I'm down."

They shook hands and truly touched for the first time.

Wiz reached under her seat and pulled out a small Ziploc with a few clips. He gave her one. "Beep me if you get hungry," he said, and handed her the key.

Crystal took the clip and the key, then opened the door.

"Hold up," Wiz told her, then reached into the back-seat and handed her the outfit. "You forgot this."

Crystal looked at the outfit with a dazed expression.

"I know you like it, yo, you picked it out yourself." Wiz smiled, letting her know he had had it planned the whole time.

She wanted to thank him, but her voice caught in her throat. She just took it and got out, feeling nothing but the weight of the gift in her arms.

THREE

For the next few weeks Wiz's plan worked perfectly. He'd get someone to rent Crystal a car, she'd go to different spots to boost, then sell it to Wiz for her high. It kept her off the streets, but Wiz wasn't really doing his part. He seldom sold the wares she stole. He gave them to his workers or kept them for himself. But then again, his point wasn't to make money in the first place.

His game was booming, and his product was moving. He kept in constant contact with Veronica in Harlem. He'd go over to buy his weight, slide by, bang her out, then get her to push it back to Jersey on the bus. It was a sweet setup, but Veronica was a strict uptown chick, and had a sweeter setup in mind. She paid close attention to the weight he was moving. So when he started picking up a kilo every two weeks, which was heavy for a spot nigguh in '86, her conniving mind began to twirl.

Crystal, on the other hand, knew she was being taken care of. Her monkey was being fed, and her womanly needs were being met, so she was content. Hell, she went shopping in the exclusive spots. Short

Hills Mall for Liz Claiborne and Fendi, Secaucus, at the Gucci and Nike outlet. Not to mention Fashion Avenue, Canal Street, Macy's and everywhere in between. The only difference was, she took what she wanted instead of paying for it. The rest of the time she and Wiz spent together. In the morning they usually had breakfast, then at night he'd come through with Chinese food, some weed and apple Boone's Farm. Then they'd chill, get weeded and a little tipsy, getting more and more comfortable in each other's presence.

"Why do they call you Wiz?"

"'Cause, when I did go to school, I was like, mad smart. I used to pass tests and shit wit'out studyin'."

"Why you drop out?"

"Got bored and the streets was callin'." He shrugged.

He found out that Crystal had gone to college. She even had him thinking about going back to school. "At least for your GED and doing something constructive with your money. Put it to good use, Wiz. Buy some old houses and fix them up. Things ain't always gonna be sweet," she jeweled him.

But the realest conversation they had was when he told her that his mother got high too. "That shit be fuckin' me up, man. Knowin' what that shit is about and I don't be wantin' to give it to her, but I don't want her in the streets gettin' it neither...I don't know, it's crazy," Wiz mumbled, then glanced away.

Crystal felt honored that he was doing the same for her as for the woman who had given him birth. He

THE "P" IS FREE... / 93

looked back at her and asked, "Can I ask you somethin'? How you get fucked up with that shit?"

Crystal was sitting Indian-style in the middle of the bed, while Wiz lay back on both pillows with his head propped up and a half-empty Boone's bottle in his hand.

Crystal shifted her weight and replied, "To tell you the truth, I don't know. I mean, I've been smoking weed and drinkin' since I was like fourteen, but I still did good in school. I sniffed a couple of times, but it ain't really do nothin' for me."

She stretched her bare leg from under the long T-shirt she was wearing and dangled it off the edge of the bed for circulation.

"At the time I was in college, had a decent job and everything, but I guess when I—" She cut herself off before she said *abortion*. It was still a painful subject, because she had never truly dealt with it.

"When you what?" Wiz inquired.

Crystal looked at him, weighing a lie in her mind. "When I...looked at my life for what it was truly worth... anyway, it was this party on Chancellor, that my girl Tricia told me about. Some guy named Skee or Skeem or—"

"Skeet," Wiz said for her, feeling his heart drop to his stomach.

"Yeah, Skeet. You know him?"

Wiz just nodded and got up from the bed. He wandered over to the mirror, seeing Crystal's reflection over his shoulder's reflection.

"They had everything. Weed, pills, cocaine and... and crack."

Wiz focused on himself, his own reflection, his own eyes. He remembered where he had seen Crystal now, and it was crystal-clear. It was his coke that had turned her out. She continued, "I just looked at it like just another high, you know? I...I...I didn't know..." Her voice trailed off and she looked at Wiz in the mirror. "Wiz, you okay?"

"Yeah," he heard his mouth say as he turned around. "I'ma jet, yo. I gotta take care of something."

Crystal got off the bed and felt his forehead. "You sure? You look sick."

"I'm straight," he lied, making his way to the door. "I'll see you tomorrow."

"Oh, okay," Crystal responded, but as he opened the door, she added, "Wiz, you, um...think you could leave me a little somethin'?" with a hint of humiliation in her voice.

He quickly reached in his pants, pulled out half a clip and tossed it to her. Then left without saying a word. Had Crystal gone to the window instead of the bathroom to get high, she would've known his car never started. Had she not gone to sleep, she would've known the car never moved. Wiz sat behind the wheel, numb, knowing the monster he hated she had was his fault all along. He sat there, head back on the rest, falling asleep from mental exhaustion.

He awoke the next morning, disoriented until he realized where he was at. Why he was still here. Part of him wanted to pull off and never come back, but he had never been a coward, so he decided to apologize. He decided to go in and tell her right then, so he got out before he changed his mind.

Wiz keyed open the door and went in to find Crystal asleep. She had the covers pulled up to her chest and she slept on her back, with one hand near her face. Wiz froze like a deer in a pair of headlights. He froze, gazing at her sleeping innocence. He moved slowly closer and sat on the side of the bed. He gently caressed the side of her face until her eyes fluttered open. He started to pull his hand away, but she took his wrist, putting it to her mouth, and kissed his palm. Then licked it from heel to fingertip. Crystal had wanted to initiate intimacy many nights but she was afraid that Wiz wouldn't see past her problem to the woman she truly was. Now that he had come to her, she wanted to devour him and be devoured by him.

Inside, both their hormones were raging but they allowed the intensity to build with touches and small kisses that made Wiz break his rule and kiss her on the mouth. Their caramel and peanut butter complexions creamed into one flavor called black love, pain and pleasure, so the moans caused by either became undistinguishable from the other's. Where sex ceases to be intercourse and becomes pure energy embodied in a total embrace...

From that moment on, they were inseparable. Everywhere Wiz went, Crystal was right there. While he handled his business, she watched his back. The only time she wasn't with him was when he went over to New York and picked up because of his arrangement with Veronica.

Nigguhs didn't understand why Wiz had this crackhead chick with him everywhere he went, but they had to admit Crystal looked nothing like the chick they remembered. Gone were the raggedy clothes and busted sneakers. Thanks to her boosting abilities and Wiz's style she stayed laced in the flyest shit, bamboo earrings and rings on every finger. And her body... it was a combination of good eating and good loving that got her weight back up and she filled out her jeans nicely.

Still, nigguhs couldn't get past her habit.

"Yo, Wiz, what up with that bitch? She trickin'?" young Nu-Nu still wanted to know.

Wiz restrained himself from tapping his jaw. "Naw and watch yo' mouth, lil' nigguh, 'fore it get bloodied."

But despite her veneer, she was still as big an addict as ever. Wiz tried to smoke weed with her more, not realizing he was only feeding her dependency.

She always promised, "Baby, I'm tryin', I swear I'm tryin'. Please, just give me a chance."

And he did over and over, numerous chances. She could go a few days, but it always ended up, "Come on, Wiz, I've been doin' good, right? Just do me right one more time." He couldn't tell her no, but it hurt him to say yes. It was his mother's situation all over again, and she was still a factor.

"How come you never home, boy?" his mother demanded to know. "What lil' hussy got you so twisted, you can't come see your mama?"

"Ain't no hussy, yo, I just be busy," Wiz would tell her, but after the ranting and raving, the guilt trips and browbeatings, it always ended like, "So you gonna look out for me or what?"

And he always gave in. He felt like he was caught in a three-way tug of war between Crystal, his moms and the game. Like he was the crackhead, hustling backward, selling drugs just to give them away.

He and Crystal got an apartment in Weequahic Towers, because keeping the motel room for months was getting too expensive. He hoped their having a place would give Crystal a home. He let her lace the place out, which kept her occupied for a few days, but after that...

"Ain't I been a good girl, Daddy?"

And the game began, until one night when it all changed.

He had taken Crystal to the movies in Perth Amboy. It was late when they went to White Castle, but the Castle was always packed. Booming systems, fat whips and Newark hardheads everywhere. Wiz pulled up in the Jetta and parked.

"You comin' in?" he asked Crystal.

Her seat was reclined and she was half asleep. "Naw, just get me what you get."

Wiz got out and went in. While he was inside, Fatty

Moo, a cat from Renner Avenue, peeped Crystal in the car. "Yo, Crystal!" he called out, approaching the car. She didn't hear him because she had dozed off, so he tapped on the window. "Yo, Crystal, it's me, Moo. Open the door." He knew whose car it was but he ain't give a fuck.

Crystal froze in horror. She knew Wiz would flip if he saw Moo at the car, and she also knew Moo wouldn't back down. She didn't know what to do, but she opted to lower the window, try and be nice and get rid of him. "Hey, Moo, whut up? I got a crazy headache."

"Oh word? I got that medicine, yo. Whatever you need." Moo cheesed.

Crystal tried to maintain a smile, saying, "I'm cool. Just let me—"

"Ay yo!"

Crystal knew exactly who that was. Wiz. He had seen Moo at the car window and he came out to see what the deal was.

Moo leaned up from the window and spoke. "Oh, whut up, Wiz?"

"Whut up wit' you all over my shit!" Wiz barked, not three feet away.

"Oh, this you?" Moo faked ignorant. "My bad, I was just hollerin' at my old friend."

"Come on, Wiz. He just actin' stupid."

"Stupid? Oh, we ain't friends? You sayin' you ain't come through the block last week and cop an O.Z.?" Moo was purposely blowing her spot because Crystal hadn't let him fuck her when she came through last week, even though she had tricked with him in the past.

Crystal covered her face with her hand so Wiz knew it was true. By then a crowd was looking on and Wiz couldn't just let Moo clown him in the middle of the parking lot. He took off his chain and his Goose Bomber and gave them to Crystal.

"Yo, Moo, bring yo' bitch ass on!"

"Wiz, no!" Crystal pleaded, teary-eyed. "Let's just go, please!"

"Shut the fuck up!" he snapped.

Moo took off his waist-length fur and said, "Nigguh, this ain't what you want, but you damn sure can get it."

"No, Wiz," Crystal muttered helplessly.

Fatty Moo outweighed Wiz by a yard easy. But Wiz had been taught by Al-Ameen, who was extremely swift with the hands. The first few blows from Wiz proved that he had been taught well. He landed a sweet left-handed jab to Moo's chin and nose several times in swift succession, which only angered the bigger Moo. Moo swung a haymaker wildly, but Wiz ducked and caught Moo with a gut shot that took the wind out of him. Moo saw he couldn't handle the smaller man toe-to-toe, so he rushed him, scooped him and slammed him hard on his back.

"Wiz!" Crystal screamed.

She didn't know what to do. Her nerves were shot to pieces. She knew it was all her fault, but there was nothing she could do about it. She wanted to get away and that want became a need. So as someone pulled Moo off of Wiz, saying, "Shoot the one, fuck all that grippin' and grabbin'," Crystal slid out of the tightly formed circle and walked the few blocks to their apartment.

Meanwhile, Wiz got to his feet. Moo had landed a few heavy shots while he had him pinned, and the effects could be seen in his busted lip and puffed eye. But he continued to fight, catching the bigger man repeatedly, but becoming less and less effective. He was tired so it slowed him down, allowing Moo to land some hard joints. Had Wiz's mind been clear, he would have danced on Moo; instead he was the only one bleeding, despite the fact he landed the most blows.

They fought for twenty minutes, until Ali Smalls and Al-Ameen pulled up in Ali's Eldorado. Someone had called and told Ali that Wiz was at White Castle fighting, so he came through. He and Al-Ameen got out and maneuvered through the crowd to the front, his huge gold plate medallion clinking with every step. He looked at Wiz circling Moo expertly, but he could tell by his footwork he was on his last leg. He let Wiz catch Moo three more times before he stepped in, threw his arm around his shoulder and said, "That's enough, baby."

Moo saw Ali and automatically assumed the worst. He didn't know who Ali was to Wiz, but he knew if he had stepped in, that was his man.

Ali looked across at Moo, then stepped to him calmly. "You straight, Moo? You got it off your chest."

Moo dropped his eyes to avoid the shorter man's gaze. "Yeah, Smalls, it's over, yo."

"Yeah? You sure? The problem solved itself?" Ali probed.

Moo knew Ali was a live wire, one he really didn't want to ignite, so he replied, "It's dead, Smalls."

"Aiight," Ali responded, then went back to Wiz.

Once the crowd saw the fight was over, and that Ali and Al-Ameen were there, they quickly dispersed, leaving Ali to deal with Wiz.

"Whut up, Cousin? That nigguh Moo owe you something?"

Wiz spit out a stream of blood and saliva, then wiped his mouth. "Naw, yo."

"You say some ol' slick shit?"

Wiz was getting aggravated because he hated to tell Ali the real. "No man, he just disrespected me. Fuck it, it's over."

"How it's over if he disrespected you? What the fuck he do?" Ali aggressively persisted.

Wiz checked his lip, glanced around, then proceeded to tell Ali what the fight was about. Ali and Al-Ameen listened to his whole Crystal story with expressionless faces. The only comments they made were mainly questions of clarification, but they held their tongues until he finished.

"So I was like, fuck it, shoot a fair one," Wiz concluded.

Ali lit a Newport and put the lighter back in his

pocket. He blew the thick smoke into the frigid night air and watched it quickly dissipate. "Nigguhs been tellin' me you been tryin' to turn a crackhead into a housewife, but I told them nigguhs, keep your name out they mouth. If that's what you wanna do, fuck it. But then, I'm hearin' how she always wit' you, even when you in the mix, and I'm like whoa. Fuck is lil' cuz thinkin'," Ali stated, and Wiz tried to explain, but Ali stopped him. "Let me finish." He hit the cigarette, then said, "Word is bond, Wiz, you in a position to see some real cheese, okay, 'cause your weight is up here. Any mistakes and shit be like dominoes. You got enough problems than to be out here fightin' over some chick! Smokin' or not, what the fuck shit you on? Huh? You 'posed to have thanked Moo for pullin' yo' coat to that triflin' shit, then took her home and whooped her ass, yo! Am I right, Ameen?"

"Word is bond, Wiz." Al-Ameen was far from a yes-man, he was just a man of few words. Wiz looked at the two men who had basically raised him in the life, knowing they were right.

"Now dig, go home and straighten that. If you love this broad like that, raise her ass like a thoroughbred, if not, turn that mule into dog food and feed her to the street. Either way, I hear you doin' this bullshit again, you gonna shoot me and Ameen a fair one, aiight?"

Wiz nodded his understanding. As Ali and Al-Ameen walked to the car, Ali stood in the open driver's door and said with a smirk, "A shame what happened to Moo, huh?"

Wiz looked perplexed.

"Oh, you ain't heard?" Ali snickered. "Don't worry...you will." And with that he got in the car and pulled off.

Three days later Wiz would find out Moo's body had been found with two to the head on the steps of his own basement. But that night Wiz wasn't thinking about Moo, he was focused on Crystal.

Crystal sat on the toilet. The floor around her feet was cluttered with baking-soda-caked spoons, empty vials and half-empty lighters. She stuffed the rocks into the end of the pipe until she couldn't stuff anymore, hoping to take a big enough hit to stop her heart. If not, to get so high she never came down, never feel anything again but cocaine's sickening comfort. Her hand was shaking so badly, she could hardly keep the lighter to the opposite end. She inhaled, eyes widening as the smoke filled her lungs, her mind and her soul. *Higher, baby...Get higher, baby, and don't ever come down!*

The words of Melle Mel's "White Lines" floated from the back of her mind. *Twice as sweet as sugar, twice as good as salt. And if you get hooked, baby, it's nobody else's fault!*

"Yo, Crystal! Where you at!"

She heard Wiz call and slam the door behind him, but she was ashamed to answer him. She sat paranoid on the edge of the toilet seat until she damn near jumped out of her skin when he kicked the door open.

"You fuckin' wit' Moo now, huh?! You takin' my money and spendin' it wit' him? Huh?"

"I...I," she stuttered, "I didn't want you to get mad."

Wiz couldn't believe the irrationality of her statement. "You didn't what?"

Crystal got up and came over to him. "I know how you hate to give me stuff all the time, so I figured—"

"You'd go behind my back!" Wiz furiously finished her sentence, then turned his back and walked a few feet away.

"No, I didn't go behind your back, Wiz," she said.

"How the fuck you didn't? Did I know? Did you tell me? Did you purposely not fuckin' tell me?" Wiz paced the floor, fuming. "Did you fuck him, Crystal?"

Her whole body stiffened like he had slapped her. "I can't believe you'd even ask me some—"

He cut her off, his stomach full of butterflies, anticipating the answer. "I ain't talkin' about last week! Did you ever fuck that nigguh?" This time her whole body went limp, and all she could do was drop her head. Wiz turned away in an anguished rage and punched the wall, causing a picture to fall. He chuckled. "What the fuck am I doin'?" He chuckled harder, then laughed to keep from crying. "Muhfuckas in the street runnin' around talkin' about I'm trying to turn a crackhead into a housewife. Fuckin'...laughin' behind my back like I'm a clown, and you gonna go and do this dumb shit!"

Crystal was crushed, but she mustered up enough to say, "Then maybe I should just go."

"Naw, maybe you should stop smokin'!" he fired right back.

"I swear to you, Wiz, I'ma try harder, harder than I ever—"

Wiz's brushing past her into the bathroom cut her words off. He went straight to her Gucci pocketbook and dumped everything on the floor.

"What are you…" Crystal started to say until she saw him start throwing full bottles of crack in the toilet and flushing it. Her habit made her blurt, "Is you crazy?" She tried to reach in the toilet and salvage one of the bottles, but Wiz pushed her back and dumped the rest. "Stop it! Leave my shit alone!" she screamed hysterically, beating his back. He stood up after flushing everything and looked at her. He could see the hysteria in her eyes. "You gonna give me some more, Wiz! Give me some more now!"

"No."

"You ain't my father, mutherfucka, you can't control me!"

"Then control yourself," he retorted calmly.

"I swear to God, I'ma suck every dick in Jers—"

He turned her whole face with an open-handed slap. He didn't slap her out of anger, so he didn't try and hurt her. He wanted to make her mad.

She lunged at his face, trying to dig her nails in, but he easily swatted her hands away and told her, "Fight."

And she did, swinging wildly, but doing no damage. He reached in and smacked her again. "Fight," he repeated.

Crystal grunted with emphasis, swinging, swinging and swinging. Wiz smacked her once more. "Fight."

She couldn't anymore, because she was exhausted. She fell into his arms, sobbing like a small child, lost and turned out. He allowed her weight to sag against him, causing them to slide slowly to the floor. He cradled her in his arms, whispering, "Fight, baby girl... you're gonna need it."

FOUR

Five...four...three...two...one...
Happy new year!!!
The ball in Times Square dropped, signaling the beginning of 1987 and a new beginning for Crystal. She had never fought so hard for anything in her life, but slowly she was regaining her spirit of self, her motivation to be her best, and Wiz was with her every step of the way.

Times Square on New Year's eve was the place to be, and 1987 was no different. Everyone came out to do it up in their own way, but Crystal and Wiz did it big. Wiz rented a cocaine-white stretch limousine and held Forty-Deuce hostage as he and Crystal fucked it up in matching full-length chinchillas, diamonds smiling for every flash. They club-hopped from the Silver Shadow to the Red Parrot and even blessed the Latin Quarters with a paparazzi-type entrance. They owned the night, so they would only share it with each other.

Back around the way, paper was steadily flowing, so much so that Wiz started selling hundred-dollar clips for fifty dollars. He changed the game and had nigguhs blowing his pager like crazy. Nigguhs who ain't have their weight up couldn't compete, and those who did had no choice but to do the same. Crystal on the other hand was on top of the world. The first couple of months getting off crack had been tough, but once they passed it had gotten that much easier. Whenever the urge did hit her to scratch that itch, she'd remember Wiz's word, "Fight," then she'd sing Alicia Myers's "I Want to Thank You." *I want to thank you, heavenly Father / For shining your light on me / You sent me someone who really loves me and not just my body.*

Wiz became her everything, her world and her new addiction. She had to have him all the time. Not just sexually, although it was liable to go down anywhere anytime, she had to have him around, close. He didn't take her everywhere as he had before, because then coke would always be in her face or in her presence. But she kept a constant check on him, beeping him and would be like, "Hey, boo! Where you at? You comin' home soon?" It irked Wiz slightly, but he understood, so he never let it show.

"Gimme like an hour."

"An hour?" she'd pout. "You gonna leave me naked for an hour," she'd purr, because she knew how to get him.

"Aiight, twenty minutes."

Truth be told, between the game and home, Wiz was happily exhausted, but exhausted nonetheless. So one afternoon, while he and Crystal were cuddled in the afterglow, he asked, "You ever think about going back to school?"

Crystal lifted her head from his chest. "You tryin' to get rid of me, huh?" she asked, only half jokingly, because she had become very possessive of him.

Wiz chuckled. "Naw, yo, I just asked, you know, 'cause I know how you told me how much you liked it."

"That's true," she had to admit. She rolled over on her stomach and rested her forearm on his chest and her chin on her forearm. "It's not a bad idea...on one condition?"

"What?"

"You go back with me."

Wiz threw his head back and laughed. "Stop playin'. Me? Go back to school?"

Crystal was feeling the idea more and more because school would mean less time in the streets and more time with her. "It'll be good for both of us. We could go to Essex County and you can just test out and get your GED, then we could take business classes together. Turn that street money legit."

"We'll see," Wiz replied, realizing his plan had backfired.

Several weeks later Wiz had his GED and he and Crystal began to go to Essex County College together. He was still in the streets, but he let Nu-Nu handle things more and more.

"Shorty got that nigguh fucked up," Nu-Nu would say, "got Wiz in school and shit, yo."

Word got to Ali Smalls and he was proud of little cuz. He even approved of shorty because she was having a good effect on Wiz. School was good, money was good and love was good, until one day Veronica beeped Wiz.

He and Crystal were home making spaghetti. So he picked up the kitchen phone and hit Veronica back. "You beep me?" he asked, cradling the phone to his shoulder and stirring the sauce.

"Wiz, I need to see you," Veronica said, sounding like she was crying.

"For what?" he questioned.

Crystal was fixing the table a few feet away. She knew who Veronica was and what she did for Wiz, but she definitely didn't know what she did *with* Wiz.

"Wiz, please, when is you comin' over here?" Her sobs were getting heavier.

Wiz knew in his gut that this was no conversation he wanted to have with Crystal right there, so he replied, "Tomorrow, as usual. You straight?"

"No!" she blurted out, "I'm pregnant!"

She said it so loud, Wiz swore Crystal heard her. He quickly glanced her way, but she made no indication she had heard.

"And?" he quipped, trying to keep his answers short.

"Please don't do me like that, Wiz, I'm not a ho. I know it's yours, please, just come see—"

Wiz cut her off. "Whatever. See you then." He hung up.

Crystal could sense something in his mood. "Everything okay?"

Wiz mixed the sauce with the noodles. "Yeah. Fuckin' Veronica want more money for the trip, that's all."

Crystal shrugged. "Can you blame her? Shit getting hot out there."

Wiz didn't really hear her, because he was already thinking about an abortion, and whether or not he could convince Veronica to have one. His or not, he was willing to foot the bill, to avoid the hassle down the road.

Before he could sit down, the phone rang again. He started to get up but Crystal was already on it. "Hello?... Yeah hold...Veronica, you okay?"

Before he knew it, Wiz had snatched the phone, yelling, "What the fuck you keep callin' for?"

"Don't be like that—"

Wiz hung up again. Crystal just looked at him.

"Wiz. What is going on?" she asked in the calmest voice she could muster.

He looked away to get a lie together, but before he could the phone rang a third time. He flinched for it, but Crystal's gaze dared him to touch it. It rang two more times, then she answered.

"Yes." Her guts were all quivery like when you expect bad news. "Yeah, go 'head..." When her eyes shut tight, he knew what she was hearing, and when she put her hand to her stomach, he knew what she was feeling. "I'll tell him for sure."

Crystal hung up and said, "Veronica says she's sorry it had to be this way, but you wouldn't talk to her. She hopes you understand." With that Crystal turned to walk away.

"Crystal! So you just gonna fall for that bullshit? That ain't my fuckin' kid, yo!" Wiz explained to her motionless back.

"So...you sayin' you didn't have sex with her, Wiz?" Crystal asked, then turned to him. "Look me in my eyes and tell me you didn't fuck her, Wiz?"

"Before, okay, before," he admitted.

"So you're telling me a female you claim you pay with money just bit the hand that feeds her because you used to fuck her?"

Crystal shook her head and began to walk away again, but Wiz admitted, "I fucked up, aiight?"

Silence.

"Aiight?" Wiz sighed.

"What you gonna do about it?" she asked.

"It's too late to get another mule, so after this last run tomorrow, I'm cutting her off, word is bond," Wiz declared.

Crystal looked at him and replied, "Do what you feel is best," and walked away.

He knew he had been set up. It all played back in his head. The phone call, the timing, the sob story. It all added up to the pistol to his temple.

"Run that shit, nigguh."

He vowed to kill Veronica. She had watched him come up from half a brick to three every two weeks. Then she had made her move. Two cats in masks pistol-whipped him until he told them where the coke was at in the car. He spit up a tooth along with three kilos of cocaine and his Jetta. They even took the measly eight hundred dollars he had on him, leaving him leaking on St. Nicholas Avenue.

*   *   *

Crystal sat at home waiting for him to return, but he had been gone all night. Too long. All kinds of things went through her mind. She thought of all the nights just like this one, when he was with Veronica, betraying her love...He was taking too long...Her thoughts turned over on themselves and before she knew it, she felt that itch. She couldn't sing it away because she felt more alone than ever before...And the urge to scratch grew. Just one...she knew where his stash was...just one...But she forgot, one is too many, and a million is never enough. One became two, two became a clip and the clip made her guilty enough to know she had gone too far. She imagined Wiz coming through the door. She couldn't let him find her like this. She had to go... get out. Wiz had about a half a kilo left, of which Crystal took at least a good nine ounces. She grabbed her coat and headed out the door.

Meanwhile Wiz tried to call collect, but he got no answer, so he tried again. Still no answer. He called four times until he accepted the fact Crystal wasn't there. He called Moe collect and finally got an answer. He told Moe he was needed in Harlem and to bring the heat. An hour later he and Moe pulled up to Veronica's building. They went to her apartment, but when they got no answer, Moe kicked in the door.

Empty.

"Fuck!" Wiz exclaimed.

Just like that, he was out a large portion of his weight.

All he had left was the half at the crib and a few bundles of clips, which all totaled up to less than a key.

"Let's go."

But his nightmare wasn't over...When Moe dropped him off, and he went upstairs, he called out, "Crystal! Crystal!" He looked in the bedroom, no Crystal. He looked in the bathroom, no Crystal there either. But there was no time for that, he was in hustle mode, and he was determined to get his weight back up.

Wiz rushed to his stash, opened it and couldn't believe his eyes. He had found Crystal—or at least where she had gone...Wiz lowered his head into the palms of his hands, thinking of Ali Smalls's words, "Any mistakes and shit be like dominoes." He felt like his whole castle had fallen in on him. But Wiz wasn't a quitter. The absence of Crystal had him sick and his loss had him boiling, but he refused to fail. He went and took a long hot shower. And washed the caked-up blood off his body.

He put on a fresh Sergio Tacchini sweatsuit and prepared to take his grind back out the block. The only problem was the one he had created for himself. Clips were no longer a hundred dollars, they were fifty dollars. But with the loss he had taken he couldn't keep up with his own prices, but it was too late because everybody was on that now, so the feens expected it.

Wiz went hard, hand to hand for a few days, getting little sleep and little food. So when Ali Smalls pulled up to him on Goldsmith, he didn't look like the man he used to be. He needed a haircut and his sneakers weren't crisp. A sure sign that a man in the streets ain't on top of his game.

Ali approached, gave him a hug and asked, "Whut up, lil' Wiz, how you?"

Wiz shrugged because he could see how he was doing in Ali's eyes. "Just tryin' to get mine."

Ali nodded. "I heard about the New York shit. Shorty just disappeared, huh?"

"Yeah."

"What goes around comes back around, you'll see her again."

Wiz just nodded, glancing around, keeping an eye out for narco.

"Whut up wit' you and ol' girl?" Ali asked, getting Wiz's complete attention.

"Ain't nothin', yo . . . nothin," Wiz told him.

"Yeah, I figured that. You know, since I see she back on the shit. I figured you cut her off," Ali surmised, knowing that it wasn't the case at all.

Wiz bit. "Where you see her at?" he questioned with too much urgency in his tone.

"Why?" I thought you said wasn't nothin'? Lil' cuz, do Ali a favor. Leave her alone, aiight?" Wiz wanted to, but he needed to see her. Talk to her, so he couldn't answer. Ali sighed. "She on Lehigh Avenue. Staying wit' some head named Tricia."

Wiz shook Ali's hand. "Good lookin' out, Cuz. I 'preciate that."

"Yeah, I bet you do."

Crystal sat on Tricia's bed, letting the TV watch her. She hated to be back around Tricia, but she had no place else to go, and when she gave Tricia a little bit of coke, she was damn sure welcome. Crystal hadn't even smoked too much of the nine ounces, but she had smoked enough to know she wasn't cured. It was still in her.

She missed Wiz, but she was hurt by his betrayal and ashamed of hers. She yearned to go back to him, but...

"Crystal." Tricia came to the bedroom door. "Somebody here to see you."

Crystal didn't have to ask who it was, because she already knew. "Okay." She didn't know what he would do or say, but it had to be confronted. Wiz walked in and for a moment they just looked at each other. "How's Veronica?" she quipped sarcastically, really wanting to say how she missed him.

"Fuck Veronica, where's my shit?" he intoned, really wanting to ask, *Why did you leave me?*

Crystal reached under the bed, pulled out some socks and pulled out more than half of what she had taken. She tossed it to the end of the bed.

Wiz stared at the white rocky substance and said, "Why?"

She began to say, "Because, Wiz, I was confused and hurt, so—"

He cut her off. "Not that, yo, why period? What about this shit make you just fuckin' abandon everything, huh? Why?" he repeated.

"You wouldn't understand, Wiz, you can't."

"This shit is crazy," he stated, more to himself than to her. "How the fuck can that shit make you just say, fuck everything, take everything, take you away from me?" Wiz probed, striking his chest for emphasis. "How?"

Crystal looked at him "Wiz... I wanna go home."

But Wiz was too focused on his rival to hear her. His pride felt challenged and his curiosity was aroused. "Gimme your pipe."

Crystal's eyes widened. "Why?"

Wiz grabbed her purse. He emptied the contents, then rummaged through them until he found the pipe.

"What are you doing, Wiz?"

"I'ma show you this shit ain't nothin', yo. Then you'll see for yourself you don't need it."

"Wiz? You don't know what you're doing."

But his mind was made up. He stuffed the pipe full and Crystal tried to snatch it away, but he moved, put the lighter to it, and for the first time he heard crack speak. *"See, Wiz... it ain't shit... only weak-minded nig-guhs can't handle me. But you ain't weak, are you, Wiz? Hell no... but let me ride with you 'cause I'ma keep you sharp. Put you back on top and give you that edge... see how open you is? I do that, me and you, Wiz, me and you. Let's get this money!"*

Crystal refused to watch him, but she heard the lighter flick over and over and over again. When it finally stopped, she glanced over and saw Wiz standing in the corner, mumbling. "Me and you, baby... me and you," but he wasn't talking to Crystal.

Six months later...

"Yo, Wiz! Wiz! Over here, yo!" Nu-Nu called out to him, snickering.

Nu-Nu, Lil Mike and Pills were chilling on Goldsmith when Nu-Nu spotted Wiz around the corner in his trademark gray sweatpants and army jacket. He wasn't coming to Goldsmith to pick up money anymore; he was here to give it away. Everybody knew Wiz was smoking, and it was cats like Nu-Nu who wanted to rub it in.

"Whut up, Nu? Pills? Mike? What's up?" Wiz asked, pulling out six crumpled-up dollar bills. "I'm a little short today, but—"

"Man, you short every day!" Nu-Nu laughed. "No shorts today."

"Come on, baby, this me. Look out, yo," Wiz begged.

"Wash my car, Wiz, I'll give you a dime," Pills teased.

"A dime? At least let me get two?"

Lil Mike watched the banter until he couldn't take it anymore. "Fuck that shit, Wiz, I got you, yo. Come on."

He and Wiz walked away from the group, then Lil Mike turned to him and said, "Don't fuck wit' them nigguhs, Wiz, they be tryin' to play you out. Here." He handed Wiz four bottles.

"Good lookin', Mike, word up. Here, you want this?" He tried to give Mike the money.

"Naw, just keep it," Mike replied, feeling sorry for the man he used to admire.

"Thank you, man, and, yo...trust me. I know I'm

fucked up, but this is Wiz, baby. I'ma bounce back. Get strong, yo, then me and you gonna sew shit up, word is bond," Wiz promised, believing his own pipe dream.

"Sure, Wiz, sew shit up." Mike shook his hand. "I'm down, homeboy." He smiled. Mike watched Wiz shuffle off, wondering how a nigguh like Wiz could fall off.

Wiz wondered the same exact thing on his way back to his mother's house. Last year this time, he was the man. Now he was just a sham. But it couldn't be the crack. Naw, he could quit whenever he wanted, he just didn't want to. For what? Crack kept him on point, or so he made himself believe.

As soon as he walked in, his mother was in his face. "They let you get the short?"

Wiz gripped the bottles in his pocket tighter and handed her the money back. "Naw." He headed for his room.

"Well, did you tell them I get my check tomorrow?" he heard her say as he closed his door and stuffed a towel under it so she couldn't smell the smoke. He pulled out the vial and retrieved his pipe from under the pillow. He loaded the pipe as he had done a thousand times, flicked up and fantasized about his master plan to come up.

He was jolted back to reality when his mother banged on the door. "Wiz! You on probation or somethin'? Some lady here to see you."

Lady? Probation? he thought. He wasn't on probation and he ain't have no lady, ever since Crystal left. "I'm comin'."

He put the pipe down carefully, brushed himself off and opened the door. The face he saw froze him. It was Crystal. She was dressed in a dark purple skirt set with black pumps. Her hair was cut like Anita Baker's and her weight was up. She looked good, damn good...too good. "Hello, Wiz."

Wiz turned away in disgust. "The fuck you doin' here, huh?" He hadn't seen her since the night he first hit the pipe. The next morning she was gone. At first he was sick, but crack quickly cured him, filled her void and became his all.

"I came to see you, Wiz...to take you home," Crystal stated, wanting to cry seeing him like this, but knowing he needed her strength.

"Home?" He chuckled. "I am home, you the one that left."

Crystal walked into his room. "I never left you, Wiz, never."

"Well, where you been all this time, the corner store? Get the fuck outta here," he hissed.

Crystal ignored his tone and said, "The way I was, the way we were...we wasn't no good for each other. You watched me destroy myself, then I saw you take the same road, Wiz. So I had to do something."

"So you left? Just, fuck Wiz, and ran off," Wiz accused.

"I went to rehab. That's where I've been. In rehab. I got out thirty days ago, and I'm back in school. I'm stayin' at home until I find a job, now here I am and I'm takin' you home," Crystal concluded.

Wiz clapped his hands sarcastically. "The end. Now if you'll excuse me, I got shit to do."

He reached for the pipe, but she grabbed his wrist. "Ay yo, take your—" His words were interrupted by a face-turning smack. At first he was shocked, but his emotions quickly turned to anger.

"Fight," Crystal commanded him, unafraid of any consequences.

"I'ma let that go, but next time—"

She smacked him again, this time harder. "Fight," she repeated more firmly.

The emotions that welled up inside him started low and bubbled up like lava.

Shit from way down, way down deep came spewing to the brink. So when she raised her hand the third time, he sprang from the bed and grabbed her, wrapping his arms around her waist. Wiz didn't have the strength emotionally or the motivation physically to do anything but fall to his knees, holding Crystal around the waist like he was holding on for dear life. The tears ran down his cheeks in torrents, so Crystal just held his head to her womb and whispered, "Fight, black man... because you're going to need it."

THE LAST LAUGH

BY BONTA

Hey, Nita, where your brother at?" the passenger of a custom-painted candy-apple-red Chevy Caprice asked.

In the streets, he was known as BoBo. One of the most notorious and most feared of the Black P. Stones of Chicago's east side neighborhood called Eighty-third or simply Eight-Trey because of its proximity to Eighty-third Street. From Eighty-first up to Eighty-fifth, from South Chicago Avenue to Commercial Avenue, guys claimed Eighty-third as their set. And BoBo, five feet ten, two hundred forty pounds of dark-complected muscle, with the stature of an NFL player, was in control of it. He was clean-cut in appearance, but grimy in character.

"I don't know! Ain't seen him," a young wide-eyed girl with plaited hair answered.

"Aiight then. Tell him I'm looking for him."

"Aiight, BoBo."

"Drive up to the park," BoBo instructed the young driver. Although it was not his car, BoBo was calling the shots. If he was instructing, you had better be following his instructions or else! He was known for wreaking havoc on his own guys as well as his enemies.

They rode up to Eckersall Park, which was situated between Eighty-second and Yates Avenue and Eighty-second and Essex Avenue. It was a fairly small park that had a big basketball court, a small court, a swing set, and a grassy area for playing football. Across the street was a stadium where local high schools played their football games and ran track.

They turned onto Eighty-second Street from Yates Avenue. Cars lined both sides of the street. Some youngsters played tag football while a full-court basketball game ran with spectators on its sides, some watching and others waiting on next. Not far from the court's edge a dice game was in session. Hustlers hoped to come up on some money while some just tried their luck. There was an older couple who had seen opportunity knocking. They had converted an ice cream truck and parked right in the middle of the park. They sold beef and turkey hot dogs, Polishes, burgers, chips, candy, and ice-cold sodas. BoBo had let them know that the selling of swine was prohibited in *his* park. Knowing his reputation, they complied. A little farther down by the swings were benches. Guys and girls sat and stood around talking, smoking and drinking.

"Drop me off right here and park up there," BoBo directed the guy driving as he pointed farther down Essex Avenue.

"Aiight."

As he got out of the car, a guy yelled out his name

from the crowd of people surrounding the benches. "BoBo."

BoBo nodded his head while keeping a serious look on his face. He walked over to the crowd, which was really broken down into smaller groups. A couple of his comrades comprised one group. He went to them first.

"All is well?" he asked while extending his hand.

The first one to shake his hand was Looney. His name spoke for itself. He was certified crazy. At six feet tall with a stocky build from various stints in prison, he had a dark complexion and body full of homemade tattoos that showed his allegiance to the Black P. Stones. The tattoos on his face were enough to cause even the most hardcore gangbanger to back off him. He was BoBo's best friend. They had grown up together and become part of the backbone for Eighty-third. "Fa sho', nigga!" Looney said.

They did their special handshake that was unique to their gang.

BoBo shook the other guys' hands as well. "What's that I smell?" he asked with his face turned up like he had smelled a soiled baby's Pamper.

"What smell?" Looney asked him.

"You don't smell that shit?"

Looney just shrugged his shoulders. He did not have the slightest idea what BoBo was talking about.

"Hey!" BoBo called out. "Hey, homie." The guy he was calling was standing several feet away, puffing on a blunt. "What you smokin' on?"

The guy did not answer. Instead, he walked over

toward BoBo and handed him the half of a blunt cigar that he was smoking. "Here, BoBo. Go ahead and kill it," he told him while smiling.

BoBo took it and smelled it. "It's straight weed?"

"Naw. I sprinkled a lil' salt on it," the guy boasted, speaking of the powder cocaine mixed with the marijuana he had rolled into the cigar.

Before anyone had even thought he would, BoBo swung and slapped him so hard he literally spun around. Dazed, he went to run but BoBo's guys were on him like hounds on a fox, catching him within a few steps. The people around all stared and wondered what the guy had done that quick and what would happen to him now that he had obviously pissed BoBo off.

A girl in the crowd mumbled, "BoBo is tripping!"

"My fault, BoBo, man. I didn't know." BoBo's henchmen held dude tight, forcing him to his knees.

"Let that nigga up," BoBo commanded..He waited for him to stand. "So you like getting high, huh?"

The guy said nothing.

"Huh?!" BoBo yelled, causing him to jump.

"Y-y-y-y-yeah," he stuttered.

"How old are you?"

"Twenty."

"Who made you put coke on this blunt?" He raised the blunt and blew on the fire to keep it lit.

"What?"

"Nigga, you heard me."

"Nobody."

"Well you see these shorties out here?" He pointed to

the little kids who were on the nearby swings. The guy glanced over at them. "You ain't finna make them smoke this shit you fuckin' yourself up with. Plus, I told your ass before 'bout smokin' this shit in this park. Didn't I?"

"I know, BoBo. I forgot. My fault. I ain't gonna forget no more. On everything I love," he cried, the fear obvious in his eyes.

"I know you ain't," BoBo told him, lightly smacking him on the cheek. "Hold this muthafucka!" He reached for the guy's T-shirt.

"BoBo, what you doing?" Dude was on the verge of panic.

BoBo ignored him as he tried to jerk himself away from the two guys holding him. "Looney, put this dope-fiend-ass nigga in a chicken wing." BoBo began blowing on the blunt, making its flame glow brighter and brighter orange with each breath he gave it.

Looney took over by getting behind the guy and putting him in a choke hold. Upon seeing BoBo coming closer to his now exposed chest with the blunt, he began jerking wildly.

"Nigga, if you kick me, I'ma beat your ass half to death out here!" BoBo told him.

He knew BoBo would do just that and stopped jerking. It was no use anyhow. Looney's grip was like vise grips.

"Now I'ma help you remember what the fuck I tell you."

The crowd oohed and aahed as the guy screamed from the burning blunt's flame being extinguished on his chest's flesh.

"And for any other primo-smokin' muthafuckas. Smoke that bullshit somewhere else!"

The guy fell to the ground in pain as soon as Looney released him.

"Get the fuck up and get from 'round here," one of BoBo's henchmen told him as he kicked him in the ass.

They laughed as they walked down to the food truck. The driver who had brought BoBo to the park had caught the end of the action, however, he was not surprised. He had witnessed worse. *BoBo was unpredictable*, he thought as he mingled with the crowd.

"Hey there, BoBo. What you want? Your usual?" the middle-aged woman in the truck asked.

"How you doing, Mrs. Brown? What's up, Mr. Brown?" BoBo spoke. "Mr. Brown," he said again.

Mrs. Brown turned around to see Mr. Brown had dozed off with headphones on. "Dee. Dee," she called while shaking him.

Startled, he jumped, snatching off his headphones. "Huh? What? What happened?"

BoBo and Mrs. Brown laughed at him. He had to laugh at himself.

"I was saying what's up to you, that's all," BoBo told him.

"Oh, hey there, BoBo. I was sitting here listening to my blues. You don't know nothing 'bout that there, do you, boy?" Mr. Brown asked him.

"Naw. That's before my times."

"What can I get you?" Mrs. Brown asked again.

"Let me get two cream sodas," he said, placing a

five-dollar bill on the opening's ledge that served as a counter. She handed him the two ice-cold cans and he walked off.

Mrs. Brown turned back around in time to watch him leave and called out to him, "BoBo, you forgot your change."

"Keep it. Put it on my bill or something," he yelled back.

Over by the basketball courts, he stopped to check out the dice game. Seeing him, the guys spoke to him.

"BoBo. My nigga. Let me holler at you," one of the guys in the huddle said.

"What's up?" BoBo asked as he finished his second can of soda.

The guy consulted with him about a problem he was having. It was a minor one he was having with a fellow Black P. Stone that he did not want to escalate into something big and end up getting them both a physical violation. Members were not allowed to fight with one another. Their punishment, or violation as it was called, could consist of their having to stand against a wall while an appointed member punched them repeatedly anywhere below the neck for a certain amount of minutes. It depended on the severity of the offense. BoBo gave him a quick solution.

A pearl-white '75 Chevy Caprice convertible with its top down, twenty-four-inch chrome wheels glistening, sounds beating and vibrating, came riding past. Passing BoBo, it stopped and backed up. The driver was a light-skinned female whose hair looked as if she had just left the beauty shop. Although the top was down, she had the tinted windows up.

"BoBo," the female hollered.

"Who is that?" he hollered back.

"Boy, quit playing."

Hearing a female's voice, he walked slowly toward the car. He saw what he thought was a familiar face. "Tasha?"

"Yeah, nigga. Who you thought it was? One of your hook hoes?" She and her passenger giggled. Her passenger was a dark-skinned girl in her late teens or early twenties. She seemed to be thick from where BoBo stood just looking at her top half. Her hair was freshly done as well.

"Pull over."

"Un-uh. Come ride around the block with me."

"Girl, what you on?"

"Nigga, get in."

He walked around to the passenger side. The girl in the passenger seat got out and hopped in the back. He now saw that she was definitely thick. She wore a tight fitting T-shirt with some words outlined in glitter on the front. She had on some blue-jean shorts that barely covered her ample backside and sandals to show off her fresh pedicure that matched her manicure. He caught a whiff of her perfume and a look at her lower back tattoo as she climbed into the backseat. He got in and closed the door.

"I see you looking at her ass," Tasha told him, although she was smiling.

"What you talking 'bout?"

Tasha was looking even better than she had the last time he had seen her. Her tight-fitting T-shirt had the words I LOVE ALPO in glitter on the front. She wore some tight short shorts as well. She pressed her Air Force 1s to the gas pedal and burned rubber as she took off. Almost everyone in the park looked at the clean classic as it sped off.

"So what's up? Where you been and whatchu doin' 'round here?"

"You ain't happy to see me?" she asked.

"I'm always happy to see you. Where your man at? I see he got you ridin' real slick."

"I ain't here to talk about him," she said with attitude.

They drove around a few blocks and caught up with each other. It had been months since they had seen each other. The last time resulted in Tasha's being seen by one of her man's friends and getting a beatdown. The black eye she had gotten made her go into hiding.

She drove back to the park.

"So when we gonna hook up again?" she asked him.

"I don't know. Sometime soon," he told her, not wanting to seem pressed.

She leaned over to kiss him. They shared a brief passionate kiss, then he got out. Her girl got back in the front seat, Tasha cranked the music back up and they drove off as the bass made the ground vibrate and alarms go off.

"Damn, BoBo. Who was that piece?" one of his guys asked him.

"This lil' broad I be fuckin' with."

"Ain't that one of the opposition's car from the Wild 100s' neighborhood?" another one asked.

"Who, Alpo?" BoBo asked him.

"Yeah."

"Probably so. That is his girl." BoBo laughed at his own sarcasm.

"Nigga, you crazy!" the guy said, laughing with him.

BoBo and his guys hung around at the park until the sun went down. Many dudes and females had come through to hang or do some business with him. It was a typical day in the Trey.

Andre was a young Black P. Stone who was now fifteen years old and destined to make a name for himself. His name was ringing around the neighborhood for his love of squeezing the trigger. He was a freshman at Bowen High School. Five feet ten and barely a hundred and fifty pounds, caramel-colored skin tone that he draped in baggy clothes. He was known for toting guns, even to school. He seemed to always be getting into something.

A couple of weeks ago, he got into a scuffle with another Black P. Stone from a different neighborhood called Terror Town. The guy was a part of the Maniac P. Stones. They were a branch of the Stones but still governed by the same rules. It started over a female from Terror Town whom Andre had tried to talk to. She paid him no mind. When he reached to grab a handful of her womanly butt cheeks, she slapped his face.

Reflexes caused him to punch her in hers. One of the guys from Terror Town happened to be walking by and jumped in.

"Nigga, you don't be putting your hands on no sista," Lil' Sam told Andre. He had pulled him off of her.

"Nigga, you don't fucking be getting in my mutha-fuckin' bidness. Fuck this stuck-up bitch!"

"Fuck you, nigga!" Lil' Sam said right before punching him.

Damn! Out of all the days to not bring a gun to school. Lil' Sam whipped his ass! Andre seemed really small as he was being tossed about. Lil' Sam was not trying to really punish Andre but he kept coming back for more so Lil' Sam had no choice but to keep dishing it out. A crowd formed. Some of the other Stones broke it up. Andre seemed to be going crazy.

"Let me go! Get y'all fucking hands off me!" Andre said, trying to snatch away from the Stones who were holding him. He was out of breath and pissed off.

"Calm down, Dre!" his guy Rooster told him.

"Fuck that! I'm killing that muthafucka!"

There was only one guy holding Lil' Sam back but a few restraining Andre.

"Come on. Let's get outta here," Rooster told him, pulling him in the opposite direction.

Word had gotten back to BoBo. He had heard several versions of the story. After Andre's version, he and the guy in charge of the Maniac P. Stones in Terror Town decided to give both of the guys violations. The violation did not sit well with Andre.

"That ho-ass nigga wanna side with them niggas, he can die with them niggas," Andre told Rooster on his way home after receiving his violation.

"You straight, nigga. Let that shit ride."

"Fuck that shit! This shit ain't over!"

"Whatever. You know I'm down for whatever," Rooster told him.

Since that incident, it seemed that Andre had been doing things just to aggravate BoBo. His latest stunt had been beating down a guy who was visiting his family in the neighborhood. Andre had claimed that he was wearing his hat to the right, which was the side to which their enemies wore theirs. He had heard that somebody had run to BoBo telling him. He was waiting for BoBo to come to him about it. The guy was not a Stone, so what could he do or say?

"Andre, BoBo came by here looking for you," his little sister, Anita, told him when he came in.

His eyes lit up. "Oh yeah?" He was headed toward their basement to bag up the half an ounce of rock cocaine he had just brought. "How long ago?"

"Earlier."

"What he say?"

"Nothing. Just to tell you that he was looking for you."

"Aiight. I'll see his punk ass later."

His little sister giggled at his remark.

"I'm telling you, girl, that nigga jumped in the car with some ho."

"Who was she?"

"I don't know, but the bitch was riding slick. One of them old-ass cars. Bitch had the top down, sounds beating." LaLa was giving Serena the lowdown.

Serena was BoBo's babies' mama. One of many, nevertheless the one he was with at the moment. She had been the faithful girlfriend of one of BoBo's workers, who had mistakenly introduced them. He'd gotten stuck on her beauty and moved in on her.

BoBo had set him up to get robbed of the work BoBo gave him, then got angry and threatened him. Now in debt to BoBo, the worker was treated as a personal flunky. BoBo constantly belittled him while making advances on Serena. When the guy caught on to BoBo's agenda he relocated, leaving BoBo with the prize. Serena was upset at her boyfriend's cowardly exit and had decided to give BoBo a chance.

Now the mother of two beautiful girls, two-year-old BaBa and two-month-old Fatimah, she still maintained a 36-24-38 frame. At five feet four with honey-colored skin tone, light brown eyes, and natural shoulder-length hair, Serena was fine. She never got a chance to show it, seeing that BoBo never allowed her to go anywhere. She knew he was not faithful, but hearing about his infidelities angered her.

"I can't wait 'til that nigga brings his ass home. He expects me to sit up in this muthafucka like I'm on house arrest or something. Then he got his ass out there tricking off," she said angrily. She called his cell phone again. It rang until the voice mail picked up.

"What happened?" LaLa asked.

LaLa was her one and only friend, and acted as her informant. Her older sister, Bianca, had been a Black P. Stone until a hail of gunfire took her life. Now LaLa hung at the park with some of the girl Stones who dated the guys BoBo hung with. Her young beauty received no looks from any of them. To them she was Bianca's lil' sister. The younger guys who tried their luck got nowhere. She dressed in baggy clothes in a tomboyish style. She was five feet seven, dark-skinned and wore braids, a cross between Foxy Brown and Queen Latifah in *Set It Off.* Revealing clothes were not her style. Had she worn them, it would have shown off her 36C cups and twenty-six-inch waist complemented by thirty-eighty-inch hips.

"Shit! Fucking answering machine picked up."

She and Serena sat talking for a while. They talked about things other than BoBo but his affairs lingered in Serena's mind. She loved him, yet this part of the relationship she could do without. If she went out for a walk with the kids and one of his friends saw her, he would throw a fit. And God forbid some unknowing guy pull over to try to talk to her and try his luck. One unlucky guy had done just that. He had gotten out of his car to speak with who he thought was a girlfriend candidate sitting alone on the porch. Before she could get him to leave, BoBo and his goon squad happened to ride past. BoBo went into a rage and dragged her into the house by her hair. The whipping she received was nothing in comparison to the brutal and fatal beating that guy received. His charred remains were found on the other side of town in the trunk of the car he had driven up in. She had read it in the paper BoBo had intentionally left out, turned to the page with the story on it. Before that incident, Serena had just *thought* that BoBo was crazy. It was no longer just a thought.

That was the first time he had put his hands on her in a threatening manner, and it had proven his point. In fact, whenever they had arguments it was how he proved his point. He would always tell her she could attempt to leave him and see what would happen. As bad as she wanted to try sometimes, knowing about the murder, she decided against it.

"Who is that calling like that? Your bitch?"

"Girl, watch your mouth!" BoBo warned. "I'm finna go."

"Un-uh. No you ain't gonna just hit it and run. Fuck that bitch!"

This was the part BoBo hated about coming over to his baby mama Carla's house. She was the mother of his five-year-old daughter Charisse. Carla was tall and thin. Five-eleven barefooted. She had lost all her weight that she had gained from the pregnancy years ago. The cocaine-laced marijuana joints had played a part also. Okay-looking in the face, she wore many scars from fights with males and females. BoBo liked their physical relationship. It was he who had made her the fighter she was. She seemed to love when he beat her. The worse, the better. The sex they would have afterward would be off the charts! So much so, he still came back for more.

He got up to put on his clothes. She jumped up too and grabbed him around his neck, choking him.

"Bitch!" was all he could get out. She was choking him with all her might.

They fell back on the bed, Carla still choking him. She wrapped her legs around him as he struggled to get free from her hold.

"Uhhhh," she gasped as he elbowed her hard in the ribs.

A couple more elbows and she loosened her grip. He broke free and turned around. He gave her punches to the stomach. She used her feet to kick him off the bed. Shocked and angry, he jumped back on top of her, this time delivering punches to her head. Her screams caused him to ease up. She saw an opening and reached up, scratched his face and followed up with a swift kick to his groin.

"Ahhhhhh!" he growled as he buckled in pain.

Carla jumped off the bed, nose bleeding, and got into her fighting stance. "Come on, nigga! Come on!" she shouted.

He was in no position to fight her anymore. "Crazy-ass bitch!"

"Yeah," she said, huffing and puffing. "I thought so." She went to her mirror to survey the damage. *Not bad*, she thought to herself. Her face was a little swollen and her lip was busted but she was okay. There had been times when she looked in the mirror after an episode of their fighting and not recognized the person staring back at her. She wiped the blood from her nose with some tissue, then went back to tend to BoBo.

"After he kicked our ass, you going to see if he's all right? Fuck him!"

"See. That's why he don't like coming over here now. I wish you would keep quiet before you ruin it for us."

There were those voices in her head arguing again. She had gotten used to them now. They had seemed to appear right after she hit her head on the bathroom sink a few years ago when she and BoBo were fighting. Sometimes she listened to them, sometimes she ignored them. This was a time to ignore them. Her BoBo was there.

"Let me see!" she told him.

"Get the fuck away from me!"

"Let me see!" she demanded.

"Bitch, go on!"

Her whole demeanor changed. She stroked his back. "Baby, I'm sorry. You know I get crazy when you about to leave." She kissed his back softly.

As mad as he was and as much pain as her kick had caused him, her kisses were causing him to get an erection. He knew what she wanted. She knew just how to get it too.

"Let me make sure he okay," she whispered while nudging him to turn over. He could not resist. He turned over and lay on his back and gave her access to his dick.

Carla massaged his groin softly. Her rubs made it grow in her hands. She gave the tip a kiss followed by a lick, then engulfed it into her warm, wet mouth inch by slow, delicious inch. BoBo sat back, enjoying the sensation. When it came to her BoBo she knew her way around. She paid homage to the same organ that had released the life-giving seeds that made her a permanent part of his life. She had never stopped loving him and felt that she would feel the same way until her death.

"I don't know why I keep fucking with your crazy ass," BoBo said as he moaned.

They both knew the reason he always came back. Her head game was excellent. She would vary from a very slow stroke while sucking hard to a breakneck speed while sucking slightly and every speed and sucking pressure in between. The combination of speeds and pressures and the sensation of her twirling tongue made his ass clench, toes curl until they cracked, back arch and funny whimpering noises escape.

Satisfied with the results of her work, she let her mouth experience other parts of his body as she got into position to insert him into her pussy. She took control of things while he lay back. As she worked his dick to get her own release, her muscles contracted, fuck faces appeared, moans got louder and movements grew fierce. She dug her nails into his chest unknowingly. The pleasure mixed with pain caused him to explode. Her movements came to a stop and she collapsed on his chest to rest. They both lay lifeless apart from their heavy breathing.

In control of his breathing again, BoBo spoke. "Get up. I gotta go." He felt himself getting sleepy.

"Go 'head. Leave," she said, although she didn't move.

"Get up then."

She rolled over.

"Give me a towel."

"Naw. Let your bitch taste my pussy too."

"Come on now," he said, agitated. "I don't say shit when you go fuck with that goofy-ass nigga."

"You the one who told me to go ahead and holler at him."

"Yeah, I did. What's up with him anyway?"

She told him all that had transpired between them. She had met the guy at the mall. As she always did, she played the game and teased him by telling him he was not ready for her. Like most ballers, he wanted to prove himself and expose his personal business. She got him to go through her to purchase his next package of drugs. BoBo provided her with them. Once he saw it was good and that he could trust her, he would make a bigger purchase. She kept the promise of sex that would knock his socks off lingering in the air and stringing him along.

Once she had worked him up to a nice amount, they would meet at a hotel to do the transaction. The plan was in effect and going just as BoBo had orchestrated it. What she did not tell BoBo was that she had given him a blowjob worth sticking around for. Unlike BoBo, she knew her head game was addictive and he would stick around just for it if for nothing else.

"That's my girl," he said proudly. "Now what room are you gonna get?"

"One in the back on the end. Damn!"

"Aiight. Now go get that towel so I can go."

"You know where they at," she said as she rolled over and got under the covers.

With his mind on the money involved in this setup, he went, washed up in the sink, got dressed and headed home.

The clock read 3:53 a.m. when he stepped into the living room of his and Serena's apartment. He did his usual routine of walking through with his gun drawn, going from room to room. Looking into his daughters' room, he saw that the bed was empty. He made his way through and went into his bedroom. The three sleeping bodies, one large and two small, soothed him. He walked softly to pick up BaBa so he could stay in their bed. He was in no mood for any more sexual activity. He barely had enough energy to shower.

While in the shower, he heard the bathroom door open. He peeked out from behind the shower curtain to see Serena sitting on the toilet. The trickling of the water could now be heard.

"Where's your phone at?" she asked, sounding fully awake.

"Out on the charger. Why?"

"You didn't get my call?"

"My battery went dead earlier," he lied. "Why? What's wrong?"

She did not answer him. He heard the toilet flush and braced for the surge of hot water he knew would come next. He went back to showering. Finishing, he cut off the water and pulled back the shower curtain. Serena was standing there with his boxers in her hands.

"What the fuck is you doing?" he asked her.

"What bitch you been with that done scratched you up like that?" She stared at his chest and face. He had forgotten about the scratches. Quickly, he went to the fogged-up mirror and wiped it. He looked at Carla's engravings. "Muthafucka!" he said, sounding pissed off. "I had to beat the shit out this dude 'bout some money. He was scratching like a bitch. Goddammit!"

"Um-hmm. Turn around."

He turned around. "For what?" he asked, knowing why.

She saw no scratches, but was not convinced. When he turned back around, she threw the boxers in his face. No evidence, however she still felt he was guilty.

Had he not been so tired and worn out from Carla, he would have given her an ass-whupping for a nightcap.

"Don't push your luck!" he warned.

It was business as usual up at Eckersall Park. Same things going on as the day before. Every car coming past received a stare from BoBo. He never knew when one of his enemies would try to do a drive-by.

The traffic got heavy around the time school started to let out. Many of the younger Stones rode past just to see who all was out there. One car stood out from all the others. He would recognize it out of the parking lot full of cars at the United Center. It was the car of his mortal enemy. An enemy made from a best friend-ship turned sour. The silver '95 Honda Accord had a dent in the driver's door, three chrome hubcaps, one missing from the back passenger's side, slightly tinted windows, fan that only worked on levels three and four, with a plug-in CD player, MY DAUGHTER IS AN A STUDENT bumper sticker on the right side of the bumper and a dented-up front license plate from misjudging distances. As it approached, his feelings of love and hate begin to stir.

"Daddy!" the little girl who had emerged from the Honda once it parked upon sighting him said as she ran and jumped in his arms.

"Hey, my little princess. Whatchu doing up here?"

This little girl was his seven-year-old daughter, named Jennifer. The driver of the car was his first baby mama, Janine. Their relationship had ended almost as soon as it started. Her becoming pregnant after a few sexual sessions introduced her to the not-so-sweet-and-loving but possessive side of BoBo. His engagement proposal was not only turned down but a restraining order was obtained. No stranger to jail, BoBo ignored it and continuously threatened her and her mother, forcing her to move. After a year's absence, BoBo had calmed down and moved on. She brought Jennifer around every now and then. He knew, like most other times, it was a money issue. Many a time he had told Janine not to bring his daughter to the park to see him. She did it anyway out of pure spite. He had come to find out over the years that she could be really evil.

"Mommy said you were going to pay for my field trip."

"Field trip? Where you going?"

"Our class got the highest scores so we get to go to the movies," Jennifer told him as she swung her hand in his while they walked toward her mother's car.

"Oh yeah? What y'all going to see?"

"We don't know yet. We have to vote on it."

"Y'all ain't going to see no rated-R movie is y'all?"

She laughed as she got back in the car. "No, silly."

"Silly?"

"Yeah. Silly. Mommy says you've always been silly."

"Oh yeah?" He looked over to Janine, who was acting like she was not paying attention as she cracked a smile. He pulled out a wad of money from his pocket. "Well, check this out. You take this and pay for your trip. Whatever's left, put in your piggy bank. Okay?" He handed Jennifer five twenty-dollar bills. Her eyes grew wide. "You do got a piggy bank, don't you?"

"Yes, Daddy." She turned to her mother. "I can pay your way too, Mommy."

"Naw. That's for you. Your mama can pay her own way or get it from her boyfriend since I'm so silly."

She looked saddened by the tension that was now in the air between her parents. "Okay, Daddy. Thank you."

"Aiight now. Give me a kiss." He leaned down and kissed his daughter. "Be good now."

"Okay, Daddy. I will."

"And don't have no boyfriends."

She just laughed as he closed the door. He walked in front of the car. Janine put the car in drive and bumped his leg. They made eye contact and if looks could kill, one of them would have been dead. He went to the driver's-side window and motioned for Janine to let down her window. She gave him the finger and drove off, leaving him standing there in the middle of the street. Hearing his daughter laughing at him made it even worse. "Fuck that stupid-ass bitch!" he muttered to himself.

A car's horn beeped and startled him, causing him to jump. He turned to see a car full of youngsters laughing and throwing up the Stones hand sign.

Andre was navigating the stolen vehicle, a clean '88 Chevy Caprice Brougham LS that one of the older Stones had ordered from his crew of car thieves. He stole cars to supplement his income as well as to provide some excitement.

"Look at his scared, punk ass jumping. I told you he wasn't shit. I shoulda hit his pussy ass," Andre said, laughing.

"Fuck that nigga. Pull over and let me drive," Rooster told him. The other three Stones in the backseat just enjoyed the ride.

"Let's find this muthafucka and get our money."

"Yeah, you right. Where y'all going?" Rooster asked the three guys in the back.

"Drop us off in the B's," one of them said. The B's was an adjoining neighborhood across from Eighty-third Street.

On his way toward their destination, he saw a young

woman in her mid-twenties pushing a double stroller. He slowed down beside her.

"Excuse me, miss. Can I get out and holla at you?" he asked her. She kept walking as if she did not even notice him.

"Ay yo, ma. Holla at a nigga."

"Boy, you better take your ass on."

"Fuck you then, ol' stuck-up-ass bitch!" he yelled out and sped off.

Rooster was laughing. "Yeah right. Like she was gonna holla at your ass."

"Fuck that ho!"

He drove to the block they wanted and dropped the guys off. He and Rooster drove to their stash garage and parked the Chevy in a hurry to stand on the block where they sold their drugs to all the crackheads who came looking.

Not long after they arrived, a car with some older Stones pulled up. "Hey, shorty, let me holla at you," the driver, who had his hat cocked to the left side, said.

Andre ran up to the window. He had recognized the driver's face from being up at the park. "What's up?" he asked as he gave them the Stones handshake.

"Let us get a couple of them thangs."

"Aiight." Andre ran to his stash.

"Make sho' they propa!" the driver yelled.

Andre ran back and completed the transaction. He had seen all kinds come buy drugs from him. He did not care who they were. As long as they had enough money.

"You saw dude in the backseat?" Rooster asked.

"Yeah. What about him?"

"That was dude BoBo slapped the shit outta in the park. Then put the blunt out on that nigga's chest." Rooster giggled.

"Lame-ass niggas. I woulda definitely killed his ass for that. I'm tired of that muthafucka anyway. You know ol' girl who had the two shorties I was tryna holla at earlier?"

"The one who played you off?" Rooster said, laughing.

"Yeah, that bitch. That's his bitch and two bastards."

"Man. Why you fucking with BoBo like that? We gonna have to fuck around and kill his ass foreal."

"Fuck him. I'm like Scarface." Andre started getting hyped up. "Come on. I'll take your fucking violations." He was beating his chest like Scarface did when he was getting shot. He stopped and walked to the middle of the street, held his hands in the air and yelled at the top of his lungs, "The Trey is mines!"

"Nigga, you done lost it!" Rooster was laughing.

Cars were driving past, the people looking at him standing in the middle of the street. He caused a car to stop and just stood in front of it, still shouting "The Trey is mines!" Rooster was laughing hard. The people in the car had started honking their horn. A few cars had lined up wondering what the commotion was.

"Man, I'm high as hell!"

"Hell yeah! I feel like just whupping a nigga's ass or something."

The driver of the car turned down the radio that was blasting Common's "The Corner." "Did you just say you feel like whupping a nigga?"

"Yeah. What's up? You got somebody in mind?" the guy said, grinning.

"Yeah, I got somebody in mind. That nigga BoBo," the driver said, serious.

The other two passengers got qiuet. They knew the shit was about to hit the fan.

"Oh, so you gonna go there, huh?" the guy said, trying to play it off.

"You damn right I'ma go there," the driver said, still serious. "You let that nigga bitch-slap you, burn you, then tell you that you can't smoke in the park. Who the fuck is he suppose to be?"

"Yeah, like his name's Mr. Eckersall or something," the guy sitting in the back with him said. He and the front seat passenger laughed but the driver and the guy who had been burned stayed serious.

"I didn't see none of y'all tryna help," the guy shot back in defense.

"Nigga, you ain't help yourself. Tryna run and shit."

"Fuck you, nigga!"

"Naw, fuck yourself. You got better pussy."

"You try it then, muthafucka, since you so tough."

"I'll beat your soft ass."

"Oh yeah?" The guy was now in his feelings. The personal comments had permeated his skin and made his blood boil. Coming from his friend made them worse. The drugs amplified his adrenaline. He swung and hit the driver in the back of the head. The car swerved as his punch startled the driver as well as the other two passengers.

The driver pulled the car over and jumped out before it had stopped moving. He ran around to the back passenger-side door. The guy attempted to get out but was rushed by the driver.

"Soft-ass nigga!"

"Show me I'm soft!"

They were exchanging blows in the backseat. The other two passengers quickly separated them.

"Straight up! The beef is with BoBo, not each other," one of them said.

"That's this nigga," the driver said.

"Fuck y'all!" the guy said, and walked off.

The guy who had been in the backseat with him tried persuading him to come back but the driver insisted he was straight.

"Ain't that that lil' nigga Andre up there?" Looney put his blood-red Cadillac Escalade in park and got out. He walked up a few cars to see Andre standing there holding up traffic. "What's up, lil' homie?"

"Shit. All is well."

"Why you holding up traffic?"

"Ain't shit else to do."

"Lil' crazy-ass nigga," Looney said while laughing. "Let these people pass."

"Aiight. Aiight." Andre moved out of their way. He walked back over to where Rooster was.

Looney was now driving past them. He pulled over by them. "Be easy, lil' homie."

BoBo leaned over with a cell phone to his ear. "I wanna holla at you later too!"

"Yeah? You know where I'm at," Andre said, locking eyes with him.

"What?" BoBo could not believe his ears. It was not so much his smart comment but the look he gave. BoBo shook his head and pointed his finger at him. "You lucky I'm on something."

Andre wiped his forehead sarcastically as if he were relieved. Looney threw up the Stones hand sign and drove off. He laughed to himself.

"What's so funny?" BoBo asked angrily.

"Hey. Don't get mad at me. Lil' shorty just standing on his. We was the same way," Looney reminded him.

"Fuck that lil' nigga! He gonna make me put a foot in his ass. Hardheaded lil' muthafucka!"

Looney drove to his woman's cousin's house. Looney had been supplying him with drugs for the past couple of weeks. On the strength of Looney's woman, Tracey, he was given a chance to prove his worth.

"What's up, Looney?"

"Hey, this my man BoBo I was telling you about. BoBo, this is Jamal," he said, introducing them.

BoBo gave Jamal a pound but still wore the mean mug from earlier. He did not say anything while they talked.

Jamal was dark-skinned, two hundred and fifty pounds give or take at five feet nine. At twenty-two years old, he had grown up in this neighborhood and knew everybody though he held no gang affiliations. He felt it was unnecessary.

BoBo saw him as a problem just waiting to happen. Unlike Jamal, he knew how gang politics went. Soon as the guys in this neighborhood got wind of him making money, they would be on him like sharks on bloody meat. He would be fair game since he was not a member of any gang.

After several minutes, BoBo felt as if he could be silent no longer. "So these niggas 'round here ain't gone say nothing when you start making money?" BoBo asked, knowing what he would do.

"Naw. It ain't like that. I know all them."

"Chill out, BoBo. Jamal got this," Looney said.

"Chill out my ass! I can't stand no losses."

Looney was agitated now. The way BoBo was making it seem, he was not his own man. He was just as much in charge as BoBo. They were partners.

"I'ma get up with you, Jamal. Be easy."

"Aiight, Looney."

Soon as they got in his truck, Looney began thinking of a way to get what he had off his chest without snapping out on BoBo. After about ten minutes, he turned down the music. "Check this out, BoBo. Let me handle mines. Just like I let you handle yours."

"Exactly. I handle mines! Nobody else. I don't know that lil' fat muthafucka."

"I'ma say this one more time. Let me do me. Aiight?"

"Whatever, nigga." BoBo turned the music back up.

They rode in silence, both of them in deep thought. It was like that until Looney pulled up to BoBo's car and they parted ways.

BoBo drove around awhile before deciding to head home. He checked his phone. Two people had called since he had been in the truck with Looney. The sounds had been so loud he hadn't heard it ringing. One number was his home number. It had been Serena obviously. The other number he hadn't seen before. It was in the area. He figured it might be a customer. He called it back.

A female answered. "Hello?"

"Who is this?"

"You called here," she replied in a smart tone.

"Somebody trying to call BoBo?"

"Yeah. Serena want you to come pick up the baby's bag she left over here."

"What? Who is this?"

"This is LaLa."

"LaLa from the park?"

"Yeah. When you coming?"

"I'm a couple blocks away. I'll be there in a minute." He hung up. The fact that Serena had been out with his kids added to his anger.

When he pulled up to her building, he called her again. "Bring it on down."

"I just got out the shower. I can't. Come up and grab it."

"Meet me at the door."

"I can't. My pores is open."

"Damn! Aiight, let me park."

"I'ma buzz you up. Three B." She hung up.

He parked and walked to her building's entrance. It was a four-story, eight-unit building. He rang her bell and waited on the series of buzzes to gain entry to the inner halls.

When he reached her door it was cracked. He knocked anyway.

"Come in," she called from inside.

He entered, closing the door behind him. He stood by the door. She came out with just a towel covering her, holding it in the back. He was shocked a little by her lack of clothing.

"Could you do me a favor?" she asked.

"Huh?"

"Put some lotion on my back?" She walked toward him with the lotion bottle in her hand. He was looking skeptical. She put some lotion in his hand and turned around. She let the towel fall to the floor to reveal her naked, glistening body. Bending over to pick it up, legs straight and slightly apart, she gave a full view of her apple bottom with a hint of her pussy.

"Sorry," she said with a giggle. She held the towel to her chest and left the backside exposed.

He had never looked at LaLa in a sexual way before now. He had a full erection from standing so close to her naked body. He rubbed the lotion in his hands and began rubbing her back. Upon his touch, she leaned forward and stuck her behind out just a breath away from his dick.

He massaged the lotion on her entire back. "There you go."

"Thank you." She walked over to the couch and sat down. She began lotioning up her legs and feet. She opened her legs and exposed her womanhood, which was covered by a thick patch of fur.

He watched intently. He had to break his stare. "Where the bag at?"

"Oh yeah. It's in there." She pointed toward her room. The towel fell and exposed her perky 36C-cup breasts.

He went into the room as she got up to lock the door. She went to her room. He was looking around. There were pictures of Bianca on her dresser. BoBo's mind reflected on the night that he and Looney had borrowed her car to go to the store. That's the reason they gave her for borrowing it, anyway. Then they drove her blue 2000 Chevy Malibu to meet a guy who thought he was gaining potential customers. They robbed him of his two kilos of cocaine.

Not appreciating being beaten up and robbed, the man had gathered up some trigger-happy thugs and hit the Trey. Spotting the car, they unloaded five clips worth of bullets from their pistols into the car, where an unsuspecting Bianca and her girlfriend sat smoking a blunt. Bianca was left dead and her girlfriend, Shon Shon, was paralyzed from the waist down. Everyone had their theories of why it happened; however, other than the shooters, BoBo and Looney knew the reason.

"Where the bag at?" he asked, as if he was getting aggravated. He felt like this was a setup.

Her phone was ringing. She went to her nightstand and picked up the cordless phone that was sitting on its base. "Hello?...What's up, Serena."

Hearing her name caused BoBo's heart to beat rapidly. Knowing he had no business standing in her friend's room with her prancing around in nothing but a towel. She put her fingers to her lips, signaling him to be quiet, as if he would say something.

"All right girl, I'ma call you back...He ain't came yet though...Don't worry, I'ma make him come." She placed the phone back on its charging base and threw the towel on the bed.

"What kind of games you playing?"

She walked up to him and was practically nose to nose with him. "Whatever kind you wanna play." She began to kiss him.

Confused and aroused at the same time, he slowly took the lead. The initial shock of her being the aggressor wore off as his hands explored her body. The pear-scented lotion he had helped to spread over her skin diffused as their body heat rose. Kissing her lustfully, he guided her backward until her thighs met the bed.

Stopping his kissing momentarily, he took a step back and began unbuckling his belt. "This between me and you. Don't have nobody in my business! Aiight?"

Instead of answering him, she lay back on the bed.

With his pants and boxers around his ankles, he climbed between her legs and inserted himself inside her. A moan escaped her mouth as he wasted no time in finding the nethermost regions of her womanhood. He

"Hand me that duct tape, breed," BoBo asked of his partner. He went to the bathroom and got a face towel. He took it and stuffed it into the guy's mouth and taped it. He got down by the guy's ear and whispered, "Now this is gonna hurt you more than it hurts me." He stood and let out a menacing laugh. The baller's eyes widened as he wondered what BoBo would do.

BoBo grabbed his ankles and dragged him into the bathroom. Without any concern he lifted him and dropped him into the bathtub. The muffled screams could be heard through the duct tape.

"Awww! Stop the bloodclot crying, tough guy," BoBo mocked in a Jamaican accent. He turned on the cold water and plugged up the tub. He flipped the guy over onto his back. He whistled the beat to the Game and 50 Cent's "This Is How We Do" as the tub filled. When the water rose above his legs, BoBo turned it off. "You cold, tough guy?"

The baller nodded his head up and down. BoBo took his hand and scooped water in his face. He jerked to the side, hoping to dodge the cold water.

"Good! Now I'ma ask your ass one more time. Where's that money?" He then snatched the duct tape from his face.

"Ahhhhhh!"

"Shhhh! Keep it down, muthafucka!" BoBo said sternly.

"M-m-m-m-man, I'm t-t-t-telling you I a-a-a-a-ain't ga-ga-ga-ga-got no m-m-m-m-m-money," he stuttered badly.

roughly picked up the speed of his pumps in and out of her. BoBo's viciousness turned her on. She wailed out in ecstasy, encouraging him.

The sloshing sounds her pussy made as his dick plunged into its wetness was music to his ears. She bucked away from him as if he were more than she could handle. The thrill of a new conquest added to obvious satisfaction and brought him to the point of no return quicker than he wanted. He tried to think of cars racing, dogs fighting, all who owed him money, anything besides his balls slapping against her butt cheeks as they were at the moment. Several seconds later, he was slumped over her body with all of his energy poured into her.

At that moment the guilt of his betrayal started to seep in. Why did he just have sex with his woman's one and only friend? On top of that, without a condom? What if she went back and told or told someone who did? Was she worth losing Serena for? Of course not, if she would fuck Serena's man. The questions kept coming.

She got up and got him a towel. He wiped up and left with the baby's bag.

BoBo could not believe the string of events that had taken place over the past few weeks. LaLa, Serena's friend, had thrown herself at him and he had caught more than a handful. Although he had felt like it was a setup, he accepted a serving anyway. He had been helping himself to LaLa's servings since then. His guilt quickly subsided.

Andre had gotten on his last nerve. His smart comments had caused BoBo to hit him in the jaw. He had to admit he admired the young guy's spunk. Andre had actually hit him back. Having to prove himself to a fifteen-year-old was the last thing he thought he would have to do that day. Tired and out of breath, he still had to showcase his skills. A few of his comrades had told him that he was wrong for it. But, like he told them, if you let the youngsters get out of hand, all hell would break loose.

He and Tasha had hooked up a few times. She was sprung on him. He tried to punish her for the way he hated her boyfriend. Alpo was a known member of the Gangster Disciples, who happened to be the main rivals of the Black P. Stones. Even though he dogged her, she seemed to love him for it. Each tryst he had with her, he thought that maybe she was setting him up for her man. He loved living life on the edge. Most of the things he did were for the thrill or excitement of it.

Business had picked up. He and Looney were making more money these days and, just like BoBo had told him, Jamal had caused problems. He stayed in a Black Disciple neighborhood. They were another street gang that were opposite the Stones. They got wind of Jamal's selling in their hood and robbed him. It was as BoBo predicted. Jamal was not a Stone nor was he trying to become one, yet, on the strength of Looney, BoBo found himself engaged in some out-of-the-neighborhood beef. In his eyes, Jamal was a fat coward who was not worth a quarter.

Carla had proven her worth once again. She had lured the young baller into a hotel with a promise of not only some top-notch cocaine but also some grade-A sexual satisfaction.

The plan had been for her to get the guy naked and comfortable. BoBo would bust in and pretend to have been watching her and plotting on sticking her up for the longest. When he kicked in the door, Carla was on top of the young baller, moaning in pure ecstasy as she rode him. Jealousy enraged BoBo and he played his part a little too well.

"Don't move, muthafuckas!" he yelled, entering with his gun pointed at them. He walked over to them where they lay frozen. The shock had scared the young baller's hard-on away. BoBo punched Carla, knocking her to the floor. "Watch that bitch, breed. She move, shoot her ass in the leg," he told his masked partner in crime. *Breed* was a nickname that members of the Black Gangsters called themselves. They were yet another rival gang of the Black P. Stones. If any retribution was to come for what they were doing, BoBo wanted it to lead in his enemies' direction.

"I got her, Gangster," the guy BoBo had brought along told him as he aimed his pistol in her direction.

They hog-tied the young baller and Carla. They were naked and defenseless, and a few smacks from BoBo and Carla pretended to break down and tell where the imaginary drugs were at in her car. BoBo had to show the young baller, who was trying to play the tough-guy role and not give up so easily, that it was not a game.

BoBo went into a rage. He hit the guy in the jaw and viciously began stuffing the towel back into his mouth. He wrapped duct tape around and around his head as the guy gagged. "You still think this is a game, huh? Fuck it! Die then!" He pulled out of his pocket a stun gun. He pressed the button and the current from the voltage showed. The guy shook his head wildly side to side mumbling what sounded like "Wait." The water was turning brown beneath him as the foul smell of human waste filled the air.

"You stanking muthafucka! I should kill your ass. What? You got something to tell me?"

The guy nodded his head frantically.

"It's about money, I hope."

He was still nodding. BoBo unwound the tape from around his head and mouth. He was so shook up, he hardly stuttered while telling BoBo how to operate the stash spot in his car to get to the twenty thousand dollars hidden inside.

BoBo dragged him back into the room. He took the guy's keys and asked him which ones he needed. "Watch them. I'll be right back."

The money was where the guy had said it would be. Taking it, BoBo put it in their getaway car. When he returned to the room, he thought about the torture he had wanted to inflict upon the guy. It was more to soothe his jealousy than anything else. Having gotten what he came for, he and his guy left with Carla and her friend still hog-tied. But not before giving his stun gun a test run. He placed it to the baller's nuts and laughed as the guy shook until he passed out. While laughing, BoBo then placed it on Carla's ass and gave her a couple of volts.

The sun was out and beaming. Since it was a Saturday, the park was the place to be. It was not packed, however there was a nice amount of people out. BoBo stood under a tree kicking it with a few other guys. They were cracking jokes and reminiscing about how it was back in the day. A group of young guys walking a couple pit bulls came past them. BoBo had his back to the guys with the dogs. The first person in the crowd of youngsters he noticed was Andre. An uneasiness came over him. He was not sure why. It was as if Andre had crept up on him.

"All is well?" one of the guys sitting under the tree asked the group of teenagers.

They all gave each other the Stone handshake. Everybody except Andre and BoBo.

"What y'all lil' niggas on?" one of the older guys asked.

"Shit. Just walking the security," one of the guys with a dog answered.

They made small talk for a minute.

"It's hotter than a muthafucka out here!" Andre said, then raised his T-shirt to wipe his face. The butt of his pistol showed, sticking up from his waistband.

"That's from all that heat you carrying," another older guy joked.

Andre as well as the rest of the youngsters laughed. "Let's ride out, y'all," he told the group.

They said their good-byes and walked past. BoBo was mad but did not feel he could show it. He felt like Andre was silently taunting him. Which he was.

Hours went by and more and more people came to the park as the sun set. It was almost dark outside when the ground began to vibrate tremendously.

"Damn! Who is that?" a female asked.

"I don't know, but they beating," her female friend answered.

BoBo and his crew wondered too. These sounds were louder than anyone's around the neighborhood. They were getting closer and closer. A moment later, a Cadillac Escalade EXT with a sky-blue metallic paint job and twenty-six-inch spinning Davin rims turned the corner and all eyes were on the truck. It slowed down by the crowd where BoBo and a group were standing, then stopped right in front of it.

The tinted window eased down as the music was turned down. A dark-skinned guy with a bald head and a face that would remind you of a chubby Michael Jordan spoke to the crowd. "Is BoBo out here?"

Guys reached under their shirts and in their pants.

"Who the fuck is you?" one of them asked.

"Whoa. I ain't on nothing." He showed both of his hands. "I'm just trying to get up with him. Tell him Alpo came through." He then raised the window and drove off. He pumped the music back up.

Everybody watched the truck turn the corner. They were so entranced by the truck that the late-80s Buick Regal now riding past was not noticed until the guy standing up and out of the sunroof snapped them back to reality with the first release of bullets from the TEC-9, as he was squeezing the trigger in their direction.

Everyone hit the ground. A woman's shrill screams could be heard. The Regal slowed, then sped off after about thirty rounds had been spent.

Making sure the coast was clear, some guys jumped in their cars to give chase but the Regal was long gone.

As BoBo got up to survey the scene, a young woman by the swings behind him started screaming. A crowd quickly gathered around her as she held her four-year-old son's limp body in her arms. His small T-shirt was covered in blood. Others had scrapes and bruises from diving on the pavement. BoBo was furious! He figured it was no doubt Alpo was behind this. He had some big balls to pull this after leaving his name. BoBo barked out a few orders to his guys. They left before the police came.

Through all the commotion, someone called BoBo's name. He turned to see Jamal of all people.

"Hey, homie. Looney around?"

"You got that money you owe, muthafucka?" BoBo yelled.

Jamal's face went from a smile to a confused look of fear. "N-n-n-n-naw. I told Looney—"

BoBo punched him in the mouth, knocking him down. He tried to get up and another guy hit him. They both kicked him repeatedly. He curled in the fetal position to protect his head and face.

"Stay your fat ass from 'round here and get that money. Fat muthafucka!"

BoBo and the guy left Jamal lying there dirty and bloody.

"Daddy, can you buy me a Barbie Jeep?" Charisse asked.

"For your birthday. Okay, baby?" BoBo told her.

"Okay, Daddy," she agreed, smiling.

"Don't believe that shit 'til you see it, ReeRee," Carla told her.

"Don't be telling her that. And what I tell your ass 'bout cussing 'round her?"

"Nigga, you her daddy, not mines."

His phone rang, stopping the argument between them.

"Damn, nigga! Where the fuck you at?" he yelled at Looney. He had seen his number on the caller ID. "Meet me at Jihad's crib. Niggas done shot up the park." He hung up.

"Where you finna go?" Carla asked.

Not in the mood for her games, he left without answering her.

There was a large crowd in front of Jihad's house, everybody talking about what had happened. Looney pulled up shortly after BoBo. He got out of his truck and walked over to where BoBo stood. Without warning, he drove his fist straight into BoBo's jaw, catching him off guard.

"Yeah, nigga! Didn't I tell you to let me handle mines?" He swung again, this time missing, but barely.

"What the fuck is up with you, nigga?"

"You didn't have to do Jamal like that. That was my business." Looney got into his fighting stance.

Everyone was in shock. These two were inseparable. Both were certified killers and here they were duking it out. No one wanted to get involved by breaking it up.

What started out as a boxing match soon turned into a wrestling event. They swapped moves. Looney would slam BoBo, followed by a few blows to the body. BoBo would work his way back to his feet, slam Looney and return the blows. Neither of them was in any shape for fighting. In fact, had it been anyone else, a pistol would have surfaced.

"Break it up, y'all. Y'all ain't even fighting no more," one of their comrades told them since they were too tired to do anything else.

"You give, muthafucka?" Looney managed to say in between breaths.

"Fuck you, nigga! We can go to the death!" BoBo said back. He kneed Looney in the ribs.

This only made their wrestling last a few more minutes. Pride and ego were their only fuel.

"Man, grab Looney's ass and I'ma grab BoBo. This shit is over with," a high-ranking member of their gang suggested.

They separated the two.

"You ain't did shit, nigga!" BoBo said as he looked at the scratches and scrapes he had acquired.

"Stay out my business, homie. Worry about these nig-gas whose hoes you fucking," Looney rebutted.

"Y'all cool out," someone said from the crowd.

"Naw. Fuck this ho-ass nigga!" BoBo snapped.

"Ho? Ho? Nigga, you see a ho, slap a ho." He began walking toward BoBo.

A guy jumped in between them. "Whoa. Y'all gone head-on. Clean up and chill out. I'll handle this situa-tion." Business had to be taken care of and this guy held just as much rank among the Stones as they did.

"I got your ho," Looney said as he was walking off.

"Give it to me then."

"I'ma see you in the streets. I put that on my mama!"

Everybody knew his mother had passed away when he was younger. His putting it on her was like notariz-ing a copy. Knowing how Looney was, it sounded like he had just given BoBo a death threat. Seeing that it was Looney, it was more of a promise.

"I'm telling you, you better keep the ice on it or it's gonna be swollen tomorrow."

"That shit is cold."

Not wanting to go home and let Serena see him with his face swollen with cuts and bruises all over, BoBo went where he knew he could relax and be attended to: LaLa's apartment. Serena would think he had gotten beaten up, the way he looked. His pride and ego would not allow that to happen. LaLa knew how the streets were and would look at him no differently. She tended his wounds silently.

LaLa was BoBo's type of woman. She had proven to be very streetwise. Serena seemed to be none the wiser to their affair. She would call sometimes when they were in the heat of passion. LaLa would take the call, see that it was her and come up with a lie so fast it sounded like God's honest truth. BoBo would even look at her twice.

BoBo loved Serena but she was not a challenge. She did what he said, when he said, where he said and how he said without asking why. She was a good girl and good to come home to. All other women just fulfilled his need for sexual variety.

LaLa was there for him. Wounds, bruises, whatever. After she nursed his body, she sought to satisfy him sexually. She eased him on his back gently and placed delicate kisses on each part of his body, removing the clothing she had not already. Pulling off his boxers, she smiled. She held his now hard dick. "I'm glad he wasn't injured." He looked down at her and smiled also. Getting head was his favorite sexual desire.

She put her all into this blowjob. Not wanting him to come too soon, she applied pressure to the base of his dick as she sucked it, not allowing any blood flow for the moment.

Still holding it, she squatted over him and let him fill her pussy. Its tightness was consoling. Tired and exhausted, he fell asleep a few minutes after his orgasm.

LaLa, grabbing her cordless phone, went to the bathroom. She soaped up a towel and cleaned up the stickiness from between her legs. Locking the door and turning on the faucet, she went by the tub and dialed.

"Yeah, this me. Call me when you ready." She then disconnected the call. She sat there and thought for a moment. Taking a deep breath, she gathered herself and went back into the bedroom. She took a towel with her.

"What the?" BoBo said, jumping up from feeling the warmth of the towel.

"Sssssshhhhhh. It's just me, baby. Get your rest."

He lay back down. She joined him as he went back to sleep.

"So it's favoritism going on? That's what y'all saying?"

"Naw. It ain't like that."

"Why y'all niggas scared, then?" Andre asked angrily. "I got violated for the same thing. I'll be goddamn if this muthafucka slide! And that's on my mama!"

"Hold on now, shorty. Calm down," said the older guy who was trying to reason with him.

"Well, check this out. If that's how y'all gonna play it, then let me tell you how I'ma play it. If y'all don't violate him, I will." Andre started to walk off. "Let's ride, y'all." Rooster and a few others walked off.

"Your ass is crazy!" Rooster said, laughing.

"Man, fuck them old muthafuckas. It's our time and they in the way."

"Yeah. That's what I'm talking about," yelled Rooster, banging on his chest.

They went and got into Rooster's beat-up '84 Oldsmobile Cutlass Supreme. Just as Andre was about to turn up the radio, his phone rang.

"Hello."

Almost as quickly as he answered it, he ended it.

"Hey. Drop me off at the crib. I'm onto something."

"Damn, baby. I thought he was suppose to be your guy?" Tracey said.

"Fuck that bitch-ass nigga! He gonna get his. That's on my mama!" Looney said, hitting his fist into the palm of his hand. He was still upset. Every time he moved, the soreness kicked in and he would get mad all over again.

Tracey tried to comfort him. She rubbed and kissed him. When he heard his phone ring, he practically tossed her to the side to answer it.

"Hello? . . . Aiight." He pressed END and got up to leave.

"Where you going?" Tracey asked.

"Not now, Tracey," he said, aggravated by her question. "I'm taking your car," he informed her as he left.

"Bitch!" Slap. "You still fucking with that hook-ass nigga, huh?" *Slap. Slap.*

"Alpo. Baby, please stop. You're hurting me," Tasha pleaded.

"Hurting you? Bitch!" He punched her in the eye, making her fall to the floor. "I'll kill your ass, ho. You wanna floss my shit for that hook?"

Tasha stood up holding her eye. "Alpo, I'm sorry," she cried.

"Alpo, I'm sorry," he mimicked her. Suddenly, he reached out and grabbed her by the throat. She wrapped her hands around his, trying to pry them from around her neck.

As she gasped for air, her life seemed to pass before her. *How in the hell did he always find out?* she wondered. The lack of oxygen plus the fear of not knowing how far he would go had her blacking out. Alpo's phone rang, luckily for her. He released her to answer it. It was a quick phone call.

"Bitch, have your shit packed and ready to go by the time I come back," he ordered as he left.

Smoking cocaine-laced marijuana joints always made Carla a hard person to deal with. She sat on the couch with a large amount of cocaine sitting on the table in front of her. She estimated the value at over twenty thousand dollars if sold wholesale. After she broke it down to smaller quantities, it would be worth even more.

Many times had she broken down packages for BoBo. After all, she was the one he trusted. Tonight she was breaking down a kilo into eight balls, quarter-ounces and ounces. There were also four and a half ounces of cooked cocaine that he wanted bagged up into dime bags. It was a tiresome job they used to do together.

As the poisonous fumes of the two drugs she'd mixed together burned and inhaled their way into her bloodstream and found their way to her brain, good thoughts and bad thoughts battled in the core of her mind.

The nerve of BoBo bringing this shit over here. Why he couldn't keep it over there with him and that bitch? She too good to take a chance on the police kicking her doors down and hauling her funky ass to jail?

BoBo loves you. You just too difficult to deal with sometimes. You ran him off.

Oh, so it's all good when he wants some ass or his dick sucked, huh? He comes over here, fuck us, then go and lay up with that bitch. Hmph.

Stop it! Soon as he comes over here, who really is all over who? Huh? Who is so quick to put they mouth on his ho-stick? We have to give him a chance. He really is a good man. He just needs a good woman. It's obvious he trusts us.

Bitch, please! If he trusted our ass, we'd be looking at stacks of money like that bitch he lays up with has and not this shit. We set niggas up for this muthafucka! Sometimes it seems like he gonna shoot our stupid ass too. Look at us. Sitting here, getting high.

Shut the fuck up! BoBo loves us! That's why he get mad when we don't do right.

Both of y'all bitches shut the fuck up! Damn! Y'all blowing our high. Let's just get high and forget about BoBo. We should be thinking of a way to kill that muthafucka. Fuck him! Go get that weed pipe and put a piece of that rock cocaine on it. Let's see what muthafuckas be going crazy for. Plus it'll shut you hoes up so we can relax.

Carla, already in flight, leaned up to grab a piece of rock cocaine. The voices in her head were starting up again. She got up to get her weed pipe. Before they could start their heated argument, her phone rang.

"Hello."

*   *   *

The ringing of her phone caused LaLa to take a deep breath. She reached over to grab the receiver, then turned back toward BoBo so he could hear. "Hello," she said in her sleepy voice. She nudged him, acting like she was lying on his chest. "What? Right now?" she said loudly, jumping up. "I mean, well, where you at?...Naw, boo. I was 'sleep." She was now shaking BoBo, who got up lazily. She motioned for him to get up. "Why the fuck would I have a nigga over here? Look, don't start. Bring me something to eat...I don't know, anything... Aiight, in a minute." She hung up before the dial tone came through the receiver showing that her caller had hung up.

"Who the fuck was that?" BoBo asked.

"My man! You gotta go."

"Go? Fuck that nigga!"

"No! Fuck you! He paying the bills. All you giving up is dick."

BoBo looked shocked. Never before had a female spoken to him like that. Seeing the look on his face, LaLa cleaned it up a little.

"Look, baby, we both know what this is. No attachments, right? I mean, I never say nothing when you go home to Serena or any one of your other hoes after taking your frustrations out on my pussy. Leaving me with a wet spot in the bed and a funny walk, now do I?"

He could only laugh. She was right. Bold and up front, but right.

"Come on now, BoBo. I done stalled his ass already. Don't fuck up mines. Please."

He got up and got dressed. Before fixing his pants, he turned to face her. With his manhood in his hands, he told her, "Come give little BoBo a kiss good-bye."

"Come on now, BoBo."

"You want me to leave, don't you?"

She jumped off the bed and knelt before him. She replaced his hand with hers. She placed a long kiss on the tip of his limp member, which was now awakening. She put it in her mouth and gave it a couple of quick up-and-downs, ending with one slow, long suck as she exhumed it all the way from the back of her throat.

"Gone 'head and finish," he told her.

"Uh-uh. I already gave you more than a kiss. Now go," she told him, smiling, as she stood up.

She leaned up to kiss him. He tongued her with a fury while palming her cotton-covered backside.

They walked to the door.

"Make sure you tell that nigga me and lil' BoBo said hi. Give him a kiss soon as he come through the door."

She laughed.

"I'm serious!" he said with a straight face.

"Boy, bye."

BoBo left out the building with his head in the clouds. He was the man and no one could tell him different. He exited the building and fished for his keys to activate the automatic starter on his two-month-old Chrysler 300C. The sound of it starting was music to his ears as he made the trek toward the corner. He never parked directly in front of her building. Not even if space was available. Seeing his car parked around the neighborhood was common but he did not want to bring any links between him and LaLa.

Lurking in the dark shadows, someone crouched aiming a .22-caliber semiautomatic pistol. The assailant was creeping fast between the cars parked adjacent to BoBo's.

Empty shell casings hit the pavement faster than BoBo's body did as two of the projectiles entered his skull, a couple his neck and a few his back.

As he lay on his back, looking into the sky, his executioner's face sent his heart into cardiac arrest. The face had been familiar to his vicious life. He had departed before the .22 spit one more bullet to his frontal lobe. Whenever the ambulance came to pick up his carcass, it would be leaving the scene without its sirens blaring.

The executioner took off into the night.

A month after Beau Bodine aka BoBo was laid to rest, the mystery of his murder still lurked with many assuming what had happened. The police were backlogged with unsolved murders just like his. It was just added to the piles on homicide detectives' desks.

Word on the street was a better source of information, but had proven to be inaccurate. Many fingers pointed in Andre's direction. On the night in question he had received a phone call while he was riding around with the guys from the park after swearing to handle his business on BoBo if nobody else did. A call from a local neighborhood female made him put his plans on hold. She had alerted him that her mother had left to go work her night shift at the nursing home and the coast was clear for him to come over.

Some fingers pointed in Looney's direction. A lot of people had witnessed their brawl and heard what they were sure was a death threat from him to BoBo. His leaving out of the house after his quick phone call, then switching cars, even had Tracey doing some pointing his way. He was never one to tell his business. Not even to BoBo. Since they were at odds, Looney was left to go for self. Little did Tracey know that her 2002 Honda Accord was not only very good on gas mileage but also equipped with electronic hiding spots he had installed in it for the purpose of transporting his dope, guns, and/or money. On the particular night in question his new connect had let him know that he was ready to meet at their agreed-upon location for a transaction to take place.

Alpo did not know he was figured into the equation. The move he had pulled earlier on the day in question was definitely gangsta! A little bird had informed him of his girlfriend's infidelities and with whom. They say that all black people are related and his messenger was a cousin who lived by Eckersall Park and who sought revenge for BoBo's slapping him and putting out a laced blunt on his chest. Alpo was pissed off about his girlfriend and the fact that she had disrespected him, not only with another man but with a rival at that. He had no intentions on killing either Tasha or BoBo. He wanted them to know though that Alpo was not to be fucked with. A call from a schoolteacher he was also having a relationship with had saved him from torturing Tasha to death accidentally.

Also suspect was Carla, BoBo's crazy baby mama. Throughout their relationship they had always fought. She had actually believed that if he did not beat her, he did not truly love her. She would provoke him until he did. Mostly, he would do so in self-defense. She might not have been crazy in love, nevertheless, she was definitely crazy! Her drug addiction made things no better. It drove her already demented mind into crazier thoughts. It is known that thought is the cause for everything. Her actions proved that. On the night in question, voices in her head told her to call up the baller whom she had last set up and tell him she knew who had robbed them. She could then use him to kill BoBo. The voice telling her to get high got the most attention. Her access to the drugs made sure she listened solely to that one. A phone call from one of her "get high" homegirls stopped her from possibly overdosing.

Serena had not taken it well. BoBo's death had left her financially stable but emotionally wrecked. She decided to move not only out of the neighborhood but out of Chicago.

The movers had packed the last of her boxes and headed toward Atlanta, Georgia. The black mecca. She climbed into her Chrysler 300C. The same one BoBo had recently purchased in her name. Her mother had her two daughters until she could get settled into her new house without having to juggle two small children. She drove off, thinking how this neighborhood would not be missed by her.

Before leaving, she had one stop to make. She stopped in front of a building by the park and blew the horn. A moment later, a female ran out. She threw her huge duffel bag in the backseat and got in the front passenger seat. She leaned over and gave Serena a friendly peck on the cheek.

"You ready?" Serena asked as she drove off.

"Hell yeah! Let's roll!" LaLa told her.

Serena looked ahead as she drove, smiling. As she drove past the spot where BoBo had met his maker, her mind went back to the night it happened.

BoBo had been mentally and physically abusive toward her. She was not to go anywhere. All her time spent thinking about her situation started her to plotting and planning her escape. After seeing how far BoBo would go when the guy was found murdered for merely talking to her, she knew there was only one way out.

LaLa had been instrumental in her escape plan. He had fallen for LaLa just as Serena had known he would. Her hearing of their passionate affair only fueled her motivation and desire for revenge. Each of their trysts was recorded on tape and used so she could stay focused. BoBo thought he and LaLa were becoming close, but actually it was Serena and LaLa who had bonded.

That night Serena had crouched in between two cars in the darkness and waited to become free. BoBo's death was her only option. Many nights of being home alone, patching her wounds, recuperating from one of many beatdowns while watching A&E's *Unsolved Mysteries* had helped her pick the perfect untraceable weapon. She wore headphones that played the tapes she had insisted LaLa make of her and BoBo's affair to use as fuel. There was no turning back. Serena having fallen in love with LaLa left BoBo not standing a chance. Each pull of the trigger released years of oppression from her.

She stopped at a stop sign. The memories caused her to shake.

"You okay?" LaLa asked, concerned.

"Yeah. Just thinking." She turned to look at LaLa's concerned expression. She smiled, then leaned over as LaLa leaned toward her. Their mouths connected and they kissed passionately while their tongues danced together. Just as Serena raised her hand to touch LaLa's face, a horn sounded behind them and caused them to jump. They both laughed. Serena drove off.

That's a wrap!

ALL FOR NOTHING

BY SHAWN "JIHAD" TRUMP

ONE

It was late. The moon was a silhouette in the cloudy sky as Jihad drove through the McKeesport city streets en route to Legends nightclub.

He stood five-nine and weighed in at 160 pounds, so appearance alone was not enough to instill fear. His pale face would make a brother in the hood quick to judge. But any brother from the hood who knew Jihad knew better. More than once, men had waged war and walked away with regrets or died from their stupidity.

He pulled the purple '72 Cutlass in front of Legends and those in the line outside stared as he exited the vehicle. Never flashy, he sported a pair of butter Timbs, blue jeans and a black hoodie with seven cornrows woven perfectly to the back. As he approached the entrance he was joined by three other brothers, and together the four young men created the clique known as Point Blank Mob.

They weren't your average crew. Most cliques were plagued with some form of jealousy or envy, but not them. They operated in harmony and were willing to sacrifice their lives for one another, and the bond of loyalty and love they shared would bring certain death to anyone who transgressed their limits.

"What up, y'all?" asked Jihad as he began to embrace the squad.

"Ain't shit," answered Crook. "Just sittin' out this muh-fucker waitin' on your ass."

"My bad, homie," replied Jihad. "I had to break out the crib. You know Monique's ass is always actin' crazy."

"Man, you's a sucka," laughed Crook as he looked at the other two men and said, "He the only nigga out here who can put a bullet in a chump and go home and bow down to some pussy."

As Jihad laughed he thought to himself how close he and Crook were. By nature, Jihad wasn't playful and the fact that Crook could clown him and get away with it said a lot. Crook and Jihad were as tight as friends could be. They had grown up in the same building and were separated by only two months in age. During their twenty-one years on this earth they, just like their moms, had been best friends.

Standing more than six inches taller than Jihad, and seventy-five pounds heavier, Crook always stood out. However, he was the least likely of the two to start any drama, but once shit jumped off, you had better duck.

"What the fuck. Y'all gonna sit·here and crack jokes or we gonna go inside?" asked the short and stocky dark-skinned brother named Teku impatiently.

"Quit crying all the time," mocked the fourth and final man, named Tree, as the two men stared at each other as if a fight would evolve from their words.

Eventually, though, the two men stood down and laughed. Since birth there had been a challenge of superiority, but only a few could have a bond as strong as Teku and Tree. They were identical twins.

Done playing games, the four men passed the crowd and made their way to the front. A woman began to protest, but was silenced as her man placed his hand on her shoulder and whispered in her ear. Jihad laughed at the gesture of fear as they nodded to the bouncer, placing some money in his palm, and made their way around the metal detector and into the club.

Once inside, Jihad and Crook hit the bar as Teku and Tree blended off to try and talk to some females. After ordering two triple shots of Henny, Crook looked over at Jihad and asked, "So how'd it go?"

"It ain't good," remarked Jihad as he stared solemnly at his partner. "The young boy is gonna have to do a bid."

Earlier that day Jihad had paid a visit to the crew's attorney to discuss the fate of one of the young soldiers named Petey, who hustled for them. A few weeks prior, Petey had taken a fall when he attempted to drop a kilo of coke on some chump. Turns out the chump was wearing a wire and now Petey, at eighteen years of age, was preparing for a mandatory sentence with the Feds. Adding insult to injury, Jihad didn't know who the chump was who had set Petey up, but he knew if he ever saw the brother again he would recognize him. Jihad never forgot a face.

"What the fuck was Petey thinkin'?" questioned

Crook, pulling Jihad out of his thoughts. "He ain't even know ol' boy like that."

"That bitch Marcy introduced them," said Jihad, frustrated.

"Which Marcy?" asked Crook incredulously. "I know you don't mean his baby's mom."

"What other Marcy do you know?" asked Jihad. Then he added, "If she didn't have his seed I would put a bullet in her stupid ass."

As the night progressed, Jihad and Crook got drunk and tried to forget about Petey and the fact that someone had crossed their organization. Although the essence of Point Blank Mob consisted of only the four of them, they had grown into an army of over two hundred soldiers. And it was not to be mistaken. When a brother rode under the banner of Point Blank Mob, it was known that if someone crossed him, there would be consequences and somebody would die.

TWO

Two weeks later...

Jihad and Crook drove on East Carson Street heading toward downtown Pittsburgh. Crook passed the leaf to Jihad, blowing smoke through his nose as he lay back and savored his high. The bitter thought of treason had not escaped either man, but some things were out of their hands. "There is no need stressing about it," Jihad had told Crook a week prior. "Sometimes we have to be patient and wait for things to find us."

Jihad was a firm believer that everything a person did in the dark would eventually come to light. Jihad pulled the ride into the car wash and hopped out to go make change.

By the time he returned to the car, Crook was leaning on the hood finishing the rest of the leaf.

Jihad snapped, "I don't know why you got out the car; your lazy ass ain't gonna do nothing!"

Unable to defend himself against the truth, Crook stood there and smirked as Jihad stepped out of the stall and into the sunlight.

It was a nice day, and although the car wasn't necessarily dirty, Jihad wanted it to shine when they drove through downtown. As he sat and thought about how good his shit looked, a white Chevy Lumina pulled into the lot and proceeded to the vacuums.

Something about the driver caught Jihad's eye, but he couldn't seem to remember. He continued to stare intently and then it all became clear.

"Motherfucker," he whispered after recognition set in. "Yo, Crook," said Jihad as he motioned for his man to join him.

Taking his time, Crook casually made his way over to his man as Jihad leaned in close and whispered, "That's the cruddy muhfucker who told on Petey."

"What you wanna do?" asked Crook as he stared.

Jihad didn't respond verbally. Instead, he reached into his waistband and withdrew the Glock .40 as he moved toward the unsuspecting victim. Without thought, Crook followed.

As they approached the car, Jihad noticed that his victim was not alone. In the front passenger seat sat a brown-skinned female with long hair and a natural beauty that made Jihad wish he could let her live. Now five feet away, the target turned and locked eyes with Jihad as realization struck and fear set in. Jihad stared without ever once blinking at the young light-skinned man's eyes. He raised the Glock and fired.

The cannon erupted, showering the young woman with fragments of her young lover's skull and dark crimson liquid. A state of paralysis overcame her as she watched the life of her man depart. Finally, as self-preservation kicked in, she reached for the door handle and attempted to escape. It was to no avail. As she stepped onto the concrete and stood, the muzzle of Crook's .44 revolver exploded. The bullet blew through her pretty little face and out the back of her neck. A fountain of blood painted the white Lumina. She slumped to the ground instantly as the life slipped out of her body.

Staring at the carnage in front of them, Jihad whispered menacingly under his breath, "That's for Petey, motherfucker." Then he turned and ran back to the car.

As they pulled from the car wash the sound of sirens in the distance hurried their retreat. They were aware that the mayhem had been witnessed by many.

Jihad knew he had fucked up. He had allowed his emotions and anger to take control. He should have waited, followed the young man to a safer spot, but he hadn't and now there would be consequences. *Ain't shit I can do now*, thought Jihad as he laid on the gas trying to make it to the hood.

While they drove, Crook sat quietly in the passenger seat clutching the revolver. Like Jihad, he knew they had fucked up, but unlike Jihad he didn't care. He was a warrior, fighting for today, never caring about tomorrow. Although he walked with a smile on his face, and tried to avoid drama for the most part, he hated his life. Knowing that one day his environment would claim his young soul. But he would never go alone. He had vowed to himself that he would make sure he shared Hell with each and every one of his enemies.

After about five minutes they were well into the borough of Homestead. By this time Jihad began to feel relatively safe as a few cop cars shot by them without a second glance en route to the car wash. However, as they exited Homestead and drove on past Kennywood Amusement Park, their luck ran short as a cruiser swung behind them and activated its overhead lights.

"Fuck," hollered Jihad as he punched the gas, causing the old Cutlass to hesitate, then jump forward.

As the vehicles accelerated, reaching speeds of over a hundred miles per hour, Jihad told Crook to pick up the phone and try to call the twins. Tree answered on the second ring and Crook began to relay Jihad's plan.

"Yo, Tree, we need y'all," shouted Crook anxiously.

"What's going on?" asked Tree.

"I don't got time to explain. The police is chasing me and Jihad and we're about to bring 'em through the hood in about five minutes. When we do...light they motherfuckin' ass up."

Hanging up the phone, Tree hollered for Teku as he flew to the closet and retrieved two AK-47s that he had purchased for an occasion such as this. Once armed, he and Teku ran outside hollering for those who were loyal to follow as they made their way to the treeline that ran parallel to the brick road that cut directly through Crawford Village. When Jihad and Crook came through Duquesne and turned onto the Duquesne-McKeesport Bridge, they found themselves trapped without an avenue of escape.

THREE

Fuck this," hollered Crook as he began to get out of the car and set it off. However, he was stopped short as Jihad reached over and grabbed his arm.

Jihad was surprised at Crook's aggressive behavior. Crook was the more levelheaded of the two and usually it would be the other way around. Jihad knew they didn't have no win. However, one thing he did know was that regardless of the amount bail was set at they could meet it with no problem. "Live to fight another day," he said to himself as he coerced Crook into laying the pistol down and getting out of the car.

"Get your hands in the air," shouted the police as they exited the car and knelt on the concrete, only to be tackled to the ground and beaten viciously until the cops believed thoughts of resistance had vanished.

After the beating subsided, the two were dragged into a police cruiser and hauled off to jail. When they arrived, they were placed in cells that were facing each other and after the police left, Jihad looked at Crook and asked, "What the fuck got into you, dawg? You all right?"

"Nah, I ain't all right," retorted Crook. "I'm tired of this shit."

"Just 'cause you tired don't mean you should let the police shoot you down like some motherfucking dog," said Jihad firmly. "You know we ain't have no win but you still wanted to play cowboy."

"Nigga, you don't get it, do you? I'm ready to go. I can't keep living with all these ghosts. Never knowing when some nigga I done murdered is gonna come back to haunt me. Every day I wake up wondering if today is the day I'm gonna die or go to jail. You act like that shit don't bother you, dawg. But I ain't you!" hollered Crook as tears of anger welled up in his eyes.

Unable to respond to his longtime friend's breakdown, Jihad placed his head in his hands and stared at the floor as he tried to figure out their next move.

Meanwhile, Tree and Teku were already on it. They began to assemble ten of their most trusted soldiers and devise the craziest, most daring plan ever conceived.

The twins had waited patiently in the treeline, but Jihad and Crook never came. They heard sirens in the distance and realized that Jihad and Crook had been caught. What for they still didn't know. After making some calls they had all the information they needed. Now here they were, ready to attempt the impossible. But had the tables been turned, there was no doubt that Jihad and Crook would have done the same. Twelve determined men walked out of the house and into the waiting vehicles.

The cars were stolen. The clique always made it a point to be prepared for drama. Part of this preparation entailed the storage of a few hot rides in various garages they owned. To be from the hood, Jihad, Crook and the twins owned over four hundred thousand dollars in property. In reality they could have all been legit had they chosen to do so. Several hours had passed since Crook and Jihad had been arrested. By the time they arrived at the police station most of the hype had died down. They could see three cruisers in the lot, the rest already returned to patrol their assigned sectors.

Inside, only a handful of officers remained. Tempers flared high as thoughts of the two criminals they had apprehended made the officers want to take justice into their own hands and do away with "this trash."

Crook was the first to be questioned as Officer Green took him into a small office and drilled him. When the interrogation first started, Green tried to play buddy-buddy with Crook, also known as Michael Drake. He started off by saying, "Look, Mike, I know you ain't pull the trigger. All you got to do is tell on your man. You know he don't care nothing about you."

"Fuck you, pig," spat Crook as Officer Green erupted into anger.

"Look, you little piece of shit. You think you just offed some petty-ass dope boy, let me bring you up to date. That dope boy was an undercover DEA agent named Percy Smith. And the woman was his fiancée."

Crook stared at the officer unfazed before he finally said, "I guess y'all bleed too."

Losing all control, Green stood over Crook and kicked him in the chest as Crook fell backward onto the floor. As Crook lay there trying to come to his feet, Green began to approach. An excessive commotion outside the door made him hesitate.

Going to investigate, Officer Green opened the door and as he did so he was greeted by a masked man wielding an assault rifle. "Back the fuck up," ordered the masked man.

Officer Green was no dummy. He didn't know the identity of his attacker, but he could see his eyes. They were cold and without mercy. He knew that if he didn't comply, his life would be over.

"Cuff that pussy and take his shit," ordered the masked man. Crook stared at one of the twins in disbelief. Unlike Green, he knew exactly who was under the mask. After standing, Crook threw a right punch square on Green's jaw, causing him to fall to his knees, following through with a kick to his face. Green lay sprawled out on the floor, lying in his own blood and piss.

After paying Green back, Crook did as the twin told him and walked out into the common area only to see eleven other masked men with guns ready for war. Jihad had already been retrieved and the unsuspecting officers had been bound with their own cuffs and stripped of their arms. They had taken over the police station with military and strategic hood precision.

"Let's go," ordered one of the twins as the young army turned and exited the station.

Once they were in the cars, things were no less tense

as the threat of opposition still hung in the air. They were almost at the garages when Crook finally looked at Jihad and said, "That nigga we killed was a Fed."

"What?" asked Jihad unbelievingly.

"You heard me," replied Crook. "He was an undercover DEA agent."

"Fuck it," replied Jihad nervously. "Ain't shit we can do about it now."

Finished talking, the crew arrived at the garages and once inside, Crook and Jihad were loaded into a waiting truck where Teku and Tree's sister, Love, waited anxiously with a smile on her face.

"Y'all niggas is crazy!" she said, not able to believe they had pulled it off. When the twins had first told her their plan, she tried to reason with them but they weren't much for reason. When they left the spot and told her to go to the garages and wait, she truly believed the next time she would see her brothers would be through bars or in a casket.

"You gonna drive?" asked Jihad as he pulled Love out of her trance.

Without answering Love began the drive toward one of the safe houses, located up the river about thirty minutes away in Donora. By the time they reached the house, both Jihad and Crook were high-strung. The trip had seemed to take an eternity, which gave them time to realize the predicament they were in. In a rush, the three of them hurried inside and collapsed on the sofa.

Love looked at the two best friends and asked, "What now?"

FOUR

While Jihad, Crook and Love thought of their next move, Tree and Teku were busy trying to clean up any evidence that might link them to the assault on the police precinct.

Once nightfall came they sent three soldiers to get rid of the cars used during the breakout. Each drove in a different direction so that the cars were scattered all over Pittsburgh. The next move the twins made was cleaning out their crib. Eventually the police were gonna come knocking and warrants would be issued and served. Nobody wanted to get caught slippin'. And just a little over three hours later the twins' door came crashing down as a full SWAT team entered the premises, preceded by a barrage of tear gas canisters.

Although expected, the police's sudden entrance startled the two brothers as the tear gas caused them to suffocate. As they clutched their throats and gasped for air, the intruders beat them viciously with their batons.

Eventually the attackers relented and the twins were

escorted into separate rooms and interrogated. However, instead of being questioned, the twins were threatened and given demands. When they didn't cooperate they were beaten. And still they didn't break, so they were left for dead.

No arrests were made. The police didn't have any evidence to hold Teku or Tree, but things were personal. As the officers filtered out of the twins' home, they vowed to break the crew "one way or another."

The twins lay on the floor in pain, knowing they had started a war. However, neither man cared. As children they had seen the police murder their father during a simple traffic stop, having mistaken him for a stickup boy who had just robbed a local convenience store. Since that day the twins had rebelled against any type of authority.

Tree was the first of the two to find his footing and make his way into the living room to check on his brother. He then cradled Teku's head in his lap, promising revenge. At the sound of his brother's promise, Teku opened his eyes and began to smile.

As time passed the twins realized they would live. With lots of bumps and bruises to mend. Teku took a trip to the emergency room to have his head stitched up, but most of the injuries were minor.

That night in the hood, all hell broke loose as any brother affiliated with Point Blank Mob was snatched off the street and questioned about Jihad and Crook's whereabouts. In all, twenty-seven brothers were arrested for firearm and drug violations due to the searches that were performed prior to questioning. By the time KDKA aired the eleven o'clock news, Jihad and Crook were the city's most sought-after criminals. The anchorwoman said, "Today, a new precedent was set in the criminal world as two men, arrested for the murder of an under-cover DEA agent named Percy Smith, were broken out of jail by members of their gang, known as Point Blank Mob. Deshawn 'Jihad' Williams and Michael 'Crook' Drake of McKeesport…"

The anchorwoman went on to explain that sources stated Point Blank Mob had been the target of a year-long federal investigation. However, no indictments had been handed down as of yet.

As Tree and Teku sat and watched the report, Jihad, Crook and Love did the same.

"We need to get out the state," said Jihad nervously.

"Fuck the state," retorted Crook. "We need to get out the country."

Jihad couldn't believe how fast shit had gotten fucked up. There was plenty of money, so relocating wasn't an issue. But now he realized that everything he knew and loved was gone.

He thought about Monique. They had been together since ninth grade. When Jihad got a year in juvenile, she wrote him every day. At nineteen he spent fourteen months in the county fighting a murder case and she never missed a visit. *Can I walk away?* Jihad thought as he turned to Crook and said, "I need to see Monique."

Crook understood. He knew that he couldn't deter his friend, so instead of arguing he turned to Love and asked, "Can you make it happen?"

"Yeah," replied Love. "But you know you're taking a chance."

FIVE

The day after the breakout, Monique sat in the passenger seat of Love's ride as tears rolled down her face. She hadn't slept and her eyes were swollen. However, all the tragedy in the world could not conceal her beauty. She had deep chocolate skin with a natural radiance that illuminated any room she entered. At five foot six, 125 pounds, she was that girl. And that girl belonged to Jihad.

As the two women drove, the tail was obvious, but they continued on without a care as they pulled into the Century III Mall's parking lot. Once out of the car they proceeded into the mall and began to shop.

As they walked in and out of the stores, Monique kept asking, "You sure this gonna work?"

Love continued to reassure her friend, but deep down inside she wasn't sure. It was time to find out, as they entered Kaufman's Department Store and walked toward the women's clothing.

While they browsed through the aisles, Love finally spotted the female who resembled Monique. Their eyes met and Love ducked into the dressing room. Five minutes later Monique followed.

In the dressing room there wasn't much time as the two women quickly switched clothes. After getting dressed, Monique exited the dressing room and headed to the register with the other woman's choices.

After paying for the clothes, Monique walked to the exit and into the parking lot, where a brand new beige Pontiac Grand Am sat waiting, just as planned.

She was a nervous wreck as she fumbled with the keys. After extensive effort, the car turned over and she pulled off.

She had no written directions because Jihad had not wanted anything in writing that could lead to the only safe place he and Crook had. Monique prayed she would find her way. Love had been pretty clear and as Monique manipulated the car through the small city streets of Donora, she became confident that she would be all right.

The trip from the mall was uneventful. Monique wasn't the paranoid type. Dealing with Jihad over the years had given her the ability to overcome stressful situations. She pulled up in front of the small yellow house on Allen Avenue. Overwhelmed with emotion she saw her man open the door.

Hurrying from the car, she made her way up the few steps as Jihad stood there waiting. Without thought she fell into his arms and opened the floodgates of emotion that she had been keeping at bay until she could see for herself that Jihad was truly safe.

Inside they walked down the hallway into the bedroom. Monique wasn't stupid. She knew that this might be the last time she would ever see her man. She couldn't follow him, he wouldn't allow it. She was in her last year of college, studying to be a teacher, and he always made her promise to graduate. It was important to Jihad that she succeed and he would help her no matter what. During her freshman year she had come up almost ten thousand dollars short on her tuition and when she explained that she would end up having to attend community college, Jihad left, only to return ten minutes later with the money, saying, "I want you to take this money and do right."

If it had been any other man, Monique would have been surprised. But with Jihad, nothing was a surprise. He had taken care of her since the first day they met and given her everything, and now she would return the favor. She looked at him and said, "Tonight there ain't no limits. I love you more than I love anything in this world and I never want another man to say I was his first anything."

Up until that point in their relationship, the sex had been relatively reserved. Monique had always been conservative when it came to sex. If needed Jihad always had a woman ready to handle his fetishes, because he never pressed her into doing something that would make her uncomfortable. But tonight would be different. Monique stepped back and began to remove her clothing.

As Monique undressed, Jihad sat back on the bed as

he felt his manhood rise to attention. He had watched her undress a thousand times, but never had her demeanor been so erotic as she caressed her firm breasts, running her fingers over her fully erect nipples, which were shaped like gumdrops. Then, almost as if she were reading his thoughts, she pushed her right breast up, taking the dark, thick nipple inside her mouth and sucking it lavishly. Jihad couldn't believe it. He sat and watched, feeling as if the swollen muscle between his legs would burst at any minute. Knowing she had her lover's attention she walked closer to the bed and lifted her leg, placing it on the bed and giving him a clear view of her most intimate spot. Unable to control himself he began to rise up off his elbows to meet her. She gently placed her hand on his shoulder and pushed him back down.

"You want this pussy?" she asked as she began to run her well-manicured finger over her clit.

Jihad was speechless as he watched in pleasure and pain as his woman played with her pussy, teasing him.

"You know this is your pussy, don't you?" Monique stated more than asked. "I want you to see that I don't need no man."

He was screaming inside as he watched Monique open herself up and curl her finger deep inside, stroking her G-spot. He watched as the nectar of her fruit reflected the dim light of the room. He wanted to taste her. To consume her taste buds with her warm, sweet juice.

"Let me taste you," he begged.

Wanting to satisfy her man, Monique climbed on

top of the bed and straddled his face as Jihad pushed his tongue deep inside her. The sense of hunger he felt overwhelmed him as he sucked feverishly on her pussy.

As he pulled her lips apart he ran his tongue along the walls of her pussy. She bucked and pressed her pussy firmly against his face while grabbing the back of his head, trying to pull him inside her. She was about to explode. Her first thought was to back away so as to prolong her pleasure, but her body's need to release won out as her core shuddered and erupted with an explosive orgasm.

For a moment she was dazed and silent as she held on to Jihad's head for support. Never had she cum so hard. Never had she felt so free, and in an attempt to make it last she began to lower herself from Jihad's face, saying, "Now it's your turn."

Monique wrapped her warm, soft hands around his dick and began to stroke him. In the past they had satisfied each other orally but Monique had always been somewhat apprehensive about it. Tonight she was anything but as she took him in her mouth, stroking and sucking him until his eyes rolled to the back of his head and he warned her, "I'm about to cum."

His words didn't deter her and being afraid that she hadn't heard him he repeated himself. This only made her more determined as she took him deeper in her mouth. Unable to hold back, Jihad grabbed her by the roots of her thick black hair, pushing himself deep inside her as he released his hot load in her mouth.

Never missing a beat, Monique savored the taste of her man, making sure she didn't leave a drop.

Unable to move, Jihad lay there as Monique curled up next to him and lay in his arms. "I know you ain't done?" she whispered as Jihad looked at her unbelievingly.

"I don't think I can move," he responded.

"Turn over," she said.

Unable to disobey her, Jihad turned lazily on his stomach as Monique began to massage his shoulders and back. Her touch was draining him of any energy he had left as she ran her tongue lightly across his skin, taking time to kiss each and every muscle. Jihad was almost asleep when Monique descended below his waistline and gently placed kisses on the cheeks of his ass. Slowly manipulating the area, she worked her way down until finally she spread his ass apart and ran her tongue through his crack.

He was fully awake now as he tried to crawl from her touch but she wouldn't be denied as she slid her tongue in his forbidden hole.

More than a few females had licked his ass, but to have Monique do it heightened the pleasure. It wasn't the act itself, but the standards she set for herself as a woman, that gave him an exhilarated sense of power. At this moment Jihad knew that she was living out her fantasies and the fact that it was with him made him feel supreme.

By the time she finished Jihad was rock-hard as she turned him on his back and mounted his hard long pulsating cock.

"You ain't never gonna forget this pussy," she said as her hips pulsated up and down. Never before had a woman exercised this much control over him. For the moment he was her slave. He had to do something. Her demeanor challenged him and his pride couldn't allow her to be in complete control as he pulled her leg underneath him and threw her on her back.

Unwilling to yield to his power, Monique continued to buck under his weight until he lifted himself up on his hands and thrust himself deep inside her.

"Oh, now you want to fuck me," she taunted, but the taunts turned to gasps and moans as her pussy expanded, allowing him to enter her completely.

"Turn over," he demanded as he pulled himself to her.

Eager to have him back inside her she quickly turned onto her elbows and lifted her ass so he could enter her.

Without hesitating, Jihad slid his manhood deep inside her as she backed into every stroke. The ecstasy was unbearable and Jihad knew he was losing control, but instead of slowing down he pushed harder, filling her with his cum.

Knowing that he had just spent himself inside her, Monique ground and gyrated her hips while squeezing her vaginal muscle, trying to hold her man inside. Surprisingly, she felt him start to rise again.

Monique was determined to not stop now as she hollered out, "I want to feel you in my ass."

Jihad pulled himself out of her pussy. He lifted her ass up roughly as he spread her cheeks apart. He licked her hole, tongue-fucking her tight virgin ass as she hollered with pleasure, "Fuck me. Fuck me now!" she demanded.

Jihad raised up and mounted himself behind her as he began to work his large cock into her ass. She was so tight he had to grit his teeth against the pleasurable ache as he penetrated her tight, juicy ass. She screamed out in pain as he buried his dick deep in her ass. Her screams caused Jihad to push deeper inside her as her muscles gripped his dick like a vise. A look of pleasure crossed Monique's face as multiple orgasms started to rock her body.

"Don't you ever forget this ass!" she screamed out. "I want to feel you cum in my ass."

As if on cue, Jihad shot his load deep inside Monique.

SIX

Three days had passed since Monique's arrival, but now the time came for her to leave as they stood holding each other. No words were spoken. They knew this was good-bye and words would only complicate things. It had been years since Jihad last shed a tear but now his stomach turned and his vision became blurry as he pulled Monique close to him and said, "You gotta live for both of us."

Knowing that was Jihad's way of saying good-bye, she kissed him one last time, saying, "I'll always love you."

With that she turned to leave, but before she went Jihad grabbed her arm, pulled an envelope out of his back pocket and handed it to her, saying, "That's twenty-five thousand dollars. I'll try to get you something more once I get situated. You know I can't keep in touch, but somebody will. Just do me a favor and graduate. Then get the fuck away from here."

Monique knew Jihad wouldn't take the money back so she didn't argue. Instead, she turned and walked out the door. Tears blurred her vision as she drove away.

*   *   *

"You all right?" asked Crook as he sat at the kitchen table watching his best friend grieve.

"Nah, but I will be," Jihad answered. "Let's just get the fuck out of here."

Over the past three days Crook and Jihad had put everything in order. It was decided that once Monique left they would be leaving right behind her.

In order to change their appearance, both men cut their hair and bought some glasses. Their little man Squirt hooked them up with some fake IDs. The two best friends were about to embark on a journey. They had a little over $150,000 between them, which was enough for a new start.

The bus station and airports would be monitored so they planned to drive a rental car to Charleston, West Virginia. From there they would catch the Greyhound. In Texas the duo would be met by Crook's cousin Chris, and from there they would see what happened.

Both men were wound up tight as a clock. They expected the police to jump out behind them at any moment. Neither man was stupid. The murder of a federal agent meant certain death. Therefore, they had already agreed that the only court they would participate in would be held in the streets. However, without incident the two arrived in Charleston some three and a half hours later and thanks to Squirt they would have five days before the rental car was reported stolen. He had paid some fiend a half ounce to rent the car and follow through with the plan. They didn't think the police would connect the car to them, but just in case, they wanted to be tucked away safely.

Once they were in the bus station, their nerves didn't get much better as the presence of the police made them somewhat paranoid. They were dirty as hell. Each man wore a vest. Jihad had a nine-millimeter Beretta tucked in his waist and Crook was armed with a .38 revolver. Under normal circumstances they would never have traveled in this manner, but this trip was anything but normal. Not to mention that the JanSport backpack slung over Crook's shoulder contained their livelihood. Therefore, they weren't taking any chances.

After purchasing their tickets and finding seats the two waited patiently for their bus, which was due at one-twenty p.m. Checking his watch Jihad saw that it was a little after twelve-thirty p.m., so he left to grab them something to eat.

After what seemed like forever, they heard the call for their bus, casually proceeding to their shuttle of freedom.

The trip was uneventful, taking about thirty-six hours. By the time they arrived at the small bus station in Kileen, Texas, their bodies were sore and their minds exhausted. Sweating profusely from the vests and tired beyond reason, they were grateful that Chris was outside the terminal waiting for them.

Jihad had met Chris at Crook's family reunion. That was five years ago but he still looked the same: dark-skinned, with a low-cut Caesar and a chubby frame. He looked like a teddy bear.

"What's up, Cuz?" asked Chris.

"Ain't nothing. You remember Jihad, right?" asked Crook.

"No doubt. What's going on?" asked Chris as he showed Jihad some love.

As the greetings continued, the trio made their way to Chris's ride and hopped in.

"So what's up, Cuz, you got some drama?" asked Chris.

"Man, if you only knew," replied Crook. "Let's just say we need to stay low...forever."

The ride to Chris's house took about five minutes and once they were settled, Chris cracked a bottle of Rémy as Crook explained their dilemma.

"Y'all niggas fucked up big!" commented Chris as he stared wide-eyed at the two. Then he added, "You know I got y'all's back!"

SEVEN

Four months later...

At first Crook and Jihad stayed hidden, never wanting to venture outside the apartment. Eventually the hot Texas weather and need for some form of life pushed them out the door.

The apartment complex they were staying in was a nice spot that was tucked away in the cut. Chris had shown the duo lots of love. Not only did he have their apartment in his name, he put both their rides in his name. And staring out the window and into the pool area, Crook had finally had enough as he said, "Fuck this. I need some pussy."

Jihad, understanding his friend, just laughed. The women in Texas were fine, thick, and he was miserable as hell without one.

They had met a few women messing around with Chris, but both had agreed not to get serious with anyone. They had to stay on point. They couldn't allow their faces to become known. However, being cooped up like an animal was starting to take its toll and

Jihad said, "Fuck it," as he headed out the door after his man.

It was Saturday afternoon, the pool was packed. Still somewhat leery about getting familiar with the neighbors, Jihad found an open table outside the pool area and watched as Crook jumped in the pool.

After sitting out under the hot sun for a few minutes, Jihad began to relax as he thought about everything that had transpired. He was so consumed that he didn't notice the woman walk up beside him until she asked, "You ain't gonna swim?"

Startled, Jihad looked up as the woman apologized for interrupting, but then regained his composure and replied, "Nah. I'm just laying back, shorty. Why you ask?"

"You look like you're lonely," she said in a sincere tone.

Jihad laughed as he thought to himself, *If you only knew.* Then he asked, "What's your name, Miss Lady?"

"Tiffany. What's yours?" she asked.

"Tony."

"Just Tony?" she asked. "You don't have a real name?"

"Let's just keep it at Tony and Tiffany right now, babygirl," he laughed as they began to talk.

The conversation was pleasant and something about her demeanor made him hate lying. She asked where he was from and he said, "New York."

She asked what he did and he said, "I own real estate." Which wasn't a total lie, but the fact that the Feds had probably seized everything in his name by now probably canceled out the truth of his statement.

Shorty wasn't stupid. She knew Jihad was a hustler so the lies he told were expected. Therefore, she didn't trip or pry too much. She figured that he probably did own some property, but that definitely wasn't how he made a living.

"What you doing in Texas?" she asked.

"Damn, babygirl. You sure ask a lot of questions," he laughed and then added, "Why don't you tell me something about you?"

She was a twenty-six-year-old single mother who was a registered nurse, which made Jihad laugh to himself, thinking, *Good, when the police shoot my ass up you can put me back together.*

For over two hours the pair sat and talked. Jihad was surprised to look up and see that Crook was gone. *He must have figured me and shorty was better off left alone,* thought Jihad.

"So what apartment do you live in?" asked Jihad, wondering why he had never seen Tiffany before.

"Oh, I don't live here," she said. "My sister does."

"I guess that means I can't stop by and check you out then," Jihad said.

"You can check me out whenever," she offered as she retrieved a pen and piece of paper from her purse and began to write. "All you got to do is call."

The conversation continued a little while longer until Tiffany excused herself. She had a job to get to. They agreed that he would call her sometime around eleven-thirty that night and they would hook up. Before leaving she gave him a hug and planted a kiss on his cheek.

After watching Tiffany retrieve her son from the pool and leave out of the complex, Jihad proceeded to the crib to see what had happened to Crook. However, when he got there, Crook was nowhere to be found. With nothing better to do, Jihad jumped in the shower and went to lie down.

It was a few hours before he finally opened his eyes and when he did, Crook was standing over him.

"What the fuck you doing?" asked Jihad.

"Waking your ass up," replied Crook, laughing. "You ain't even get the pussy and she put you to sleep."

"Fuck you!" replied Jihad, laughing. Then he asked, "Where you been?"

"Unlike you," Crook said, "I was in some pussy."

Jihad just laughed as the two began to discuss their day. After they were through and Jihad had told Crook about Tiffany, Crook looked at Jihad seriously and said, "Yo, dawg, she ain't Monique so don't go falling in love."

Jihad blew the comment off but Crook knew better. You could look in Jihad's eyes and see the pain. There were so many nights that he had wanted to call, to run to her even, but in the end he knew it wasn't possible. This was his life now and Jihad had to make the best of it. Crook didn't want to see his friend get caught up trying to fill the void in his life that losing Monique had created. He knew in the end it could only bring about trouble.

EIGHT

As the months passed by, Jihad and Crook began to relax and returned to the game. They weren't playing all out, but they were eating a slice of the pie.

Kileen, Texas, was a military town, sitting right next to Fort Hood army base. One night while ballin' out in City Lights nightclub, Jihad got to talking to a few soldiers who after a few drinks got loose with the tongue. They liked to get high. But finding good blow wasn't easy. "I'd pay whatever for some good shit," stated one brother, causing the rest of them to agree.

After leaving the club that night, Jihad sat Crook down and after some planning they decided to try their hand. Jihad had a connect in Houston, via Tiffany. He had met her cousin Dom at a cookout a month prior and at that time Dom had passed Jihad his number...just in case.

After a few phone calls it was settled and the next day Jihad was driving down Interstate 35 South en route to Houston.

Jihad hated driving. If he got pulled over there was no way his ID could stand a check. That would prove fatal to either him or the cop.

Once in Houston, Jihad followed the directions southeast. He was to meet Dom at Sharpstown Mall. When he arrived, Dom was waiting and after some small talk they were en route to Dom's crib.

The drive took only a few minutes. They pulled into a nice gated community. After getting out of the car, Jihad followed Dom into his town house and got down to business.

After all was said and done Jihad got what he came for, four kilos. Knowing they might have to sit on the work for a minute until shit got poppin', he and Crook had reasoned that sitting on it would be better than driving back and forth on the Interstate. Prices were damn near half of what they had paid at home. It made perfect sense. As a matter a fact, during the drive home Jihad wondered why he hadn't copped more. At $12,500 a bird, he could have copped at least eight of them. *Fuck it!* he thought. *There's always next time.*

After he arrived safely at the crib, Jihad and Crook put everything up and left the house, going separate ways.

The plan was that Crook would talk to his cousin Chris and Jihad would discuss the work with a young brother named Sweets, who was messing with Tiffany's girl.

Over the past few months, Jihad and Tiffany had become somewhat serious but Jihad still couldn't get over Monique. Tiffany would get on his nerves by pestering him about quality time. However, she helped to pass the time and dull the ache of losing Monique.

In the end, everything came together. Chris and Sweets agreed to step the game up and copped only from Jihad and Crook. In return, they were blessed with the sweetest prices they could find without having to make a trip. Crook and Jihad were only making about six thousand dollar profit off each brick. It enabled them to live comfortably and not hit their nest egg.

For three months everything went well. Money came regularly and Crook and Jihad were able to establish a limited social life. Jihad spent most of his time with Tiffany, and Crook with his cousin Chris, but they never strayed far from one another. They were together every day and this morning was no different as Crook swung past Tiffany's house to get Jihad since his car was in the shop. After eating breakfast they decided to get an early start on their day, pulling into the Winn-Dixie supermarket to grab a case of Heineken. As he got to the register, Jihad realized he didn't have his ID. "Shit," he mumbled under his breath. He asked the clerk to hold the case while he ran to the car. Outside he told Crook to grab the beer while he searched the car.

By the time Crook returned, Jihad still hadn't found it. He picked up the phone to call Tiff.

"Hello," Tiffany said as she answered on the third ring.

"Tiff, did I leave my ID there?" questioned Jihad.

"Yeah, I got it. But I'm about to leave for work," she said.

"Leave it in the mailbox or with your brother. I'm on my way," said Jihad.

"Boy, if I leave that shit, I won't see your ass for another three days. At least now I know I'll see you later."

"Look, Tiff, I need my ID. I'm on my way," he said, getting irritated with her games. She didn't know that he was on the run. Therefore, she didn't understand how important it was.

"You'll get it later. I get off at eight o'clock tonight. See you then!" she said, ready to hang up the phone, but was stopped short by Jihad's anger.

"Bitch. I'm coming to get my ID now and if you keep playing with me I'm gonna fuck your ass up!"

Tiffany was about to snap, but instead all she heard was dial tone. Jihad had already hung up. "Who the fuck does that nigga think I am!" she snapped as she went to get her brother.

By the time Jihad and Crook pulled up to the house, Jihad was steaming. Crook tried to calm him down, but he wasn't trying to hear it.

Walking up the path to the house, Jihad saw the door begin to open as Tiffany's brother appeared in the doorway. "Nigga, what the fuck..." His words were cut short as Jihad pulled the nine-millimeter Beretta from his waistband, grabbed him by his shirt and jammed the barrel in his mouth, knocking out some teeth in the process.

"You think this is a motherfuckin' game!" screamed Jihad as Tiffany came out of the kitchen, horrified at the drama erupting.

Seeing Tiffany only escalated Jihad's anger. He withdrew

the pistol from Smitty's mouth, bringing the cold steel crashing down on his head.

As Smitty fell, Crook ran around Jihad and began to stomp the shit out of him. Jihad walked toward Tiffany saying, "Where's my shit?"

"I ain't giving you shit, motherfucker!" she hollered. "Get out my house!"

Unable to control his anger, Jihad reached out and snatched her by the throat. He heard her son screaming, but he didn't relent. She tried to back away and fight for air, but her attempts were futile as he backed her up against the wall and tried to choke the life out of her.

Jihad didn't realize Tiffany's supply of oxygen was running out as her dark complexion turned purple and she went limp and slid down the wall. Finally letting go, Jihad stepped back and watched as her seven-year-old son ran to her, trying to revive her while crying hysterically.

Jihad had thought she was dead. He raised the pistol to eliminate any potential witnesses. And was surprised to hear Tiffany gasp for air and begin to vomit.

Her son clung to her as she looked up into Jihad's eyes. She had seriously misjudged him as being just another hustler with a few dollars. Seeing the rage in his eyes she knew she had fucked up. He was a stone-cold killer.

Tiffany struggled to her feet and reached into her pocket, saying, "Here's your ID. Now get the fuck out!"

He reached for his property and he and Crook walked away from the house. Once they were gone, Tiffany ran to her brother. He lay there in a puddle of blood, unconscious but breathing. Through tear-streaked eyes she dialed 911 and let them know her brother had been beaten, then hollered out after Jihad and Crook, "You niggas is going to jail!"

NINE

Being involved with Tiffany had made Jihad take certain precautions. They had rented another apartment. You always had to have a backup.

When things began to get somewhat serious between Jihad and Tiffany, Crook had warned his friend, but Jihad wasn't trying to hear him. It wasn't that he loved Tiffany. She was just convenient. "It ain't like you think," Jihad had told Crook. "I'm just having some fun."

"What did I tell you?" shouted Crook. "Leave the bitch alone. But you had to be hardheaded."

"Man, fuck that!" retorted Jihad. "That bitch served her purpose and now it's over."

"That bitch is also gonna call the police," stated Crook, trying to control his temper.

"And tell them what?" asked Jihad. "That some brother named Tony Spears fucked up her brother? She don't even know my name and don't have no pictures of me. The most she can tell them is the type of car I drive and there's a hundred other people driving the same shit. Like I said, that bitch served her purpose. I got almost forty grand out her girl's man so now she can kiss my ass."

"Dawg, you're not looking at the big picture! We're on the run. And now we're down here running again. This shit got to stop."

As Crook continued to berate him, Jihad listened. Crook was right and Jihad knew it. He had a habit of overreacting and given their situation he was gonna have to chill. He was also gonna have to lay low for a minute. He wasn't trying to get sucked up behind some stupid shit.

After about ten minutes of driving Jihad's cell went off and the caller ID showed a number he didn't recognize, but he answered it anyway. "Hello."

"Is this Tony Spears?" asked the caller on the other end.

Hearing his alias made Jihad laugh as he asked, "Who's this?"

"This is Officer Wilson from the Kileen Police Department. I think we need to talk."

"I don't got shit to say to you," laughed Jihad.

"I think you do, son. You beat Smitty Montgomery up pretty bad and his sister called the police. She also said you probably got a gun and some drugs on you."

"Fuck you, pig. You want me? Come and get me!" laughed Jihad as he hung up the phone and stared at Crook.

"I know that wasn't the police?" asked Crook, looking at Jihad in disbelief.

"Yeah, but fuck 'em!" replied Jihad. "I'm just gonna lay back for a minute. Just get me to the crib. We can send your cousin to the other spot to grab the rest of our shit."

Crook couldn't believe the shit Jihad got him into sometimes. He looked at Jihad and laughed, saying, "You know your ass is going to Hell, right?"

"Probably!" mumbled Jihad as they pulled up to the apartment they used as a stash spot.

The two friends sat back for a minute. Eventually Crook broke the silence when he asked, "So what now?"

"I really don't know," answered Jihad. "But we'll figure it out. One thing is for sure. We just lost our connect."

As the conversation continued it was decided that they needed a break anyway. They still had plenty of paper. Losing the connect didn't mean much. Once Chris went through the last two and a half kilos they could take some time off, letting things cool down a bit.

With that out of the way, the topic of conversation changed and instead of their predicament their thoughts shifted to home as Crook asked, "I wonder how Teku and Tree is?"

"Man!" said Jihad. "I think about the twins all the time. Those is some crazy muhfuckers, running up in the police station for our ass."

"That's something I definitely won't forget," remarked Crook as he sat back laughing.

"You know, dawg, I wish I would have never pulled that trigger at the car wash that day. I really fucked up!"

"Ain't shit we can do now, homie. Just pray for the best," replied Crook.

"I feel you, dawg. It's just...we lost everything. The crew, property, our family, Monique."

At the sound of Monique's name, Crook became silent. He knew that without her Jihad could never be truly happy and he wanted to somehow help his friend.

"Why don't you call and check on her?"

"I can't call her! You know the Feds probably got her shit tapped," Jihad replied in exasperation.

"Don't call her, then. Call Love! While you're at it, check on the twins."

As Jihad thought about it, he knew he would be taking a chance. But after weighing the pros and cons he decided to give it a try.

It had been almost a year, so when Jihad punched in Love's cell phone number and she answered, it kinda threw him off as he uneasily said, "Hey, babygirl, you miss me?"

"Holy shit!" cried out Love. "What you doing?"

"Checking on the hood, I guess," replied Jihad.

"Boy, shit is real fucked up!" she stated and she began to fill Jihad in on all the drama. As she spoke his heart sank and his stomach turned. Teku, Tree and sixty-three other brothers from the hood had been indicted for RICO violations. "After that police station shit the Feds tore this muhfucker up. They still lookin' for y'all's ass! I seen y'all on Crime Stoppers the other day."

Jihad couldn't believe what he was hearing. The

empire they had created had crumbled and now every-one he loved was jammed up. However, he couldn't pos-sibly be prepared for what was about to come as Love challenged him, "And guess who is telling on everyone?" she asked.

"Who?" asked Jihad.

"That cruddy-ass nigga Petey," replied Love.

Jihad felt as if his whole world had just collapsed. He wanted to believe that he had heard her wrong. That it was some kind of mistake. Petey. The one who had started this whole fucking mess. "I killed a Fed for that coward," whispered Jihad, not realizing he spoke out loud.

"Boy, I don't want to hear that shit!" she cursed over the phone.

"Look! That's my bad, Love. This shit is just too much for me right now," replied Jihad. "Anyway...how's my wifey?"

"Oh, I forgot. Congratulations, Daddy!" she said cheerfully.

"What?" asked Jihad, not sure he had heard right.

"That's right, big brother. You and my girl have a brand-new baby boy," Love stated, as Jihad almost dropped the phone.

"Love. Are you telling me I got a son?" Jihad asked incredulously.

"I wish she could have told you, Jihad. He looks just like you."

As tears began to well up in his eyes Jihad was left without words. He told Love that he would call her back.

A son! thought Jihad. He knew he could never be a father and it crushed him. He had planted a seed in the woman he loved, then abandoned them both. All for Petey, who was a motherfucking snitch. Now he knew what he had to do.

TEN

After hanging up with Love, Jihad began to relay the news to Crook. The two friends sat quietly in the living room, each of them feeling sorrow and loneliness.

"What can we do?" asked Crook.

"I don't even know! I can't even think right now. Between the Feds and hearing about my son, this shit is killing me. I need to see my son, Crook."

"Is you crazy? If we go back there, the only people we're gonna help is the Feds by making it easier for them to catch us," replied Crook.

"Dawg, we already decided that we wasn't gonna get caught," retorted Jihad.

"But you need to decide if this shit is worth dying for."

"I already have!" Jihad said firmly.

Crook knew his friend's mind was made up. However, he also knew what they were doing was by far the craziest thing yet. But that was his man. They had been brought into the world damn near together and that's how they would leave.

*   *   *

Later on that night, after dropping the rest of the work off with Chris, Jihad and Crook jumped in the ride and hit the highway.

They would have to be careful as they made the long journey across the country. As they drove, Jihad prayed he would reach his son. To be pulled over meant somebody would die. He didn't want that. He only wanted to hold his child. There were so many obstacles in front of them. Passing from state to state without resting, the duo passed through West Virginia and into Pennsylvania before Jihad began to believe they had a chance.

By the time they reached McKeesport it was almost eleven o'clock at night. Aware of the danger, they were on guard.

Monique lived in an apartment building off Versailles Avenue that Jihad had bought and placed in his mother's name. As they pulled around the back, Jihad prayed she hadn't moved. Stepping out of the car, Jihad noticed the light in her living room was on, but he couldn't see through the window to make sure she was inside.

Fuck it! he thought. He looked over at Crook and said, "Let's go!"

As they entered through the back and began to ascend the stairs, Jihad felt the butterflies in his stomach, just like the first day he and Monique had met. Staring at her door he froze, unable to raise his hand to knock.

"Nigga, what you gonna do?" asked Crook, becoming somewhat impatient.

Finally, coming out of the zone, Jihad raised his hand and knocked lightly on the door.

He heard her coming and he began to sweat. "Will she be happy to see me?" he asked himself as the door began to open and Monique stared at him from the other side.

Without hesitating she ran into his arms and he held her tight. He wanted to feel like that forever, to never let go, but Crook brought the two lovers back to reality when he said, "We need to go inside."

Once safely behind closed doors Monique began to cry, not believing that the man she had thought she lost had returned. She had given herself to him entirely and as a reward he had given her their child.

Love had informed Monique that Jihad had called and deep down inside she knew the only reason he had come. She asked, "You want to see our son?"

"More than anything!" replied Jihad as Monique grabbed his hand and led him to their son's room.

As Jihad entered the room he saw a reflection of himself, curled up in his crib as if the world were entirely perfect. He wanted to run to him and hold him, but the thought scared him. Working up the courage, he began to slowly make his way across the room. Before reaching his son he stopped, pulled off his shirt, undid the straps on the bulletproof vest and removed it. He wanted to feel his son's heartbeat next to his own.

While Jihad reached into the crib and touched his son for the first time, Monique watched through tears as young Deshawn opened his eyes and smiled at his father.

The reunion lasted for almost a half hour as Monique presented Jihad with her college degree. He became aware of the pictures she had of him scattered about the house. He thought happily to himself, *She never left me.*

Then without warning Crook looked up from the window and interrupted Jihad's thoughts, saying, "We got drama."

Jihad didn't have to ask as he kissed his son and passed him to Monique saying, "Take him and go to the back." Then he added, "I want you to know that no matter what happens, you're the only female I ever loved."

With that Jihad motioned for Crook to follow him out the door as Monique ran to the back, holding her son tightly.

"Somebody must have seen us come in," whispered Crook as the two men exited the second-floor apartment and ducked into the shadows of the stairwell, while Jihad began to whisper his instructions.

They had to catch them off guard. The police probably believed they had them trapped inside Monique's apartment, giving Jihad and Crook the advantage. Then, hearing the sound of the heavy steel door open up and admit their attackers, Jihad and Crook became silent.

From where they stood, they couldn't see, but they could hear the sound of footsteps gently creeping toward them. Seconds seemed like hours until two officers stepped up to the second-floor landing, one right after the other.

It was as Jihad had planned. The police, being completely focused on Monique's apartment, never saw them coming. Jihad and Crook stepped out of the shadows behind the staircase. The two officers never had a chance as Jihad caught the second man, placed his nine-millimeter Beretta to the back of his neck and fired, pushing the cop's spine through his throat and onto the wall in front of him. The first cop had an equally tragic ending as he turned and tried to fire, but was cut down as Crook placed his .45 behind his ear and pulled the trigger.

The sounds of gunshots echoed through the empty hallway with a deep resonance. Then there was nothing but silence.

"Bang! Bang! What the fuck's going on up there?" screamed one of the officers.

"He's dead, motherfucker...and you're next!" yelled Jihad as he turned the corner and fired down the stairs at his attackers. "I'm a motherfucking G, you fucking pussies!" hollered Jihad after he emptied the Beretta and slid back around the corner. "Y'all don't want no war for real!" he screamed, reaching out to grab the dead officer's AR-15.

"Deshawn, drop your gun and come out. We can all get out of this alive," hollered a cop, praying that Jihad would listen. Jihad answered him with two shots that slammed into the wall inches from his head.

"Ain't no talking, motherfucker, we beyond that shit now!" screamed Jihad as he turned the corner and opened fire once again, with Crook stepping out to join him only to be rewarded with a bullet through his head.

Backing away from the line of fire, Jihad saw that his friend was gone as he stared into Crook's unseeing eyes.

"Motherfucker!" Jihad screamed as he burst out from behind the corner firing, catching one of Crook's killers off guard and opening himself up for attack.

The first bullet struck Jihad in the leg, causing him to fall down on one knee. Trying to lift the rifle again he felt the lead tear through his bare chest and exit through his back. As he collapsed, he thought about the vest lying on his son's bedroom floor and smiled thinking how it felt to have his son next to him. He had exchanged his life for that moment with his son. It was well worth it.

As he lay there dying he thought of how everything had started. *Fucking Petey.* Jihad had murdered for him. He had abandoned everything he knew and loved. Every man who was ever his friend was now either dead or in prison. And now he was about to give up his life for a coward who didn't deserve it.

In the end, as Jihad's eyes closed and his heart stopped beating, his last words were, "This shit was all for nothing."

EPILOGUE

After attending Jihad's and Crook's funerals, Monique decided she had had enough and moved to a nice little town outside the city. She had enough money now to start a whole new life. She found a JanSport backpack stowed away under her kitchen sink. Inside was $183,000. During that final visit Crook must have stashed it, knowing deep down that his and Jihad's run would end that night.

She and Love were still friends. That would never change. They had lost so much together and that misery would forever serve as a bond, holding the two together.

As for the twins, after hearing of Jihad's and Crook's deaths, they set off a riot in the county jail and murdered two corrections officers. That along with their RICO violations earned them a trip to the United States Penitentiary in Terre Haute, Indiana, where they are sitting on death row. The only regret they have is being taken alive and allowing the system to cage their physical bodies. But their minds are their own and, regardless of how many chains the enemy forces around their necks, they will never be mentally conquered. They may die in prison, but their spirits are free, and will remain that way forever.

MAKIN' ENDZ MEET

BY WAHIDA CLARK

ONE

Nigga, you busted!" *Pop!* My girl Nina punched this nigga Cream dead in the mouth. "That's what I'm talkin' 'bout!" She had had her suspicions for over two months and tonight her suspicions finally paid off.

"Nina, baby, I ain't do nothin'! I just gave the bitch a ride home."

"Nigga, these are my wheels! You could have at least had enough respect to ride the bitch in your own fuckin' car! Give me my keys, Cream!" she yelled as she tried unsuccessfully to snatch them out of the ignition.

"C'mon, baby. Get in the car," Cream demanded.

Here it is three in the morning and Nina just got done dragging a ho outta her whip and then stomping her in the street. The bitch went limping down the block. Now we on Hermitage Avenue, she's screamin' mad, hurt, embarrassed and trying to get her car back. The nigga's Beemer is in the shop because he was in an accident, and he had a ho in the car then.

Even though it's three in the morn the block is HOT. The ghetto food chain is highly visible. The hustlers are posted up, the fiends are pacin' back and forth, circling the hustlers as if they are the prey, the boosters are tryna unload the goods, the crack hoes are struttin', and a couple of systems are boomin'. Shit is all the way live. This nigga Cream is crusin' in my girl's ride at five miles per hour, while she's walking along the driver's side crying and shit, trying to get her keys. My feet in these damn Manolos are killin' me, and this short-ass Chanel skirt is not protecting my ass from the cool breeze. I'm walking along the passenger side for moral support and daring my girl to give in to this no-good-ass nigga.

"This is your last warning, Cream. Get the fuck out and give me my keys."

"How I'ma get home?"

"That's not my fucking problem! Get that bitch to give you a ride! You can ride on her fuckin' back for all I care!" Then she looked over at me. "Yo, M, dial 911 and tell them I'm getting jacked for my ride."

"You ain't got to tell me twice. It's about fucking time." I pulled out my celly and dialed. "Let's get this bullshit over. We got an early day of hustling scheduled for tomorrow."

Cream looked over at me and saw the phone up to my ear, cut the car off, got out and slammed the door. Nina snatched the keys out of his hand and we both jumped in.

"Finally!" I spat. I was tired as hell. Thank God she lived right up the street. I took my shoes off and said, "Fuck him! Let's roll!"

"Fuck you, Michelle! Find you some business, ho!"

"Fuck you too, Cream! That's why your bitch ass is walking! You ho-ass nigga! I ain't scared of your black Michael Jordan–lookin' ass!"

He looked at me as if to say, *Bitch, when I catch you by yourself, I'ma fuck you up!* before turning his attention back to Nina. He started begging, "Yo, ma, lets handle this like adults. Just give me a minute. Let me talk to you for a minute."

"It's over, Cream. It's a wrap! Do you, nigga, 'cause I'm damn sure gonna do me from this day forward." She turned on the engine, backed up, made a wild-ass U-turn in the middle of the street, damn near running niggas over, heading to her crib.

NINA

I can't believe this nigga! Here I am catching cabs and buses while he joyridin' hoes around in my shit. He got me fucked up! But you know what? Everything happens for a reason. And that shithead nigga is officially dismissed. I don't need no dead weight. Shit! I'm tryna come up. This is a new day.

Oh, by the way, I'm Nina Coles. I'm twenty-one, your typical ghetto girl. I was an honor roll student, prettiest, most popular chick in school. I'm a five-four Janet Jackson look-alike. All the niggas was and still is sweatin' me. But for some reason I just have to settle on the dogs. The lowest of the low. That's how I got hooked up with Keith. He was the high school jock, most popular and most wanted fine-ass basketball star. You know the type, had all the hoes sweatin' him. But I was the one most determined to make him mines. What a stupid-ass mistake that was! My hot ass got pregnant with my daughter Daysha the first time we fucked. I would have gotten an abortion but Keith promised me the world: marriage to an NBA star, ticket outta the hood, stability, house with the white picket fence, you know, the all-American dream. Sheeitt! That nigga got ghost as soon as I began showing. My meal ticket outta the hood—gone. My plans for college—gone. My plans for becoming the next wife to an NBA star—gone. My moms even had the nerve to put me out. Here I was on my own, forced to survive with a baby and the few little clothes we had and armed with a high school diploma. Luckily for me I had Michelle, and my aunt Sheila worked for the Mercer County Board of Social Services. She got me an apartment with Section 8 and helped me get put on welfare and food stamps.

Speaking of Michelle, that was my girl Michelle Martin y'all met earlier. She has been there for me since day one. She even talked her moms into letting me move in with them when my evil-ass mom first put me out. We grew up together. We have been in the same classes since the first grade. She doesn't have any children and still lives with her ma dukes. I don't know what I would have done without her, especially when my moms cut me off.

I have three big-head brothers but they are doing their own thing. I'm the baby of the crew. First, there's Derrick, who's a crackhead, then there's Blue, who's doing a bid in Northern State Prison, and Peedie. He's the only sane one outta the bunch. He got a wife, a chick on the side and two kids. He is also cheap as hell.

So anyways, after I get on my feet and get kinda used to this being-on-your-own-with-a-baby thing, here comes Jermichael. Fine-ass nigga. My prince in shining armor. Bam! I get pregnant again. And once again I get promised the world, stability, the house with the picket fence, the all-American dream. I really believed in Jermichael. He was a hustling-ass nigga. Everything was going well, and all the way up to my seventh month, Jermichael was right there. Then one day I get a phone call that Jermichael got robbed and wet up by some stickup kids. By the time I catch a cab up to Helene Fuld Medical Center my second baby daddy is dead. He never even got the chance to see his first son, Jermichael Jr. So now it's me, Daysha and Jermichael Jr. Once again here comes my aunt to the rescue. She helps me get a two-bedroom Section 8 apartment and now I get a bigger check and more food stamps. Wow!!! Yeah, right!! That shit is for the birds.

After I get situated and accept the fact that I now have two mouths to feed, here comes Supreme. Once again, fine-ass nigga, full of charisma and could fuck a bitch into a coma. But this nigga was jealous as hell and would beat my ass if I even looked at another nigga. His temper was wicked. So when I got pregnant with my third child I was devastated. I feared that I would be tied to this mean-ass nigga for life. So I explained to him that I wasn't ready for another baby and didn't want to keep it. No surprise to me, he flipped the fuck out and threatened to kill me if I ever thought about killing his seed. Needless to say, I was stuck; I didn't get the abortion so he didn't kill me, but he did kill some other nigga he was robbing. At least that's what I heard. To this day I still don't know what the real deal was. Now he's in East Jersey State Prison doing seven years. Wow! Seven years for killing a nigga? Fuckin' unbelievable! If he got caught with some dope he would be doing twenty-seven years instead of a measly seven. But hey, that's how fucked up the system is. Meanwhile, I gave birth to his daughter Jatana while he was locked up. Not one of my babies' daddies was present for the birth of his child.

Now here I be. Twenty-one years old, three kids, stair steps at that, three babies' daddies and on welfare. Believe it or not, Supreme, the baby daddy on lock, is the only one who offers some help. Keith, Daysha's father, is working and in the free world but don't do shit for his seed and is an expert at dodging the child support people. Some niggas are just plain triflin'! Jermichael, may he RIP, I wonder what he would be doing and how different my life would be if he were still alive.

Anyways, Supreme introduced me to his cousin Charli. An older sista, fly as shit, from Brooklyn. He told me she would teach me a hustle that would be so good, I could tell the Board of Social Services to kiss my ass. His only request was that I break him off a little sumthin'-sumthin' for the commissary every now and then and bring Jatana down to see him. I said, "Bet.

What do I have to lose?" Having three kids, broke as hell, and on welfare definitely wasn't my original game plan. Living check to check, month to month is for the chickens and I'm far from being a chicken.

I had to pick Charli up from the Trenton train station at five p.m. She instructed me to alter my appearance. I had to dress in business attire, put a wig on, makeup, the whole nine. She emphasized, "Don't let a hair be outta place! You are on your way to being independent for real." I was excited, curious, anxious and nervous all in one. I was about to learn just how slick this sista really was.

To get my feet wet we drove to Philly, where some outlet stores were. On our way there she gave a crash course, lecture style. She explained that our weapons were an ink pen, checkbook, credit card and driver's license. She said the strongest weapon was confidence. She also told me that most stores will have a personal check limit sign posted and if not to ask one of the employees or even the manager what the check limit was. The homeliest, most naïve and friendliest worker was whom we were to seek out to service us. I was like, "All righty then!"

Our first stop was a Toys "R" Us. In the car she showed me a driver's license, employee ID, credit card and checkbook. Everything was inside a Coach wallet. All the identification read Kathleen Dixon of Matawan, New Jersey. She even had a home and work telephone number that she had me memorize.

Once inside the Toys "R" Us she told me to grab a cart and she did the same. We began cruising the aisles and she told me to get what I wanted. I filled that bad boy up with pajamas, underwear, socks, winter clothes, Pampers and a toy for each of the kids. She grabbed a couple of things but my shit filled up both of the carts. When we finished she told me to pick a cashier. I looked around and chose the one who had the shortest line.

She snapped, "You're not paying attention! If you're not going to pay attention, I'm not going to waste my time on you. Remember what I told you in the car? Try again."

Needless to say, I axed the one with the shortest line. My eyes went to a young, snobby girl, who looked like a high school student. There was a black woman who looked as if she would take a bullet for her job, an old white lady with cat glasses on and finally there was a doofy-looking nerdy dude.

"Which one?" She was testing me.

"I guess we can go to the old lady or the nerd."

"Which one?" she shot at me again.

"The old lady who seems nice and can barely see," I humbly answered, while praying that I was right.

"Nah." She shook her head no. "But not bad. My gut is telling me the nerdy-looking fella."

"Why? So we can flirt with him?" I was now beginning to pay attention and peep game.

"It always works for me," she said as she maneuvered the shopping cart toward him. "I'm glad you learn fast. Just make sure you *always* pay attention."

When we made it up to the register Charli put on her Ms. America smile and sang, "Good evening, Bob! How are you?"

Bob flashed a yellow grin and said, "Fine." He immediately began unloading the cart and ringing up the items. When he was almost finished Charli diverted his attention by asking for a price check on a pair of jeans for Daysha.

As he did, the customers behind us were getting fidgety as they impatiently moved around and let out sighs that screamed, *Hurry the fuck up, Bob!* This caused nerdy Bob to rush. Charli whipped out her Coach wallet filled with someone's stolen identity and began to fill the check out. I watched her as she expertly and swiftly wrote in the home phone number, the job number, the date and Toys "R" Us and then signed it.

"Seven hundred ninety-four eight-nine," nerdy boy anxiously said as he grabbed a rubber stamp and twirled his ink pen. "I need a major credit card and your driver's license please."

"No problem." Charli wrote in the amount of the check and handed him the check and two pieces of ID. I watched Bob stamp the back of the check, then fill in the blanks with her info. I was holding my breath, my right eye was twitching and my palms were sweaty. Shit, I really wanted, as a matter of fact, I needed all the shit that was in both carts.

I let out a sigh of relief as he passed back her credentials, stuck the check inside the register, handed her the receipt and said, "Thank you, Mrs. Dixon. Have a nice evening." We grabbed the bags, loaded them into the carts and strolled out.

That was my first experience. By the time the stores closed for the night we had so much stuff in the car there was hardly any room for us to be seated. Charli taught me to always hook the babysitter up first. You gotta keep the babysitter happy. I picked out some leather boots from Nine West and a leather trench from Wilsons for Michelle. For me, a comforter set from Bed, Bath & Beyond, a couple of outfits and then we went grocery shopping. All on a book of stolen personal checks and fake ID.

At this point, my new motto was, "Fuck welfare! Who said crime doesn't pay?"

That lesson with Charli was two years ago. Now I am a master of the check game. I even train people to go out and do what I do, how I do it, for a fee or percentage of course. Daysha is now five, Jermichael is four and Jatana is three. I live in a three-bedroom house that I rent, still taking advantage of Section 8, of course. No more barely makin' ends meet from month to month. I'm actually ballin'.

TWO

itch, you should have killed that ho!" Michelle spat as soon as Nina finished the wild U-turn in the middle of Hermitage Avenue.

"I wasn't messing up my shit! You know how much money I'm wearing? I'll catch that bitch another time."

"I'm talking about Cream! He's the one who needed his ass stomped!"

"Girl, fuck him! It's over. And you know what? I'm glad the shit went down the way it did and how it did, because now I have no ties here. I'm getting ready to put my dough to good use. I can stack for real now and get the fuck outta Dodge. I'm sick of Trenton. I'm sick of these ghetto-ass streets. Look at this shit!"

"Say word?"

"I've got almost enough loot saved. I just need to go on a couple more missions."

"Where to? Why you ain't never say nothing?"

"Charlotte or Atlanta. I'm getting my kids outta the fuckin' ghetto. Gonna find them a good private school, get a house with a backyard, a white picket fence so they can play without a stray bullet hittin' them. I'ma

fulfill that all-American dream for my own damn self!
Fo' real. I'm out!"

Michelle got quiet as Nina parked the car. She had
never even thought about leaving the hood. But then
again she didn't have any children. It had always been
about her. Hell, she still lived with her momma. *BOOM!*
The sound of the brick cracking the front windshield
broke her out of her trance and scared Nina half to
death. Neither had seen Cream coming.

"Nina, let me talk to you," he ordered as he snatched
the door open.

"Call five-o, Michelle, now! Nigga, what the fuck is
wrong with you? Look at my shit!" Nina screamed. "You
done lost your damned mind?" Nina jumped out of the
car with her fists balled up.

"Where was you at, Nina? Why you just getting home
at three in the damn morning?" Cream had the audacity
to grill her.

"Nigga, don't try and flip the script. I had already told
you I was going out with Michelle. So don't even try it.
Just because you got busted with some ho in my car
don't try to snake your way out of this. You busted,
nigga! So accept it. It's over! That was your last chance."
Nina got all up in his face now that a police cruiser was
pulling up. She was like, *Nigga what?* The two officers
were getting out of the squad car.

"What seems to be the problem, ma'am?" the taller of
the black officers inquired. The shorter one rested his
hand on his nightstick and kept his eyes on Cream.

Pointing at her cracked windshield she said, "He

threw a brick at my window and he's now threatening me."

They both were now focused on Cream. "Sir, step over here." The short officer pointed to the tree as his hand rested on his holster and his fingers twitched. Cream walked over defiantly, wearing a fuck-the-police smile. "Place your hands up over your head and spread them. You got any weapons or firearms in your possession? Any drugs or paraphernalia?" he rattled off.

"No I don't." Cream stood there.

"I'm not going to ask you again. Hands up over your head and spread them," the short officer repeated.

By the time the charade was all over it was four in the morning. Nina and Michelle had to be up and out by nine to go on a mission.

At nine a.m. sharp, Michelle and Nina were looking tired as hell but ready to take care of business. Michelle had been promoted from babysitter to driver and partner. The new babysitter was old lady Ruthie from across the street. She would come over and watch the kids, cook and clean. Some days Nina would let them go over to her house. Ms. Ruthie lived solely off of her Social Security and food stamps. So whatever extra money she got from Nina was greatly appreciated. Plus she enjoyed the kids' company. She didn't mind working hard for her money and Nina felt she deserved every dime.

Nina and Michelle both had on their disguises, which consisted of wigs, makeup, moles and glasses. They looked like entirely different women. The conservative clothing added the finishing touch. Today was not a shopping-at-the-mall day. This was strictly a get-money day. Michelle had gotten a hold of some insurance checks. She had the personal checking account info of a Tina Machurley. The account was drawn on a bank with at least fifteen branches in the South Jersey area alone. Nina had from nine to five to hit as many drive-through windows as possible. The check-cashing limit of the drive-through window was a thousand dollars. So Nina typed out seven insurance checks, each for $975.00, payable to Tina Machurley.

She was looking over the checks one more time. First she combed the front of the check to make sure everything looked legit and perfect. She then turned the check over to its back. She had a photocopy of Tina Machurley's canceled check and she carefully matched her version of Tina's signature against the original. Once satisfied that it was a perfect match she carefully stuffed all seven checks in the Coach checkbook holder that she carried. Being that the banks she had planned to hit were all deep in South Jersey she estimated that they should be able to cash all seven of them. Give or take one or two.

Map in hand, Michelle yelled, "Let's roll!"

Nina nodded to her partner in crime, locked the front door and on foot they went to find the stolen vehicle that she had Derrick cop. He had said it was a white-on-white Acura Legend and the keys would be under the mat. Nina never used her own vehicle, it would always be a stolen one or some crackhead's who didn't give a damn what she did with their car as long as she supplied them with a couple of rocks to smoke. That way, when the bank cameras or employees caught the plate number, the joke would be on them. After the banks were hit, she would ditch the ride by giving it back to the hood. Someone would happily take it off her hands.

They walked two blocks before spotting the pearly white-on-white Legend. "Damn, I was beginning to think somebody had stole it back from us! I might wanna hold on to this for a few days." Michelle lusted after the new vehicle as she jumped in the driver's seat and began feeling under the carpet for the keys.

Nina tapped on the window. "Unlock the door." Michelle popped the lock and when Nina jumped in she warned, "Don't even think about it. This shit is history after today."

Michelle grinned. "You know I was only playin'!"

"Yeah right. Your ass look mighty happy to me." Nina watched as Michelle adjusted the seats and mirrors and found something on the radio.

"Let's do it!" Michelle was hyped up as she pulled out and headed for the highway.

An hour and twenty minutes later they were pulling into the first bank parking lot.

"Damn," Nina pouted. "This country-ass bank don't even have a drive-through! I should walk my ass right on in, shouldn't I?"

"Hell fuckin' no!" Michelle snapped as she rolled right

back out of the bank's parking lot. "Your black ass ain't walking up in there talking about give me 975 dollars! They'll lock your black ass up, Mrs. Machurley!"

"Whateva, bitch. You know I look the part, I can pull that shit off if I need to." Nina snapped her neck back as she pulled out her list of the bank branches. "There should be another one on this same highway. Turn left and we'll just cruise until another one pops up."

Sure enough, after they drove for another ten minutes they came to another branch. The same rule applied just as if you were mall shopping: *go to the easiest-looking mark*. It was tricky, because the black folks were such Uncle Toms and harder on their own people than the white folks. There was a sister at one window and an older white woman at the other. "Go to the sister," Nina ordered.

Michelle did as she was told. The sister smiled at Michelle and nodded as she counted a stack of bills. Michelle flashed her own Ms. America smile as she rolled the window down, grabbed the glass tube and handed it to Nina. Nina confidently stuffed the check and license inside the tube and handed it back to Michelle, who stuck it in the slot, pressing the green button that sent the tube sliding to their lick. Sister girl opened up the tube, took the check out, eyed the front, turned it over, eyed the back and began punching some keys on the computer. Nina and Michelle were slyly keeping an eye on the sister as they indulged in idle chitchat. A minute later they both let out a sigh of relief as sister girl asked, "Mrs. Machurley, would you like that in large bills or small?"

"Large, please." Nina smiled as she went back to conversing with Michelle.

When sister girl finished counting she stuffed the bills into a bank envelope, placed it in the tube and sent it back. She then smiled and said, "Have a good day."

"Thank you and you have a good one," Nina said as Michelle took the envelope out of the tube, handed the envelope to Nina and placed the tube back. Nina counted the money to make sure it was all there as Michelle put the car in drive and they headed off.

"All praise is due to the Most High," Nina said.

"Amen to that," commented Michelle. She was happy because as the driver, her take was twenty percent on each envelope.

At bank two they collected 975 dollars as well as at banks three, four and five. When they arrived at bank six the bank was stashed at the back of the shopping center. It was very busy and had lots of traffic.

"This should be a piece of cake. This spot is jumpin'. It's like we back in the hood. Obviously, this must be where all the black people shop," Michelle cracked as she pulled up to the drive-through, snatched the check from Nina and placed it in the glass tube.

"Sho' you right!" Nina said. They kept an eye on the teller as they indulged in their usual chitchatter.

After about three minutes Michelle said out the side of her mouth, "What the fuck are they doing? Who is he at the window?" A young guy had appeared next to the teller servicing them. He was talking to her and looking at the check and ID in her hand.

"It's probably her supervisor. You know how some branches gotta get approval when it's over a certain amount." Nina didn't want to go into panic mode.

"Fuck that! Let's roll." Michelle's hand was already on the gear.

"Hold up," Nina said. "Don't panic. How many times we went through this and everything turned out copacetic?" she said as she smiled at the teller. The supervisor rushed back inside. "Aw hell no! Hit the call button." Michelle hit the button.

Nina leaned over Michelle and said, "Excuse me, miss. Is there a problem?"

The teller looked up and gave a fake smile and said, "It'll be a minute, we don't have your signature card on file."

"Oh, okay." Nina relaxed because that was a normal response and plus she knew that she had the woman's signature down to a tee. "See what I mean?" she assured Michelle.

Just then the supervisor came back out, looked over at the car and ran back in.

"Aw, hell no!" Nina said.

"You ain't said nothing but a word!" Michelle said as she threw the car in drive and pulled off.

When Nina looked back the teller was writing the tag number down. Michelle swerved recklessly, trying to get the hell outta Dodge.

"Ain't this a bitch?" Nina yelled. "We only had one more spot to hit! Slow down, girl we don't want to get pulled over for speeding." They both knew the drill and began pulling off the wigs and taking off the jackets, cleaning the makeup off their faces, thus giving themselves a totally new appearance. Nina ripped up the check, cut up the ID and tossed everything out the window. She watched the fifty-five-mile-an-hour wind blow everything away. Two police cruisers passed them and Nina and Michelle both watched as they turned into the shopping center.

"Step on it, Michelle. Hit the fucking turnpike! Or should we ditch the ride and hop a bus?"

"Naw, fuck it! I got it. I think we can make it. We won't get on the turnpike, we can take the back roads." Michelle mashed the gas until she hit seventy. Both of them had an adrenaline rush. When Michelle looked again in the rearview mirror she saw lights flashing. "Damn it!" They both saw another shopping center up ahead.

"Hurry, quick Michelle. Pull into that shopping center," Nina ordered, as she gave Michelle her share of the money. Michelle slowed down as she pulled into the huge parking lot of a Target. There was no need for words. They stuffed the wigs under the seat and then split up. Nina headed for the bus and Michelle flagged down a cab as a police cruiser turned into the parking lot.

Two buses, three hours later and 4,390 dollars richer, Nina was putting the key into her front door. The first thing she noticed was the stillness of her house. "Ms. Ruthie," she called out. She walked to the back of the house and saw that the back door was swinging off the hinges. "Oh shit!" Her heart began to race as she grabbed a butcher knife outta the kitchen drawer. "Fuck!" she cursed as she ran to one of her hiding spots for her loot. She frantically snatched the garbage bag out of the way; the box with 8,200 dollars was gone! The tears immediately began streaming down her cheeks as she ran to her second spot. The 14,400 dollars was gone! "Oh my God!" Her knees were turning to mush as she saw her ticket out of this hellhole fly out the window. She snatched open the door to the attic and climbed the stairs and as soon as she saw the closet door off the hinges, she knew the safe was gone. She sat down, balled up into a knot and let out gut-wrenching sobs. "I hate this place!" she screamed out into the silent air.

THREE

Ms. Ruthie had taken the kids to the park. Nina was sitting on the porch with a baseball bat waiting on Michelle to pull up. She had paid the sitter an extra hundred dollars to stay with the kids. She was also waiting on her neighbor Mr. Jimmy to fix the back door. He had said he would be right there but that was an hour ago. Nina had steam coming out of her ears and if she could have spit hot boiling blood she would have.

"Damn, shorty, who yo' fine ass plannin' on fuckin' up?" Nina ignored the two niggas in the silver Porsche. Any other day and time she would have been ready to get her mack on and hone her pimpin' skills, but not today. "Yo, shorty, come here!" the dude on the passenger side yelled. "Why you lookin' so mean?"

"Nigga go 'head. If you ain't trying to help a sista out by fixing her door or replacing my shit that was stolen then I suggest you keep it movin'." Nina rolled her eyes and kept looking up the street for Michelle's ride.

Ol' boy shocked Nina by getting outta the car. She gave him a *nigga what!* look as she gripped the baseball bat tighter.

"You're not planning on using that on me, are you? 'Cause I just want to get your name and number."

"Nigga, didn't you just hear what I said? If you ain't ready to fix my door or replace the shit that was stolen outta my crib, then I suggest you keep it movin'."

"I heard you, ma. Where's the door?"

Nina hesitated before answering as she gave this fine specimen of a man before her the once-over. "Go right around back and you'll see it."

He surprised her again by going around the back of the house. She used this opportunity to further scope this nigga out. He was definitely from New York, the accent was a dead giveaway. From the ice on his wrist and in his ears she knew he was ballin'. The crisp Air Force 1s looked like they were fresh out of the box. The Rocawear sweatsuit looked brand new. The Porsche was pimped out. He was her complexion and about six feet two. He reminded her of Alonzo Mourning of the Miami Heat.

"Damn," she mumbled to herself. Then her attention went to the nigga in the car, who was looking at her while he was licking his lips. He was finer than his partna. "Fuck him!" She said to herself, *His ass ain't get out and offer no assistance. Which would say a whole lot for the brotha.*

"Yo, Nick, pop the trunk and see if my toolbox is in there." Dude came back from behind the house.

"Ump, looks like the whip belongs to the passenger after all," Nina mumbled to herself.

"Yo, shorty, I can fix the door but you still need to

replace the locks. The bottom one is busted up." He disappeared again. Nick closed the trunk and was carrying a medium-size gray toolbox.

"Yo, my boy don't be going around assisting damsels in distress on the regular. He must see something in you," Nick told her.

She turned her glare in the opposite direction to make sure her body language said she wasn't falling for the bullshit. *This big ass, perky tits and pretty face. That's all the nigga sees*, she mumbled under her breath.

"What was that?"

"I said, don't be trying to big your boy up on my account."

"I'm serious, ma," he said as he carried the toolbox to the back.

Nina opened up her cell phone and hit seven, Michelle's speed-dial key. Michelle answered on the first ring. "Yo, I'm turning down Hermitage now. I had to get ma dukes some Rolaids, a Pepsi and a pack of Kools. You know how she do."

"Yup. Some things never change," Nina responded drily before turning her phone off.

Three minutes later, Michelle was making a U-turn in the middle of the strip. She was oblivious to the traffic she was holding up. She pulled her dark green Land Rover next to the Porsche, then rolled the passenger window down. "I thought you was ready? Let's roll! Why you just sitting there?"

"Park the car. I got something for you to check out."

Michelle did as she was told, backing up and sliding

in the spot behind the Porsche. "I hope what you got for me to check out has something to do with this piece of expensive machinery right here." She was sweatin' the Porsche.

Just as she walked up onto the porch, Nick and his boy were coming from the backyard. "Yo, shorty. Your door is fixed," ol' boy said as he set the toolbox down and dusted his hands off. "So what was stolen?"

"Just my hard-earned cash."

"How much?"

"You don't want to know."

"Oh, it's like that?"

"Yeah, it's like that." They remained staring at each other. In the meantime Michelle decided to interrupt the staring contest by introducing herself to Nick.

"Well, can I finally get a name and a number? I'm Reese."

"If you have something to write with," Nina snapped but then caught herself. Shit, the nigga had just helped her. "I'm on my way to take care of something."

"That something requires a baseball bat? What, you got a game today?" Reese asked.

"Oh, so you got jokes!" Nina snapped. "But to answer your questions, yes it's gonna require a bat and no I don't have a game," Nina said as she eased off the front porch and headed to the Land Rover.

"Damn, shorty. It's goin' down like that?" He was becoming more intrigued by the minute. She ignored him as he watched her get into the Rover. He then pulled out his keys, opened the trunk, placed the toolbox inside and threw the keys back to Nick. He came around to the passenger side of the Rover and said, "You gonna give up a name and number?"

"I told you to get your pen and paper."

"I don't need a pen and paper. That's how niggas get in trouble."

Nina gazed in his eyes before deciding he was serious. "Nina, 609-396-3732."

"Nina," he repeated. "Aiight then. You gonna be safe or what?"

"Oh, I'ma be fine. One." She rolled her window up. Michelle started up her ride and they pulled off.

Reese jumped into the Porsche and said to Nick, "Yo, son, follow them sistas. I need to know what shorty into."

"Who the fuck was that?" Michelle pressed. Nina was in deep thought.

"You heard him. His name is Reese. I know just as much as you."

"I ain't talking about him. I'm talking about that nigga he was rollin' with. Where did you find them?"

"You was talking to the nigga. They was just out on the block; ride down Stuyvesant first." Nina was trying to focus on the business at hand.

Michelle, not being slow, knew what time it was. "Shit, Nina. Foreal, foreal, if Derrick got your loot we ain't gonna find him today. Right now he holed up somewhere suckin' on that almighty glass dick."

"I don't give a fuck! That means we are gonna roll up into every hole until I find his punk crack-smoking ass.

He can't smoke up thirty-five thousand dollars in one day. Even the biggest of feens can't do that."

Michelle shrugged as if to say, "I ain't sure about that."

Michelle pulled up on the corner of Hoffman and Stuyvesant. They looked around. Nina rolled her window down. "Yo, Father Master Divine, you seen my brother?"

"What up, Ni?" he said, looking like a walking skeleton. "Naw, I ain't seen him. I need to get downtown. You got a coupla dollars?"

"I got you as soon as you find my brother for me. I'll spot you a twenty."

"Go through Roger Gardens," he wasted no time snitching. "He was over there earlier. He got jumped and robbed."

Michelle skidded off before he could say another word.

"You hear that shit!" Nina screamed. "The nigga gonna rob me, then turn around and get robbed! I swear I'ma kill his ass!"

"That's fucked up. Find him and then let's go after the niggas who robbed him! Fuck them feens!" Michelle was amped up. That's why she was Nina's roadie. She was always down for whatever. Three minutes later, they were rolling through Roger Gardens. Michelle didn't even notice Reese and Nick a few cars behind them as she parked the car.

Nina rolled her window down when she saw Rob, another feen. "Rob, where my brother at?"

"Who dat?" Rob had the biggest, ashiest nigga lips you ever saw.

"It's me, Nina, nigga. Where my brother at?"

"That nigga out east. He spending with Horace and them over on Tyler. I got some checks for you. You want them now?"

"Nah, get at me tomorrow."

"Hold up." Rob was trying to bum-rush the Land Rover.

Michelle put the car in gear and headed for Highway 29, the quickest way to the east side of town. As she was driving and changing lanes, she thought she saw that Porsche rolling behind her but nixed it off when it dropped back. They pulled up on Tyler Street, creepin' along, trying to spot Derrick. The strip was busy as usual and Horace's porch was full of niggas as usual.

"What you need, Nina?" a hustler named Shawn asked her.

"My brother. Tell Derrick to come here."

"Yo, Tone! Tell Derrick his sister is out here!" he yelled. He turned back to Nina. "That's all you need, ma?"

"Yeah, that's it. Thanks."

Ten minutes passed and still no Derrick. "If that nigga snuck out the back door, I'ma fuck his ass up, watch!" *Tap. Tap.* Nina turned and Reese was tapping on her window.

"Yo, shorty, who you waitin' on?" He was dead in her face.

"What? Are you following me?" She couldn't mask her surprise.

"Yeah. I'm trying to make sure you gonna be aiight."

"I'm cool. This is family business, and thanks. But I suggest you go back to your car before you get jacked."

Reese lifted up the front of his jacket and revealed a shining Glock. "Holla if you need me. If anything, I'll be doin' the jackin'." He headed back for his Porsche and both of the ladies started giggling.

"Damn, M, I'm starting to like this nigga," Nina said as she watched him go back to his ride.

Five minutes later Derrick came out of the house. He looked smoked out as he peeked up and down the block, obviously paranoid and geeking. When he stepped off the porch Nina grabbed her bat and jumped out of the car. "Yo, D, come here." Michelle jumped out of her side, snuggling with her two boys, Smith & Wesson, in her hand. She leaned up against the front of her ride watching Nina's back.

"Ni, what you doin' out here?" He looked as if he had two black eyes.

"You thought I was gone, didn't you? I'm looking for you, nigga, where my money, D?"

"What money? I ain't got your money."

Swooosh! You could hear the bat slice the air as she hit him on the backs of his legs, causing him to fall. "AAAGggg! Nina! What the fuck is your problem?" Derrick screamed out, obviously shocked and in pain.

Swoosh! She hit him on the legs again. "Where my money, Derrick?"

"Aw shit, y'all! D gettin' his ass whipped by his sister!

A fuckin' girl, y'all!" Tone yelled as everybody started laughing and began gathering around.

"Ouch! You see that shit, Nick? Shorty ain't no joke," Reese said, enjoying the show.

"I see her. Yo, what the fuck son do? That's her man?"

"I don't know. He's a pussy if he is!"

"Where my money, D?" *Smack!* She came down on the backs of his legs again.

"Oowww! Damn, Nina. You broke my leg! Stop it! What the fuck is the matter with you? Fuck! Somebody call an ambulance!" He was squeezing both legs while groaning in pain.

Nina began digging around in his pockets and socks and pulled off his sneakers. All three spots he had wads of money. The more money she pulled out, the madder she got. She threw the money to Michelle.

"You punk-ass nigga!" She began stomping him and kicking him in the face. When she went to pick up her bat, he pulled her legs out from under her, causing her to slip and fall. She then sent her foot smashing into his nuts.

"Uuugg oooweeee, damn!" His screams echoed into the air. He grabbed his nuts with both hands as he rolled around on the ground. All the spectators began to groan, as the fellas felt his pain.

She crawled over to the bat, stood up and began swinging. "Where is the rest of my money, D? Who robbed you? I want my money!" She kept hitting him and he kept screaming out in pain.

"Yo, ma, you gonna kill him." Horace came out on his porch. Just then, the po-po was coming up the street, yelling on the horn to break it up. Their lazy asses wouldn't even get out of the car.

"Let's roll, Nina." Michelle jumped in the Rover and cranked it up. "Come on, Nina," she yelled out the window. "He ain't got no more loot on him."

Nina grabbed her bat and kicked D in the face one more time, causing the crowd to moan, "Oww!" She jumped in the Rover and Michelle pulled off. Nina began to cry as she counted the few dollars that were left of her hard-earned stash.

"Fuck!" she screamed out like a madwoman. "All my hard-earned money, Michelle. Why niggas don't want to see a sista progress? And this nigga 'sposed to be family. I can't take this shit no more, M. I feel like I'm about to lose it. I got to get the fuck away from here. But how the fuck can I? I get one step forward then get pulled ten steps backward. What part of the fuckin' game is this? This is the third time that I almost reached my goal only to have a major setback." She put her hands in her face and cried some more. Michelle was silent as her best friend released her frustrations.

When they pulled up in front of Nina's, Nick and Reese pulled up behind them. Nina hurriedly dried her tears.

Reese came up to the passenger side of the Rover. "Yo, ma, that was really gangsta back there. You aiight? You need anything?"

"No. What's up? Why you still following me?"

"Just wanted to make sure you was aiight. Can I hit you up later?"

Nina nodded her head yes.

"Bet. I'm out."

FOUR

Nina sat Jatana down on the chair while straightening out her clothes for the umpteenth time. *I don't see how mothers go through this shit with more than one child,* Nina thought to herself as she looked around at all the kids running around like wild Indians, ignoring the threats of their mommas.

Supreme stood quietly admiring his baby mama's fat ass as she fixed his daughter's clothes. Nina was bent over and right now he would give anything to hit that the way he used to. He was grateful that they were on good terms. Not as good as he wanted because he still had mad feelings for her. She had made it clear from the gate that she wasn't doing time with her own daddy, definitely not her baby daddy.

When she stood up, Jatana saw him and screamed out, "Daddy!" She wiggled out of her chair and ran to him.

He scooped her up and gave her a big hug and kiss. "Hey, baby. How are you? Can Daddy have another kiss?" She gave him a kiss and kept on hugging his neck.

Nina sat quietly as she watched the exchange between her daughter and the man she used to love. She had wasted no time burying those feelings as soon as he came to prison. She knew it was no sense in frontin' because she was not cut out for playing the role of a prisoner's wife.

As soon as Supreme sat down he asked, "So to what do I owe this pleasant surprise?" He had the right to be sarcastic because his moms or sister was the one who brought Jatana down to see him almost every other weekend. He could count the times on one hand that Nina had brought her down.

"How you doin', Supreme?" she asked, ignoring his sarcasm.

"Better than some, worse than others, but I'm here. How are you, Nina? You look good."

"Thanks. You look good too."

"So what's up?"

"Where do you want me to start?"

"Oh. You came down here just to use me to vent?"

"You said I could do that whenever I needed to. You forgot all about that, huh?"

Supreme just stared at her. His mind drifted to how badly he wanted to tap that ass. He finally said, "So what's on yo' mind?"

Nina let out a long sigh. "I feel like I'm suffocating. I can't stand this city. The air stinks; it's too crowded, too noisy. All I hear at night are screams, sirens, gunshots, car chasings, niggas out on the block. I can't take it anymore."

"Then move, Nina. It ain't like you can't find a place somewhere else."

"My punk-ass brother broke into the house and took all my money, so now I'm damn near back at square one."

"What?"

"He broke into my shit and smoked up almost every dime."

"Damn. I know you handled that nigga. If you didn't, just say the word, Nina. He taking food outta my daughter's mouth. I knew I should have wet his ass up when I had the chance."

"I've got to move, fast. Fuck everybody! It's all 'bout me and my kids. I need you to hook me up with something big. I'm moving South."

"South where? South Trenton? South Jersey? South Philly? Where the fuck is south?"

"Down South, Supreme. I'm going to Atlanta or Charlotte."

"For how long?"

"What you mean for how long, Supreme? I'm going to live. Have you been listening to anything I've just said? I'm relocating."

"Not with my daughter you're not!"

"What the fuck you mean your daughter? She's mines too!"

"You can go down South but leave my daughter right here."

"Supreme, I—"

"Nina!" he interrupted her. "I'm not asking you, I'm

telling you." He hugged his daughter and blew on her cheek.

"Daddy," she giggled.

Nina could only stare at him in disbelief. She was so heated she couldn't create enough spit to form a word. Her silence to Supreme meant that she had conceded to his demand. "Supreme," Nina managed to say through gritted teeth. "As long as you are locked up, I have the final say-so concerning the welfare of our child. Now when you get out, we can talk and work something out. Do *you* understand me?"

Supreme looked at her and said, "Nina, if my baby wasn't sitting here in my lap, I'd bust you in your fuckin' mouth! You do know that, right? I don't know who the fuck you think I am. And let me say it one more time. You are not taking my daughter no-goddamn-where!" Supreme didn't say what he was really feeling. He not only wanted his baby to stay close by, but the baby's mama as well. He felt that if she went way across the country he would lose her to someone else for sure. They hadn't broken up on bad terms but Nina always made it clear to him that she was not sticking by a nigga who was doing time.

Nina reached over and grabbed Jatana. "Tell Daddy bye-bye, Jatana."

Supreme grabbed her back. "Nina, I know you gonna let me spend some time with my daughter!"

"We're ready to go, Supreme. C'mon, baby." She was visibly pissed as she grabbed Jatana and stood up. "Tell Daddy bye-bye."

Jatana covered both of her eyes with her little hands and said, "Bye, Daddy."

"Nina, you know you fucking with the wrong nigga, right? And you should know better than anyone that I ain't the one to be fucked with. Bye, baby." He turned his attention to Jatana and leaned over to kiss her on her fat cheeks. "Daddy loves you. You know that, right?"

Jatana vigoriously nodded her head up and down as her mother carried her out of the visiting hall.

"Girl, shit is sooo fucked up for me right now."

Nina and Michelle had just finished winding it down. Nina had put the kids to bed while Michelle cleaned up the kitchen. Now they were sitting in the living room, feet propped up on the coffee table, smoking a joint.

"I mean, for real. Can shit get any more fucked up for me?" Nina continued to cry the blues as she blew smoke rings up toward the ceiling. "I mean damn, my own flesh and blood kicks my door down, steals my life savings and then smokes it up. My baby daddy don't want me to do the main thing and only thing that I'm focused on doing, and that's relocating. He's threatening me with Lord knows what he has up his sleeve. On top of that, I don't have a man. I mean damn, what about me?"

"Obstacles are only temporary and just like ali the other ones you'll get over this one, my sista," Michelle assured her best friend.

"They sure don't feel temporary."

Bzzzzt! Bzzzzt! "I hate that bell! Who the hell are

you expecting?" Michelle got up to peek out the front door. "It's damn near midnight."

"I ain't expecting nobody. Fuck it, don't even answer it," Nina said.

"Girl, you ain't gonna believe this shit! It's your crack-head brother."

Bzzzzt! Bzzzzt!

"Tell him to stop ringing my damn bell. He ain't related to me no more."

Michelle cracked the door and yelled out, "Your sister said get the fuck off her bell. Y'all not related no more!"

"Tell her I got something important to tell her," he yelled loudly enough for Nina to hear.

"I don't want to hear it, you thieving-ass fiend!" Nina snapped.

"Ni, I got some work for you. Just hear me out. I promise it'll be worth your while. Please, yo, let me in for a minute."

Nina thought about it before finally yelling, "Let him in."

Derrick came through the door limping on one crutch. His head was bandaged up and he immediately began apologizing. She gave him the hand. "I'm so mad at you that *killing* your skank ass won't even give me the satisfaction I'm seeking. So save the fake-ass apologies..."

"Yo, Ni, I don't care what you think, I ain't rob you," he mumbled through swollen lips. "Mommy asked me who did this to me; I didn't tell her it was you. This is fucked up, you fractured my kneecap." He pointed down to the cast that was encasing his knee.

"You fractured my pockets! What the fuck makes you think I care about your fuckin' kneecap?" Nina had jumped up off the couch and started throwing flurries at Derrick's face.

"Nina!" Michelle screamed as she went and pulled her off of Derrick. "Don't wake up the kids with this bullshit." She had both of Nina's arms behind her back.

"Get the fuck outta my house, Derrick!" Nina was screaming at him.

"I got something to tell you, damn it!" he said, guilt obviously not allowing him to give up. He wiped the blood from his nose onto his sleeve.

"Tell me, then get the fuck out! I hate you right now."

"Canada's mom got access to a bunch of checks from Columbia University. She don't got nobody trustworthy that can get the ID to cash the motherfuckers, then give her her cut. They are in different people's names for different amounts. She wants to meet with you tomorrow because she don't know how long she's going to have access to them."

This did get Nina's attention and she managed to calm down a tad bit. "What she want out the deal?"

"Half."

Both Nina and Michelle burst out laughing. "Half? What the fuck that bitch been smokin'? I supply the IDs, get the team together and take all the risk? And she want half? That ho must be crazy! And you even crazier for bringing me some shit like that. Get the fuck outta here!"

"It's okay, Sis. Let her get that."

"Nigga, you smokin' too much. And I am not your sis. Get the fuck outta my house before I shoot you!"

"Ni. Listen to me. After y'all cash the checks, she will come to collect and when she leave, we gonna rob that ho. That bitch ain't gettin' nothin'!" Derrick stuck his chest out as if he was proud and wanting an award for his master plan.

He had Nina's attention once again. She thought about it for a few minutes, finally concluding that it could be done. But then it hit her: "I'ma be the first person she accuses of setting her up."

"No you won't. At the meeting with both of y'all, that's when we gonna get dirty."

"So you think I'ma trust you with my half, nigga? You got me fucked up! I'll talk to her and see what she working with but that's all. Robbing her with your crackhead ass will probably get me killed."

"Think about it at least, Ni. I'm telling you it'll work. And fuck her! You shouldn't care if she know you had something to do with it or not. You bouncin', right? Here's her number." He handed her a business card. "Call her tonight."

Nina took the card and pointed to the door.

"I'm out, Nina, damn!" he cursed as he limped out the door.

The next day, after the meeting with Canada's mom, Nina was explaining to Michelle that it was something they could do real quick and it would just about put her stash amount back to where it had been. Canada's mom had a stack of freshly dated checks for different amounts. She wasn't sure if they were financial aid checks, tuition reimbursements or what. Her only concern was that they were fresh, meaning only two to three days old and good. They hadn't been reported stolen and were scheduled to go out to the payees in that day's mail.

Michelle thumbed through the checks one by one, calling out the amounts. "Twelve hundred forty-six eighty-seven, 2,468.43, 682.90, oh shit! This is what I'm talking about, 9,087, oh yeah! Seven thousand, two hundred and forty forty-seven. Damn, Ni, I think we can do something with this, 4,321.03. If we bust all of these, that's what? Twelve thousand dollars? Then if we rob this ho, now that's twenty-four Gs. She didn't have any over ten grand?" Michelle was talking a mile a minute.

"She did but I didn't want them. So we gonna do this or what?"

"You know I'm down. We gonna go to the banks or check-cashing spots?"

"We gonna have to do both, unless you wanna get some more help."

"This is only six checks. That's three apiece. We'll be done with that in an hour."

"She had more but they were in a man's name. We don't have any trustworthy men for this mission. I can't afford no fuckups."

"C'mon, Ni. Crack the fuckin' whip, put your crackhead-ass brother to work and his little posse. Give them a rock, and get this money. We might as well get it while we can, especially since it's been thrown right in our laps."

Nina ran over in her mind everything that Michelle had just said. She was still pissed off at Derrick, but she reasoned that she needed to put her emotions in check and get this money. The thought even crossed her to *rob him*. Give him a taste of his own medicine.

Two nights later...

Nina let out a loud yawn as she turned off her computer. She grabbed the pages off the printer stack and carefully inspected each driver's license. Tomorrow her crew would be out cashing the checks she had gotten from Canada's mom. After she gave the last ID her final approval she decided to call Michelle.

"What up, chica?"

Nina heard a beep for the other line. "Hold up." Nina clicked over. "Hello."

"What up, bat girl?"

Nina was caught by surprise but tried to play it off. "Who is this?" she asked, even though she never forgot a voice or a face.

"This is me. You got some time to talk?"

"Yeah, hold on." She clicked back over to Michelle. "Sorry about that. You straight for tomorrow?"

"Who was that on your line?"

Nina couldn't help but laugh. "None of your business! Are you straight for tomorrow?"

"Yeah, I'm straight. Is it that nigga from New York?"

"Why?"

"Why? Why you gotta be all secretive and shit?"

"Bitch, don't be tryna keep tabs on me. I'll call you back." Nina clicked back over to Reese. "So what's up?"

"Getting straight to the point, huh? You ain't got time to just shoot the breeze?" Reese was smiling.

"Yeah. I just wanted to know what's up."

"I'll be down that way tomorrow afternoon. I wanna get with you."

Nina spun around in her swivel office chair. "No fault of yours but your timing is really off. I shouldn't have given you my number."

"That was in exchange for me fixing your door, remember? We had an agreement. I earned that."

"Like I said, I apologize but I do got a lot on my plate right now, lot of shit I got to deal with and tryna do. I know you can understand that? Right?"

"Oh yeah, I understand, but what does that have to do with us getting together for a dinner or something?"

Okay. I see this nigga can't take a hint, Nina thought to herself. "Look, Reese, right now, I got a lot of drama. I got three kids, three babies' daddies and I'm tryna make some moves for the kids and my future. Now I know I look real good to you and all that but nine times outta ten you just want to fuck. Maybe, if you would have caught me at another time, just maybe, I would have been with it. But not right now. I don't have the time. Especially not to play."

"Why are you so defensive? I don't know what makes you think I want to play. Shit, I got three kids and three babies' mommas my damn self. I'm always tryna make moves to secure their future. So I got drama, probably way more than what you got. I only want to take you to dinner, not jump the broom or no shit like that."

Nina smiled. She hadn't been prepared for that response. So she kept twirling around in her swivel chair. She could faintly hear Floetry playing in the background. She finally conceded and said, "Call me around this time tomorrow."

"I'll see you around this time tomorrow." *Click*.

Nina was left listening to the dial tone.

FIVE

On a mission . . .

Everything went like clockwork. Nina had a carload of peeps in her car that she drove to the banks and check-cashing joints. After each stop she collected the money on the spot. Michelle had a carload of folks whom she oversaw and did the exact same thing.

Both crews finished up a few minutes before the banks closed. They were scheduled to meet up at Nina's brother Peedie's spot at three-thirty, which was the designated meeting place. This was his day off and Nina knew no one would try anything stupid in his presence.

When she arrived on his porch he yanked the door open and yelled, "Yo, Sis, take that shit in the basement and I'm charging a hundred dollars by the hour, ya dig?" Peedie stood hovering over her. He was so black, all she could see was his teeth.

"You got that. But can a sista get some light? You did pay the bill, didn't you?"

"Lights are fifty dollars extra."

"Nigga, go 'head with that bullshit. I ain't no damn

feen." She went back outside and motioned for everyone to come in.

Peedie stood in the doorway mean-muggin' everybody as he forced each one of them to squeeze by him.

"Everybody down to the basement," Nina instructed. "And don't touch nothing!" She rolled her eyes at her brother before slamming the door behind her.

"Slam my door again, and that's your ass!" she heard him yell.

Once they were downstairs the payout went like clockwork. She paid the fiends their fifteen percent for their work while Derrick escorted each one out one by one. She gave Michelle twenty percent of each check that she had cashed. She counted out Derrick's five percent and held it out for him.

"Yo, what's that, man? Looks rather light to me," he said, looking at what she was holding.

"What the fuck it look like? It's your cut. Take it or leave it!"

Derrick snatched the stack of bills out of her hand. "This is bullshit, man!"

"What the fuck you mean? You just robbed my motherfuckin' house, I shouldn't give you shit!" Nina was poking his forehead.

"Calm down, Nina." Michelle was pulling her back.

She pushed Michelle away. "No, fuck that!" She pushed Derrick, causing him to fall back onto the tattered loveseat. "Why should I even let you live, nigga?"

"C'mon, y'all, before Peedie come down here. Plus we still got business to take care of. What time Canada's mom want you to meet her to pick up her money?" he asked. Nina didn't respond. She just stood there mean-muggin' Derrick.

"C'mon, Ni, why you trippin?" Derrick pushed himself up on his elbows and Nina pushed him right back down. "Stop trippin', Ni!" he yelled. "Let's get this money...What time?"

Getting her composure together, Nina said, "She told me to page her as soon as I'm done on my end. Just be ready, fool." She smacked his head. "I'll call you. If you don't pick up the phone the first time, it's your loss. So don't go running off on no crack binge with all your little buddies that just ran outta here. Y'all get a few dollars and the glass dick is all y'all know."

Derrick got up. "Aiight. I'll be on point." He limped up the basement stairs.

Nina sat down on the couch, pulled out all the money and began counting.

"Your brother is a piece of shit," Michelle said with disgust apparent in her voice.

But Nina shook her head no, to tell her to shut up and not to interrupt her counting the money.

By the time she finished counting, there was 44,700 dollars. She was giving Canada's mom 22,500. Using Derrick and his fiend crew had been worth it. She had practically doubled her take. Now, if they could finish it off, her stash would almost be right back to where it had been. Not quite, but close enough so she could get the fuck out of Dodge. She felt that she couldn't get away fast enough. That's why she had agreed to Derrick's plan. She was desperate. After paging Canada's mom she stood up, ready to go.

"Let's roll, chica." Nina felt that she could finally see the light at the end of this ghetto tunnel.

"Aiight, boy. Don't fuck this up. I'm meeting her at the Red Roof Inn at ten-thirty," Nina told her crackhead brother.

"Chill, girl. Let me do what I do. One!"

"Why did I get thrown into this dysfunctional family?" she asked Michelle.

"I don't know, trick. But I do know you need to come on, we got stops to make. Plus, I need to know what's up with ol' boy from NY?"

"Nothing's up yet. He said he was swinging by later on this evening."

Earlier, they had taken Daysha and Jermichael across the street to Ms. Ruthie's house and Jatana over to her grandmother's house. Supreme was Ms. Della's baby boy and Jatana was her only granddaughter. All of her other kids had boys, bad-ass ones at that. Ms. Della loved it when Jatana came over. Jatana loved how she would get spoiled whenever she went to spend time with her grandmother.

At ten-fifteen Michelle and Nina pulled up in the parking lot of the Red Roof Inn. Michelle cocked her two boys, Smith & Wesson, and placed them on her lap. Nina backed into a parking space and cut off the engine of the stolen Escalade.

"This ho had the nerve to ask me why she couldn't meet me at my house. I said let's meet at your house. She then got all quiet and shit. I was like, 'That's what I thought.'"

Michelle laughed at what Nina had just said. "Bitch, it ain't like y'all don't know where each other live, so it really didn't make a difference."

"Ho, it's the principle of the thing. Plus, I don't want her near my crib when them fools try to jack her."

"Try?"

"Yeah, try. You know my brother is the biggest fuckup! So be ready."

"Yeah. You got a point there."

"However, if he pulls this shit off I'm leaving next month. I'm making reservations for next week to fly down and find a spot to rest my head and then it's a wrap."

"Word? You bouncin' that fast?" Michelle was shocked because she really didn't believe that her dawg was leaving her.

"You thought I was playin', didn't you?" When Michelle didn't respond Nina sucked her teeth and rolled her eyes at her in disgust.

"It wasn't that I thought you was playin', it's that I was hoping you was just running your mouth because you know I don't want you to go," she pouted. "The fuckin' country? What the fuck you gonna do down there?"

"Get a job. I'ma be legit." Her eyes landed on a Honda Accord with three niggas in it. They all had on dark clothes. She was sure one of them was Derrick.

"You peep that Honda?"

"Yeah, I got it."

Then came the burgundy Q45 that Nina had been expecting. There were two females in the front and two males in the back. Nina flashed her parking lights and the Q came over and got in a spot a couple of cars down from them, just as planned.

"Don't get out; make that ho come to you..." Michelle ordered as she fingered her boys.

"I got this." Nina was making eye contact with Canada's mom, Serita, who was getting out of the car. Nina cracked her window. "What's good, ma?" she said as she popped the lock to the back door. "Get in. I got something for you."

Serita looked just as young as her daughter. She hung with the youngens and even fucked the young niggas. She was a hustler, just like Nina, trying to make ends meet. As she opened the back door the two niggas she had with her stepped out of the Q. The short one got in the back with Serita, the other one leaned against the car. No one said anything as Michelle handed a Gap bag over to Serita.

Serita turned on her small penlight and immediately began counting the cash. Nina watched through her rearview mirror as Michelle was turned around in the front seat glued to each dollar that Serita fingered. When Serita folded the last bill Michelle said, "We straight?"

"Man, y'all roll better than most niggas. If I come up again in a day or two, y'all down?"

Nina said, "Not for half. I gotta round up too many people. Too many mouths eating outta the pot. I need seventy percent. I only did it this time because niggas and hoes was starvin'."

Serita sighed. "I don't know about seventy percent, there are a lotta folks tryna eat on my end as well. I gotta holla at my peeps."

"Aiight. Just hit me on my cell." And right on cue Michelle turned on her lights to let Derrick know they were done. She then turned the ignition on before unlocking the back door. As soon as Serita and her man stepped out of the car she put the gear in drive and was out, all the while looking at her rearview mirror. As she turned the corner, the Honda Accord gunned out and blocked the Q45 in.

Nina and Michelle pulled up to Ms. Della's and parked. Nina's celly vibrated. She looked at the caller ID and smiled when she saw it was Reese, but didn't answer it.

"What's taking your brother so long to call back?" Michelle kept looking at her watch.

"We just left ten minutes ago. Damn, give the nigga time to jack some muthafuckers! Plus you know how trifling Derrick is. They all probably taking a hit off that glass pipe right now."

Michelle couldn't help but laugh at her girl. She was truly pissed big time at her crack-fiend brother. They got out of the car, climbed the porch and rang the bell. "Damn, is everybody on CP time tonight?" Michelle cracked, after four rings and no one coming to the door.

Nina began knocking. "Ms. Della is probably asleep. You know how old people are." Nina peeped in the front window. "Here she comes now."

"Who is it?"

"It's Nina, Ms. Della." They stood and listened to Ms. Della unlock the dead bolt and two other locks.

"Damn. Where we at, Fort Knox?" Michelle cracked again.

"Bitch, chill with the jokes," Nina snapped.

Ms. Della opened the door and said, "It's late, baby. Why don't you let her spend the night and get her in the morning?"

"I would love to, but she has a doctor's appointment at nine."

"Well, come get her at eight."

"It's no way I'll be on time with getting two other kids ready and driving way across town at rush hour. Where is she?" Nina said, walking through the house.

"Well, um, her daddy called and, um, said you was taking her South so he had his friend to um...err... um...come pick her up."

Nina froze in her footsteps, her heart sank to her stomach. "Wait a minute. Who did you give my baby to?" Michelle was seated at first but she had jumped up.

"Her daddy's friend came and got her."

"Who is this friend? Call her and tell her to bring my daughter over here right now. I'm not leaving here until she comes."

"I don't know her name or number. Butchie"—which was Supreme's government name—"called and said for me to give Jatana to her until you came back from down South."

"Ms. Della," Nina screamed. "Where is my daughter? Michelle, call the police!" she frantically ordered. "Y'all ain't gonna play no fuckin' games with my child! Ms. Della, you and your son got me fucked up! You can play games with him if you want to but your ass will be sitting right in the cell next to your son if you don't get my baby back! I'll have you arrested for kidnapping."

"Butchie said he'll be calling you in the morning."

"Fuck Butchie!" Nina was about to lose it. "I want my daughter with me tonight. Call the police now, Michelle!" she screamed.

"That's what I'm doing. Bastards got me on hold."

Ms. Della snatched the cell phone out of Michelle's hand and turned it off. "No, this old lady didn't do that!" Michelle gasped in surprise.

Bbrrring. Nina's cell phone rang. "What!" she screamed into it.

All she heard was heavy breathing. "Sis. I got shot. Come pick me up. I'm walking down Olden. Hurry up. I think I killed Canada's mom."

"You what?" Nina yelled out in disbelief.

"I got your money, though. I'm bleeding bad. Hurry and come get me!" The phone went dead.

"Oh shit!" She looked from the phone to Ms. Della. "Ms. Della, I gotta go but I'll be back in an hour. I swear, if my baby is not here your ass is goin' down! Come on, Michelle!"

Michelle snatched her cell phone outta Ms. Della's hand. They stormed out of the house, slamming the door so hard the whole house shook.

SIX

"What the fuck?" Michelle commented as she trailed behind a frantic Nina.

"Why is he doing this?" Nina screamed as she yanked the car door open.

"Who? Supreme?"

"Of course Supreme! I told you that nigga said I better not take his child no-damn-where." She zoomed out of the parking spot as if she were a NASCAR driver.

"Nina! Watch where you going! Shit, you need to slow the fuck down!" Michelle was pressing her foot to the floor as if she were the driver hitting the brakes.

"My baby, Michelle. How he gonna take my baby! I swear to God if something happens to my daughter I'm killing him and his whole damn family. I put that on everything," she snarled through clenched teeth.

A few minutes later they were riding down Olden Avenue. "Where is this clown? Nina snapped. "I gotta get back and get my daughter." She was straining to see in the dark.

"Slow down. Is that him?" Derrick was in the middle

of the street limping toward them and holding his side. "That is him." Michelle said.

"Fuck! He's bleeding," Nina yelled out, as if it was just sinking in what he said over the phone about being shot. Nina had jumped out of the car.

"Get me to a hospital, Ni."

Michelle also jumped out of the car and opened the back door. She and Nina helped him inside. He threw the bloody Gap bag up front before stretching out onto the backseat. "There, I got your money back." He breathed a sigh of relief. "Damn, it's burning bad, Nina."

"What the fuck happened, Derrick?" Nina yelled as she slammed the door and gunned the gas pedal.

"What do it look like, Nina?" he responded between short breaths. "It wasn't a fuckin' cakewalk! Owww, damn! Don't hit no more potholes! Fuck!"

"I'm trying to get you to the fuckin' hospital before you bleed to death in the back of my car!"

"This ain't your car and I'ma be dead before I get there."

"Don't say that, nigga!" Nina pleaded.

Michelle was busy counting the money in the Gap bag. It was stained with blood, causing her to think of the term "blood money." "D, after you got shot you counted the money?"

"I wanted to know how much it was," he groaned.

"What happened to Canada's mom? Where is she?" Nina was trying to see Derrick in her rearview mirror. "Derrick! Can you hear me?"

Michelle stopped counting and looked back at him.

"What is he doing?" Nina said in panic mode. "Is he dead?"

"He's not moving. I think he is dead." Michelle grabbed his wrist to see if she could feel his pulse. "Hurry up! We gotta get him to a hospital! Shit! We gonna have to drop him off and jet."

"Girl, is you crazy?" Nina screamed.

"What are you gonna tell five-o, Nina? Shit, you stay if you want, as a matter of fact let me out here. I'll find me a way home."

"This is my brother, Michelle. Derrick, hang in there. I'm sorry, okay? That's my brother, Michelle!"

"I know that. But what are you going to say to the police?"

"What? What do you suggest, Michelle?"

"I told you, let's drop him off and get ghost. That's what you need to do, Nina." She looked at the blank stare in Nina's eyes. "Do you understand me, Nina? Yes or no? We are gonna pick him up and drop him off at the emergency room entrance." Nina nodded her head up and down. "Aiight then," Michelle said as they turned the corner heading toward St. Francis Hospital.

"Derrick," Nina called his name.

Michelle thought quickly about it. "Let me out first and I'll get a stretcher, wheelchair or something."

When they pulled up in the emergency room drive-way, Michelle did just that: jumped out, ran and got a stretcher. Nina's heart was pounding as she got out of the car and opened the back door. She grabbed under his arms and got a good grip on his shoulders.

"Oowww," he groaned, causing Nina to fall back in fright when she heard the sounds of pain escape from his mouth.

"He's not dead, Michelle! Derrick, we got you at the hospital, hold on, okay?" She breathed a sigh of relief.

"C'mon, let's get him moved," Michelle ordered. Even though he weighed about one hundred and fifty pounds soaking wet, it was still a struggle to get his scrawny body off the backseat and up onto the stretcher.

Nina kissed her crackhead brother on the forehead. "Hang in there, Bro."

"Move the car!" Michelle ordered as she began pushing the stretcher with all her might toward the emergency room entrance. "I'll meet you up the street," she hollered back, as she was going as fast as she could. "I think this man has been shot! Excuse me, Doctor, I believe this man has been shot!"

"I'm not a doctor, I'm just an orderly," a young black guy looking like Ruben Studdard announced.

"Can you call a fuckin' doctor?" Michelle screamed out.

He flicked his cigarette across the driveway and took off yelling, "We need a doctor out here!"

Two ladies who appeared to be nurses came over to the stretcher. As soon as one of them felt his pulse and saw the blood, she yelled, "C'mon, guys, we don't want to lose him!" As they rolled him through the double doors,

Michelle turned around and began jogging up the street looking for Nina. She ran right past her. Nina beeped the horn, causing her to almost jump out of her skin.

"Why the fuck are you parked?" a startled Michelle barked as she jumped into the car.

"I was trying to see what was happening, plus two squad cars rolled right past me."

"Let's get the fuck away from here. Let's go to my mom's. We gotta change cars. And we both got blood on our clothes. This is fucked up!"

"What did they say?" Nina wanted to know.

"The nurse's last words were we don't want to lose him."

"That's what she said?" Nina looked at Michelle in bewilderment. Michelle nodded her head yes. "This is all my fault."

"Naw. It's your crackhead brother's fault. He shouldn't have stole your money and when you told him don't jack Canada's mom, he insisted. You didn't make him do it. Or did you?" She looked at Nina, daring her to say yes.

"No. I didn't make him. I'm the one who told you he was gonna fuck up. But I didn't anticipate it being this bad."

"Well then. So why the fuck you talking about it like it's your fault?"

"I don't know." She started crying. "I just don't want him to die. Especially over something involving me. I hate him for stealing my money but I don't want him to die."

"He'll be all right. You know crack fiends don't die, they multiply."

"Why the fuck you want me to clean a stolen car?" Peedie cursed as he grabbed a bucket of water and other stuff with plans to clean the stolen Escalade.

"Because of blood, DNA, fingerprints. How was I supposed to know he was gonna get shot?"

Beep. Beep. Michelle was outside beeping the horn. They had changed clothes, washed up and gotten Michelle's Rover. Now they were ready to go back over to Ms. Della's.

"I gotta run, Peedie."

"Tell Supreme if he don't send my niece home, I'ma do something to get arrested and come where he at and fuck him up my damn self. Ya heard?" Peedie hollered at her.

Nina ran outside and jumped in the car. She grabbed her celly and dialed Ms. Della's. After four rings the answering machine kicked in. "No, this old lady don't have the machine on! I don't disrespect old people but I swear, she's itching for me to tap that old ass!" Nina was forcefully redialing Ms. Della again. This time on the fourth ring she answered. "Ms. Della, I'm on my way to pick up Jatana."

"She's not here yet, baby."

"Ms. Della..." *Click.* All Nina had was some dial tone ringing in her ears.

"No, this bitch didn't hang up on me!" Nina screamed.

"What the fuck is the matter with her?" She dialed Peedie.

"Yo!" he answered on the first ring.

"I'ma need you to come over to Ms. Della's, ASAP. Call Mommy and tell her to go to Ms. Ruthie's and get the kids. I am not going to be responsible for my actions tonight."

"Nina, don't do shit until I get there! Do you hear me?" he warned.

"Fuck that! How they gonna take my child?" she screamed. "That's my baby, Peedie! And you telling me to don't do shit!"

"I said wait for me, Nina! You gonna need somebody thinking with a level head to have your back."

She clicked Peedie off, rested her head back onto the headrest and let the tears fall. "I can't believe this shit! I really don't believe it."

Michelle remained silent as she squeezed her ride into a parking space. After she cut the engine off she looked up at Ms. Della's house and all of the lights were out.

Nina hopped out and ran up to the front door. She began knocking and ringing the doorbell at the same time. When Ms. Della didn't come to the door, Nina began yelling threats about her calling the police and getting her arrested for kidnapping. Ms. Della still didn't respond. Nina dialed 911 on her cell phone and told the operator what was going on. The operator told her to stay where she was and a squad car would be there shortly.

*   *   *

Two and a half hours later, Peedie was hugging a defeated Nina. "We'll get her back. Trust and believe that," he assured her. "I know Supreme don't want his moms to go to jail. So he'll have her brought back." As his cell phone rang he motioned for Michelle to come get a sobbing Nina.

Michelle led Nina to her car. She didn't know what to say. She had no children of her own so she could only imagine what Nina was feeling. All the police had done was tell Nina that she had to wait twenty-four hours to file a missing person's report, since she had dropped the baby off at a relative's. Michelle hugged her sobbing friend. They both turned toward Peedie when they heard him getting loud.

"Calm down, Mommy. What are you talking about?" He waved Nina over to him.

Nina's heart was beating at a pace of one hundred ninety miles per hour. Her intuition had already told her what her mom was all frantic about.

"Here, talk to Mommy." Peedie shoved the phone into her face as he turned his back and knelt down on one knee as if he was about to pray.

"Ma, what's the matter?" Nina's voice was trembling.

"What are you into?" she screamed. "What are you into, Nina, that could get my son killed?" She was hysterical. "You the devil, girl! I raised you better! You are the devil!"

"No, Moooom!" Nina screamed.

"I didn't raise you to do like you doing," she continued. "Now you got your brother's blood on your hands! Nina, you got these kids to raise. Do right by 'em. Lead by example. Do right. Live right." *Click.*

"Mommy," she mumbled into the phone. "Mommy," she said again. "I'm sorry," she kept repeating as she dialed her mother back. All she got was the answering machine. Nina sat on the curb and cried like a baby.

Michelle was still in silent mode as she watched Nina and Peedie mourn his death.

She was an only child so again she couldn't relate one hundred percent. But everyone knew that however she could help she would be down for whatever. After about a half hour five-o cruised up the block.

"What's going on? Is everything all right?" the officer on the passenger side inquired as his partner looked on.

Since Peedie and Nina didn't respond Michelle said, "We just found out a few minutes ago that we had a death in the family, sir."

"Well, it's late and I suggest you people take it inside."

"Whatever," Michelle mumbled as they cruised off. "C'mon, y'all. You know them clowns will be back."

Peedie came over to where they were, pulled Nina up and gave her a hug. "We gonna bounce back," he whispered to her. "You aiight?" He felt her shaking her head no.

"Well, you gotta remain focused. Stay on your mission and get the fuck outta New Jersey. Ain't shit here. Plus Canada's mom was announced DOA."

"What?" Nina and Michelle both gasped at the same time.

"Yeah. So shit's gonna be hot for a minute," he told them. "You gonna be all right?"

"What you think, Peedie? My baby has been kidnapped, my brother is dead, and my own mother just disowned me for the second time. Mommy has put all the blame on me. She even said I'm a bad mother in her own little way. Shit, that's why I'm out here struggling. Because I'm trying to be a good mother. I'm trying to give my children the best so that they can grow up to be good adults. She never gives me any credit."

"You know how Mommy is. Don't take that shit personal. You need to stay on point and get the fuck outta Dodge. You understand?" She nodded her head yes. "Michelle, you gotta make sure she stay focused. You hear me?"

"I hear you."

"Y'all both gonna end up in prison if y'all don't. Plus y'all don't know who Canada's mom is connected with."

"Jatana..."

Peedie cut her off. "Let her stay with Supreme's folks for now. I'll stay on top of that. You need to be getting the fuck outta Jersey, Nina! This ain't no game."

"I'm not leaving my baby," Nina cried. "I can't, Peedie. How do you expect me to do that?"

"Well you might as well be prepared to not see none of your children, 'cause your ass is going to prison. Call Ms. Della, tell her to keep Jatana until you get situated. You need to leave, Ni. You in a lot of trouble."

"I didn't do anything."

"What the fuck is two bodies?" When she didn't respond he said, "Aiight. Play stupid if you want. When you ready to act like you ain't stuck on stupid holla at me." He walked away.

SEVEN

Four days later...

Nina had been staying at or rather hiding out at Darlene's, Peedie's chick on the side. She had a four-bedroom house out in Ewing Township. For the last two days she and Michelle had been back and forth at Nina's packing up everything Nina wanted to take with her down South. Michelle had a big truck in front of Darlene's almost full with everything that she would be driving. Nina and the kids would be flying down. Because she had to leave town so soon, she had never had the chance to go looking for a place to move into.

In the evenings she and Michelle had been out writing checks for furniture, appliances and all the other household items she would need for the move to her new house down South. Plus all the shopping helped to keep Derrick's death off Nina's mind.

As Nina put Michelle's Land Rover in park she told Michelle, "Just one more night of shopping and one more bank job and that should do it. Don't you think?"

"Shit! One more night? Anything from here on out is gravy, why you bullshittin'."

"Whatever. So you gonna be here first thing in the morning?"

"Yeah. Don't try to get rid of me. I need to come up and get my shoes and those earrings we got last night. You tryna steal my shit on the sly?" Michelle teased.

"Girl, please."

They unloaded the car and proceeded to take the bags in the house.

"What up, Darlene?" Nina and Michelle simultaneously said as they walked past a half-asleep Darlene. She was curled up on the couch watching TV.

"Hey," she drily responded.

"What's her problem?" Michelle whispered to Nina.

"Who gives a fuck? In three more days, I'm outta here and she can be miserable all by her damn self. I got enough shit to deal with."

"I know that's right."

After they made the last trip from the car, they settled into the bedroom that Nina was claiming and opened up all the shopping bags. They had three piles. One for the household goods, another for clothes and the last for the stuff Michelle had gotten for herself.

"You gonna help me put this stuff in the truck?" asked Nina.

"Yeah, but first give me my Jimmy Choos from last night and my platinum earrings. Let me find out you tryna be slick with my shit. I've had to ask for my shit too many times."

"Girl, let me get your little fake platinum earrings so you can leave me the hell alone. You obviously forgot that I got my own shit!" Nina headed for the closet where she stashed all the stuff she didn't feel safe storing outside in the truck.

"Be right back, Ni. Let me take some of this stuff down to the truck." She skipped down the stairs, and walking past Darlene she said, "Your hair looks good. I like that color on you."

"Thank you, girl."

Siiiiiike, Michelle laughed to herself. On her way back past her, Michelle eyed her as she tried to figure out why was it that she had never liked Darlene.

"What the fuck?" she heard Nina yell among a bunch of commotion. When Michelle went back into the bedroom, Nina was pulling everything out of the closet.

"What's the matter with you?"

"My shit is gone! That what's the matter!" Nina yelled.

Michelle ran over to the closet. "What's gone?"

"All of my jewelry, my Gucci bags, four pair of shoes including your Jimmy Choos and my leather coat. This bitch got me fucked up! I put my freedom on the line for this shit. I'll be damned if I'ma let some lazy, broke-ass ho take it from me! I'ma beat that ass right about now!" Nina was running toward the bedroom door.

Michelle dived for it first, blocking it, and had her hand on the knob. "Hold up, Ni. What are you doing?"

She grabbed Michelle's shoulder and yanked her off the door. "Move, bitch!" Nina ran out the door with

Michelle right on her heels, but not before she grabbed her Smith & Wesson out of her purse.

When they got downstairs, Darlene was still chillin' on the couch as if she hadn't heard all the commotion upstairs. "Bitch, where is my shit?"

She looked at Nina as if she was crazy, then lazily yawned, "I don't know what you're talking about."

Nina turned around and ran upstairs to Darlene's bedroom. Michelle came behind her, closed the door and locked it. They both began ransacking the bedroom. Nina in the closets, Michelle in the dressers.

Boom! Boom! Boom! Darlene was banging on her bedroom door. "If you don't come the fuck out of my motherfuckin' bedroom, I'm calling the police," she warned. "You in my fuckin' house, remember?"

When she said that, Nina snapped. She ran to the door, snatched it open and punched Darlene in the face, again and again.

"Bitch...don't...you...ever...threaten...me... with...the police again! I'll call my brother and tell his wife where you live and I'll...tell...him... about...that...nigga...you fuck with named...Dre."

"Nina! Save some of that ass for me!" Michelle grabbed Darlene by her collar and stuck her gun in her face. "Where is our shit, bitch?" Darlene began screaming as if she were getting raped. "Shut that fuckin' noise up!" Michelle smacked her in the face with the gun. "I'm not going to ask you again," she warned while placing the barrel over Darlene's already swollen eye.

"Okay. Okay," she cried. "Don't shoot me. I'll give you your stolen shit back."

"Where is it?" Nina yelled.

"In the basement in a trunk."

Michelle yanked her up and pushed her out of the bedroom. Nina was right on their heels. A petrified Darlene led them to the basement and over to a large black trunk. She popped it open and sure enough all of their goods were right there. Michelle made Darlene carry the majority of the merchandise while she and Nina carried the rest. After they put everything back in Nina's closet, Michelle turned to Darlene, put the gun in her face and cocked it. "This stays right here, am I right? In other words your ass-whipping never happened, comprende?"

Darlene was nodding her head up and down so hard, it looked as if her head might pop off her neck.

"I know where you live, bitch. You're free to go." With that said Darlene ran out of the room.

Nina slammed the door behind her. "Ain't that some shit?" she said in disbelief.

"That bitch just messed up my plan. You know I can't stay here no more, right?"

"Yeah. I know."

Nina flopped on the bed and buried her head in the pillow. Michelle began gathering everything together. Nina turned over on her back and said, "Damn, I don't want to call this nigga Reese."

"Yo, you gots to do what you gotta do."

"Fuck!" Nina grabbed her cell phone and dialed Reese. When he didn't answer she said, "Ain't this a bitch!" as she listened to his voice mail. She thought about hanging up but then figured what the hell. "Reese, this is Nina, let me hear from you."

"Now, that wasn't hard, was it?" Michelle teased. "He ain't nothing but a trick, so I don't know why you nuttin' up."

"Whatever. Let's pack this shit so I can get outta this ho's house. She'll have me under the jail for real."

An hour later, when they were almost done loading up Michelle's Rover and Nina's Jetta, Nina's celly rang.

"Hello."

"What up, shorty? Don't tell me you finally got time for a player! You must be ballin' outta control, 'cause a nigga can't never get with you. What's good, ma?"

"What you mean you can't never get with me? You ain't been trying."

"Girl, I came by your house several times. You know you dodging a nigga."

"Trust me. It ain't even like that."

"Then why you keep havin' me come by and you don't be there?"

"I apologize for that but trust me it was not intentional. My shit is so fucked up right now, you don't have a clue, hell I don't have a clue!"

"I told you. Whose shit ain't fucked up? I know you know how to bounce back."

"My shit is so fucked up, bouncing back is a joke to me."

"What? You need some more doors fixed?" he joked. "I can do that for you."

"I wish. That door was just the beginning of this major setback I'm having."

"What about the beatdown you gave the nigga with the baseball bat? What was up with that?"

"That was the second event. The nigga I beat was my brother and now he's dead."

"Damn, shorty."

"Yeah. So now you have a little idea of what's up. I've been laying low these past few days…"

"I still want to see you. What you need?"

"Well you told me if I ever needed anything then you was that nigga. Well, nigga, I'm in a big jam. For starters I need a spot to chill in ATL or Charlotte. You got something that way? I need it like yesterday."

"You ain't said nothing but a word. Can I swing through a little later?"

"I'm not at that spot anymore. I…"

"Nina!" she heard Peedie yell. He slammed his car door. "Why in the fuck are you still here? You think this shit is a game?"

"Reese, let me call you back. Keep your line open."

"Is everything aiight?"

"No. Give me about ten minutes." *Click*.

Peedie snatched her by her arm, almost yanking her shoulder out of the socket.

"Why are you still here?"

"I'm leaving in a couple more days, Peedie. I told you I don't even have a house yet."

"You big-ass dummy! That's why they got hotels! You don't even know, do you?"

"Know what?"

"Your fucking house got burnt down, Nina! You done stole money from them niggas and now they out to get your ass. Then on top of that, five-o been questioning peeps in the hood and you know them niggas are talking. It won't be long before your dumb ass will be charged with being an accessory to a murder." He looked at all of the bags in both cars and flipped. "I know your ass ain't shopping for clothes!" *Smack!* He slapped her across the back of her head. "You leaving right now." He grabbed her by the back of her neck and pushed her toward her car.

"Wait, Peedie! I got a few more things in the house," she pleaded.

Just then they heard a car screeching around the corner and before you know it the Chevy Impala was right up on them. "Get down!" Peedie yelled and whoever it was began spraying bullets.

When it finally quieted down Nina raised her head. "Are they gone?" She looked behind her and Peedie was patting his arm. Blood was seeping through his shirt.

"Peedie!" Nina screamed at the top of her lungs.

"I'm good. It's just a flesh wound."

A few feet over, Michelle's brain matter was splattered all over Nina's Jetta. "Nooooo! Oh God whyyyy? Call an ambulance somebody!" Nina was screaming as she stood up. She ran over to Michelle's body and then back to Peedie's.

"She's dead, yo. Get the fuck in the truck and go. You know they comin' back."

Peedie watched as Nina frantically jumped in the big truck. He hoped that she could drive that thing. A sharp pain caused him to grit his teeth. "Go, Nina," he yelled.

The truck finally turned on and was gone. "Shit," he gritted. Peedie got up and headed for Darlene's porch.

"Darlene!" he screamed as he ran toward her porch. Nina turned around at the sound of screeching tires. "Open the door, Darlene!" He stood in the doorway, separated from her by a screen, astonished at the sight of blood. "Open the door, bitch!"

Splat! Splat! Splat! Darlene stood there in shock as the bullets caused her lover's body to twist and jerk before slowly sliding down the screen door.

"You bitch!" were Peedie's last words as blood gushed out of his mouth and his blank stare rested on Darlene.

READING GROUP GUIDE

BLACK IS BLUE

1. Did you already know Kaseem was a snake?
2. What was your response to Desiree and Polo getting together?

THE "P" IS FREE...

1. Do you think that Wiz overreacted when he saw the guy (Moo) at the car talking to his girl?
2. Do you think he should have chased a crackhead (Crystal) and wifed her?

THE LAST LAUGH

1. Should the best friend find out that BoBo was involved in her sister's death? And if so, should she take vengeance on his baby's mother, her now love interest?
2. Should the gang send someone after them, and how?

ALL FOR NOTHING

1. Do you think that Tiffany, the woman Jihad messed with on the run, should come up pregnant? If so, should she see his downfall on the news and go after his real family?
2. Do you think Jihad, being on the run, should have gone to see his son, or should he have put together a visit the way he did with Monique before he left?

MAKIN' ENDZ MEET

1. What do you think about the relationship between Nina and Reese from NY?
2. Do you think Nina should have left without getting her child back?

ABOUT THE AUTHORS

WAHIDA CLARK was born and raised in Trenton, New Jersey. She began writing fiction while incarcerated at a woman's federal camp in Lexington, Kentucky. Her first novel, *Thugs and the Women Who Love Them*, and the sequel, *Every Thug Needs a Lady*, appeared on the *Essence* bestsellers list. Since her release, Wahida has achieved much success with her follow-up, *Thug Matrimony*. Her most recent work, *Payback With Ya Life*, made its way onto the prestigious *New York Times* bestseller list. Wahida continues to amplify the urban landscape from her home and office in East Orange, New Jersey.

VICTOR L. MARTIN is the author of four published novels: *A Hood Legend*, *Menage's Way*, *For the Strength of You*, and *Unique's Ending*. He is currently incarcerated in a North Carolina prison.

LASHONDA "L. L. DASHER" SIDBERRY-TEAGUE is a Wilmington, North Carolina, native, coming into her own as an up-and-coming author. She is the wife of author Kwame

"DUTCH" Teague, one of the hottest street writers, and the mother of five children. She has found her calling in writing, and has her first novel, *Kiss*, coming soon. LaShonda lives by the motto "Be a blessing and you will be blessed."

BONTA was born and raised on the mean streets of Chicago's southeast side. After graduating high school and a brief stay in the US Army, he answered the streets' calling. The cost of chasing the mirage of fame and fortune was a 151-month federal sentence. While he was there, the legendary Joe Black inspired him to get serious about writing. Since then he has written two novels and a few short stories.

SHAWN "JIHAD" TRUMP was born in Pennsylvania. In November 1999 Shawn was arrested and subsequently indicted by the federal government and sentenced to eighty-four months in prison. During his time he learned to channel his emotions through writing. Since being released, Shawn continues to write and is also partner in an up-and-coming indie label, South of the Burgh Entertainment. Shawn is married with two daughters.

THE GOLDEN HUSTLA

By

WAHIDA CLARK

CHAPTER ONE

GBI

"Congratulations, Bob! You did it! Are you sitting down?" Alexis Greenspan shouted in excitement. She could feel Bob's adrenaline rush through the phone.

"Oh God, Alexis. Did I really do it?" Bob could barely contain his breathing.

"You did it, Bob Tokowski! You have just won your fair share of one million dollars of American Eagle Gold Coins! One million!" Alexis screamed out. "I told you to hang in there, Bob. The road was rocky, but you did it. Your perseverance paid off. Again, congratulations to ya, Bob. You deserve it! You finally hit the big time."

Bob was now crying tears of joy. "Thank...you, Alexis. Oh, my God. Thank you."

"Now, Bob; I need you to grab your pencil and paper. You must write down this claim number. Go ahead, Bob, grab a pen and a pad."

Alexis could hear Bob piddling around in the background. Then she heard a moan and then a thud.

"Bob!? Bob!?"

The excitement must've gotten the best of him.

Click.

Agent Houser turned off the recorder. Houser had been the lead investigator for the past two years, heading up the Georgia Bureau of Investigation. Two more years and Houser, who reminded you of the undercover detective played by Robert Blake in the 1970s hit *Baretta*, could retire. However, he was ready to retire now. His impetigo was spreading, and pus was oozing out of the skin infection on his legs. But he told himself it would all be over soon.

Retirement, here I come!

The bright side of his gloomy lining was that he lucked up and got an interview with Erica McCoy, aka Alexis Greenspan. She was one of the top salespeople at WMM advertising, aka We Make Millionaires. All of law enforcement knew that this was one of the biggest and hardest-to-penetrate fraudulent telemarketing firms in the state of Georgia; they knew how to operate in that gray area.

Houser had screamed at his team of four, "Screw the FBI! We can do just as good a job as they can."

He had pulled one of the not-so-oldest tricks in the book, but old nonetheless. He sent Erica an official-looking certified letter explaining that she had inherited some money, to the lovely tune of $250,000. The letter stated that she would have to come and get processed to see if she was eligible to claim it. When she pulled up to the Bureau's fictitious office, which they had set up just a few blocks away from WMM, Houser flashed his badge, introduced himself and told her to follow him.

She did. To the Bureau's main office.

"Why are we at the GBI?" Alexis's curiosity was piqued.

"We have to make sure that you are claiming what's rightfully yours," Houser simply stated.

As they walked past the front desk and down the long, bright white corridor, Erica got really curious. "Are you sure I'm here to claim some kind of inheritance?"

Houser smiled. "Depends on how you look at it."

"How I look at it? What does that mean? Don't have me down here on no bullshit! I got better things to do with my time," she spat.

Houser pulled out his keys and unlocked his office door. He moved to the side and motioned for Alexis to step inside. He then flicked the light switch.

"Please have a seat, Ms. McCoy. Would you like a cup of coffee? Tea? Bottled water?"

"No. I just want you to tell me what this is really all about." Erica was growing agitated.

Houser sat his six-one, two-hundred-pound frame behind his desk. He lifted his spectacles off his nose and rubbed its bridge. He then leaned back into the chair, resting his hands behind his head. Erica cringed at the patches of impetigo on his chin and elbows. He obviously picked up on her discomfort because he hastily sat up, resting his arms on the chair's armrest.

He hit the intercom button on his phone. "Doris, tell Parker and Radcliff to bring the WMM file."

"WMM? What is this about? You fucker! You tricked

me to come to your office under false pretenses. I should sue your ass!" She stood and grabbed her purse. "My name is Erica McCoy, not WMM." She turned to leave the office.

That's when Houser hit the play button on his recorder. Booming through its speakers was the conversation between her and Bob Tokowski. Erica abruptly turned around at the sound of her sales voice and stood frozen in place.

Agents Parker and Radcliff entered the office. They both slid several folders in front of Houser and took their seats. Agent Parker looked as if he had a blond toupee sitting on top of his head. His wrinkled plaid suit drooped over his scrawny frame. He reminded Erica of an anorexic Bart Simpson. Radcliff was grossly overweight and sloppy looking. His oily black hair was slicked back into a ponytail. He looked like a goldfish.

After they listened to Alexis yell "Bob!? Bob!?" Houser turned off the tape recorder.

The room grew silent, except for Radcliff's heavy breathing.

"Please have a seat, Ms. McCoy."

Erica clutched her Gucci bag tighter.

"Fuck you! I am going to sue your ass for deceit and for wasting my time. Kiss my ass!" With that said, she stormed out of the office.

Houser jumped from his chair and headed for his office door. He stood in the hallway in front of his office and said, "Murder, Ms. McCoy! If you don't get your ass back in here, you're going down for murder."

Erica spun around and practically ran to get in Houser's face.

"Murder!? You wannabe FBI agent! I ain't got nothing to do with no murder. You people have really lost your minds. Find someone else to hassle," she said through clenched teeth.

"Ms. McCoy, your client Bob Tokowski, he died. Dropped dead of a heart attack, right while you were trying to scam him with your 'millions' in gold coins."

Houser motioned with two fingers from each hand to emphasize quote unquote "millions."

"That's right, we know all about the scamming and scheming of WMM. We know your boss, Rinaldo Haywood, aka Brian Stout, aka Tommy Green, aka John Bennett. We know about his office in the Florida Keys run by his cohorts Brandon Ingram and Charlie Adams. We know your phone name Alexis Greenspan. Very catchy. We—"

"Hold up, you asshole. I don't give a fuck what you know. I'm a sales associate. A damned good one at that. I sell to business owners. If the client decides to patronize our firm and at the same time gamble at a chance of getting a bunch of gold coins, so the fuck what? That's not illegal!" Alexis ranted as she turned to walk out.

"Alexis or Erica, whichever character you're in right now," fat boy chuckled as Houser began his negotiations, "this is your only chance to help yourself. You know what's going on over there is against the law. All I have to do is say the word and the feds'll be all over that place. And not only will you go down for money

laundering, conspiracy and fraud, you also have a murder hanging over your head."

Parker finally decided to put his two cents in.

"Look, Alexis. The company is going down whether
you help yourself or not. If I was—"

"Look," Alexis sighed as she stepped back into the
office and shut the door. "If y'all had something then
you wouldn't need me."

Alexis snatched open the door and then slammed it
shut behind her.

Vote for your favorite story at
www.wclarkpublishing.com.